A WICKED KISS

Serena looked narrowly at Nicholas. " 'Tis clear you do not respect me."

"I will not permit you to ride roughshod over me," Nicholas said, his tone dry.

" 'Tis you who wishes to ride roughshod over me," Serena said angrily.

"If that is what it takes," Nicholas said, grinning. "You've thrown off every other rider, Serena, but you won't throw me. I believe I've shown you my horsemanship before. And on our wedding night I'll gladly show you it much better."

"Why you . . . you low, despicable beast," Serena gasped. Enraged, she snatched up her glass of punch. She meant only to take a cooling sip, but then Nicholas laughed at her, with such an intimate look in his eyes, that before she knew it, she had dashed its contents directly into his face.

The red punch dripped down Nicholas's cravat and shirt, staining it pink. He sat perfectly still, not flinching a muscle. He only said in a low, mild tone, " 'Tis the second outfit of mine you've ruined, Serena."

He reached down, grabbed her wrist and hauled her from her chair. Serena didn't have a moment to object, for he jerked her to him and kissed her ruthlessly. It was as if she were a lightning rod, and a bolt of lightning, white hot, came out of the morning skies and shot straight through her.

Books by Cindy Holbrook

A SUITABLE CONNECTION
LADY MEGAN'S MASQUERADE
A DARING DECEPTION
COVINGTON'S FOLLY
A RAKE'S REFORM
LORD SAYER'S GHOST
THE ACTRESS AND THE MARQUIS
THE COUNTRY GENTLEMAN
MY LADY'S SERVANT

Published by Zebra Books

My Lady's
Servant

Cindy Holbrook

Zebra Books
Kensington Publishing Corp.
http://www.zebrabooks.com

ZEBRA BOOKS are published by

Kensington Publishing Corp.
850 Third Avenue
New York, NY 10022

Zebra and the Z logo Reg. U.S. Pat. & TM Off.

First Printing: June, 1998
10 9 8 7 6 5 4 3 2 1

Printed in the United States of America

One

"Faith, I am exhausted," Serena sighed, leaning her head back against the squabs of the coach as it rocked back and forth.

"It's your own fault," Lady Lucille said. "Why you had to go herring off from Brussels like this is beyond me."

Serena closed her eyes. "I told you, I did not intend to remain one moment longer in the same town with Darrel Applegate."

"Why these dramatics I don't know," Lady Lucille said. "It was you who jilted Darrel, and not the other way around." Lady Lucille sat up suddenly and her face showed a spark of interest. "Or did he do the jilting? Is that the truth?" She leaned closer. "Tell me, dearest, did you catch him at something? Never say you caught him in an affair."

Serena lifted a brow. "Darrel? Are you serious?"

Lady Lucille fell back against the cushions. "No, I suppose not. How absolutely disappointing."

"Yes," Serena said with a chuckle. "I knew you would see it that way. No, I jilted Darrel because I found him a dead bore. The man had no conversation, unless it was to pinch at me over some silly thing."

"Well, dearest," Lady Lucille said, leaning back, "I told you when you accepted his proposal he was a dull fellow and would drive you mad."

"Yes," Serena agreed without much heat. "But after Alfredo's histrionics, Darrel seemed just the type of man I wanted. He seemed so sensible."

" 'Tis because he is," Lady Lucille said, laughing. Then she sobered. "No, you need a different type of man than Darrel Applegate, my love."

"Lucille, I've been engaged five times and jilted every one of them," Serena reminded the older woman. "I doubt there is a type of man I *haven't* met. No," she said, shaking her head. "I am through with men. They are far more trouble than they are worth."

"No, dear." Lady Lucille's eyes sparkled. "They are most definitely worth the trouble . . . if you find the right ones. Your problem is, you have always dallied with nice boys."

"Boys!" Serena exclaimed. "Roger was all of twenty years older than I."

"And everything that was polite and correct." Lady Lucille nodded. "He was still a boy, despite his age. What you need is a man. One who won't be bowled over by your beauty, nor intimidated by your obscene wealth. One who won't let you play your tricks on him like you do."

"Lucille," Serena warned, narrowing her eyes. "If you say I need a man to tame me, I'll . . . I'll . . . well, I don't know what I'll do, but I assure you, it won't be pleasant."

"Tame you?" Lady Lucille laughed. "Gracious, no. Such an archaic thought. Besides, it is always the woman who must tame the man. The men you've been engaged to were fully tamed before you met them. Well-bred lap dogs, to be exact. There is no passion in that. And you," Lucille said as she pointed a finger at Serena, "are a passionate woman."

"Me? Passionate?" Serena stared at Lucille and then laughed. "Evidently you haven't been listening to the gossips. Don't you know I am a heartless jilt and careless flibbertigibbet?"

Lady Lucille waved her hand. "You know I never listen to gossip. Society as a collective is imbecilic. It never ceases to amaze me. People can be quite intelligent individuals when in the singular, but put them together as a group and let them come up with a notion and, I assure you, they will have it all wrong. They'll have a horse's legs on his back and his rump where his head should be." She looked closely at Serena. "I thought I taught you better."

"Yes, you taught me better," Serena affirmed. In truth, Lady Lucille lived her instructions. As a widow of many years, she'd had so many affairs that even society forgot to be scandalized. "But I fear in this instance, society is correct. I am far more heartless than passionate. And as for taming or being tamed, it sounds like so much hog slop to me."

"Serena." Lucille sighed. "I abhor your choice of words. So indelicate. But you still do not understand. 'Tis not that a man and woman should tame each other. Once again, how boring. But 'tis their passions they tame together, until they run well in tandem." She smiled. "My Ivan and I did that. We made a wild and glorious team."

Serena stared. Lucille rarely talked about her one and only husband. "Do you miss him?"

"Miss him?" Lady Lucille smiled. "If Ivan had lived we would have been the swiftest and surest of teams, and oh the miles we would have covered. Yet he had to go and kill himself in that race. I must confess that at first I did not forgive him for dying. But I soon did. Being angry at a dead man is so very exhausting, not to mention futile."

The smile still played upon Lucille's lips. "And then I grew to realize that I have been, and am, a singularly

blessed woman. I have had one passionate and true
love. So few do. And since Ivan left me, I have had other
delightful experiences. Small passions, admittedly, but
each one different. When you add them all up, they
make a wondrous whole." She shook her head. "No, I
have had my one and true love. I need not ask for more.
'Tis you who still need to find yours."

Serena shivered. She wasn't certain why. "No. I don't.
I am finished with men, and that is that."

"Hmm, yes," Lady Lucille murmured. "But are the
men finished with you? That is the question."

Serena chose to ignore that comment as the coach
slowed. "Thank God we are here. I am so exhausted I
could cry. I cannot wait to sleep in my own bed again."

The door opened and Callens, their coachman, stuck
his head in. "I'm sorry, Lady Serena, but there might
be a problem."

Serena was already moving toward the door. "Whatever it is, Callens, it can wait until the morning." She
waved him aside and alighted. Then she stopped and
stared. The townhouse in front of her was dark. Nary
a light shone, and no doubt the knocker was removed.

"What is it?" Lady Lucille asked, from behind.

Serena stamped her foot. "Oh, blast. I totally forgot.
Robby has had the townhouse closed up."

"What?" Lady Lucille cried.

"He had written that he intended to do so," Serena
said, glaring at the darkened abode as if it, itself, had
purposely betrayed her. "But I thought it nothing more
than a jest."

"Whyever would he close up the townhouse?" Exasperation tinged Lady Lucille's voice as she questioned
Serena.

"I have no notion. Some nonsensical drivel about
practicing economy. He planned to send the servants to
Chesmire."

"Economy? Robby?" Lady Lucille raised her brow. "A man with his kind of wealth should never practice economy. It is indecent and blasphemous." She sighed. "I fear the military has addled the poor boy's brains. Well, what are we to do? Go to the Grillons'?"

Serena snorted. "That should create quite a nice brouhaha. 'Tis three in the morning. The gossipmongers will have enough fodder without us adding to it by appearing in such disrepair at a Grillons'. They will think I was routed from Brussels."

"And weren't you?" Lady Lucille asked.

"No, I wasn't. I simply didn't wish to remain and suffer Darrel's long face and wounded sensibilities." Serena sighed. "Though I own I had hoped for a few days of peace and quiet before everyone became aware of our arrival in town. No," she said, stepping forward with sudden determination. "We will stay here the night."

"Without servants?" Lady Lucille exclaimed.

"Without servants." Serena laughed. "You can survive it for one night, Lucille."

"Just because I *can,*" Lady Lucille said, her tone severe, "does not mean I wish to do so."

Serena prodded her forward. "Oh, do come on. My bed is waiting for me. That is all that matters."

Serena walked up the stairs, lifting her candle high. She was exhausted to her very bones, each and every one of which she could readily identify by their particular ache and pain. A well-sprung carriage was nothing but a myth. She'd left Lucille downstairs. That lady had declared she was famished and intended to discover the kitchen and forage. What she hoped to find there was beyond Serena's comprehension, but Lucille had sworn that if there was even one piece of cheese left in the larder, she'd do battle with the mice for it.

The mice were in for it tonight, Serena thought. Chuckling, she opened the door to her room. The chuckle died in her throat and she froze. She blinked hard and then blinked again. It was no hallucination. There was a man in *her bed,* comfortably arranged beneath *her* covers.

"Good God!" Serena exclaimed, frustrated to the breaking point. All she wanted to do was sleep and now there was some infernal man in her bed. There was no escaping the insidious creatures! "What the devil are you doing here?"

"Sleeping," the man said, sitting up. The covers slipped down, exposing a broad, muscled chest, totally unclad by anything such as a nightshirt. Only the length of his blond hair cloaked his bared shoulders. "What are *you* doing here?"

Serena choked. "What am *I* doing here?"

"Yes," the man said, his tone sharp. His arm moved from beneath the cover. Suddenly he leveled a pistol unwaveringly upon her. "Who are you?"

Serena started back, her mouth dropping open. "Who am *I*?"

"That is what I asked."

"Since you ask so politely," Serena said sarcastically, her gaze scathing as she focused upon the gun, "I will tell you. *I* am Serena Fairchild. This is my house, this is my room, and that is my bed." She lifted her chin imperiously and stared him down in her most autocratic manner. The man might have the pistol, but she had the right. "Now sirrah, what is your explanation? And please be swift about it. I am quite weary and wish to go to sleep in my bed. Once you have vacated it, that is."

The man's brows flared and then he laughed. He tossed the pistol down upon the blanket. "You're Serena Fairchild, 'tis clear."

"I am so glad I didn't need to bring my cards of introduction with me," Serena cooed. "I simply didn't think I required them in my own room." He merely chuckled and Serena stiffened, misliking the laughter in his dark brown eyes. "Of course I am Serena Fairchild. Who else would I be?"

"You could have been a burglar."

"A burglar?" Serena asked, indignant. "Do I look like a burglar?"

"Why have you returned from Brussels?" the man countered.

"I beg your pardon?"

"You are supposed to be in Brussels," the man said in a patient tone. "Why have you returned?"

"I . . ." Serena halted, flushing. She glared at him. " 'Tis none of your bloody business."

"Let me guess," the man said, his tone dry. "You threw that last fiancé of yours over. Appledorp? Or Appleface. Or was it Pineapple?"

"It was Applebee," Serena snapped. "Er . . . I mean, Applegate. And I did not throw him over!"

"He threw you over?" the man asked, his brow raising.

"No, he didn't throw me over." Serena lifted her chin. "I—I merely terminated our engagement. Now who in blazes are you?"

"Temper, temper," the man said, smiling.

The candle in Serena's hand shook. "I asked, who are you?"

"I'm Tom," the man said, smiling. "The overseer. Your brother hired me."

"Robby hired you?" Serena asked, stupefied. "I don't believe it."

"Well, he did," Tom said. "I'm to take care of the townhouse. It *is* closed up, after all."

His tone clearly implied she was an unwanted inter-

loper. "No, it *was* closed up. I am here now and I intend
to open it up."

"Do you?" The man positively glowered at her.

Serena glowered right back. "I do. And as such, I will
not require your services anymore, my good man."

"I beg your pardon?" Tom asked.

"You certainly may and should," Serena said, tartly.
"I have never heard of an overseer being so . . . so impudent as to appropriate the mistress's bedroom."

"Well," he drawled, "it does have the best view of the
street. And you weren't here. I thought there would be
no harm."

"No harm? I return home tired and weary to find
you in my bed, and you say there is no harm?"

He shrugged. "It's not as if you were in it. Now, *that*
I could see you objecting to . . ."

Serena flushed. "And y-you held a pistol upon
me . . ."

"Merely protecting the premises," he murmured.

"Protecting the premises, my . . . my foot!" Serena
said, and stamped that foresaid appendage. "You are
sacked, do you hear me? Now, get out of my bed! I want
to go to sleep."

"Serena!" Lucille's voice called. "You'll never guess
what I found . . ." Lady Lucille appeared in the doorway,
a chicken leg within her hand. She halted abruptly, her
green eyes widening as she took in the scene. A slow
smile crossed her lips as she surveyed Tom. "Rather, look
what *you've* found." She lowered her voice. "Dearest, I
thought you said you were through with men."

"Th-this is not a man," Serena sputtered. "He's the
overseer."

"Not a man?" Lucille asked, looking Tom up and
down with an appreciative eye. "My dear, he looks like
one to me."

Tom laughed. "Thank you, madame."

"Lucille," Serena said, pushed beyond her limits, "quit flirting with the jackanapes."

"Jackanapes?" Lady Lucille laughed. "He's displeased you, I see."

"Of course he has," Serena said. "He's in my bed . . ."

Lucille widened her eyes. "That is displeasing?"

"And he held a loaded pistol upon me!" Serena gritted.

"Did you?" Lady Lucille asked Tom, her lips twitching. "Which loaded pistol are we talking about?"

Tom laughed and lifted the pistol. "This one"

"Oh, *that* one," Lady Lucille said. Her eyes twinkled. "Not as intriguing, but most definitely a novel approach."

Tom laughed. "I thought she was a burglar."

"Well, I am not," Serena snapped. "I am the mistress of the house and you, sirrah, are sacked!"

"No, I'm not," Tom said, and actually settled back more comfortably upon Serena's pillows. "Your brother hired me and only he can fire me."

"What?" Serena all but shouted.

"He does have a point, Serena," Lady Lucille chuckled.

Serena turned and stared at Lucille. "You cannot agree with him!"

"But I do," Lucille said. "If he is Robby's man, you cannot sack him."

"Yes, I can!" Serena shrieked, her rage fueled high. She stalked over to the bed and slammed the candle down upon the bedside table. "Since I am here, and Robby is not, 'tis I who order the servants. I'll not tolerate insubordination. Now, get out of my bed this instant!"

Tom's eyes narrowed. "That is an order?"

"Yes," Serena said.

"Very well, *my lady,*" Tom said. He swiftly flung the covers back.

Serena saw a flash of lean naked male as he swung his legs over. Awesome, stunning male. She snapped her eyes shut as an inexplicable heat flashed through her. Surely it was from embarrassment. "Wh-what in God's name are you doing?"

"Just following orders, my lady. You did say upon the instant, didn't you?" Tom asked sharply. His voice seemed perilously close. Frightened, Serena opened her eyes. The man stood before her with only the sheet pulled over his narrow waist. She skittered back. He pinned her with an insolent gaze. "I wouldn't wish to be insubordinate."

"He follows orders admirably, I'd say," Lady Lucille murmured. "Quite admirably."

"G-get out of this house," Serena said, her voice shaking. "G-get out."

"No, my lady, that is one command you cannot give me," Tom said. "Now I'll gladly leave your bed. I've discovered 'tis the last place I would ever wish to be." Serena gasped at the patent insult, even as she heard Lucille chuckle. The man's angry eyes darkened to almost black. "But I'll not leave this house nor my post as overseer. I'll only accept that command from your brother."

Serena could only stare at him. He was nothing but a servant, and a naked one at that. By rights it should be he who was in the weaker position. She couldn't fathom why it was she who felt so terribly vulnerable.

She swallowed hard. "Get out. Do you hear me? Get out!" He started to move and she added hastily, "And take the damn sheet with you!"

He bowed. "You are too kind, mistress, but as your humble servant, I'd never be so impudent as to appropriate your fine sheet."

Serena's eyes widened. "Y-you w-wouldn't . . ."

The man did. He dropped the sheet in the most negligent of manner. Serena's mouth dropped open far less negligently. Her gaze flew to the man's face, for she daren't look anywhere else. He quirked a taunting brow and then, as bold as you please, and as naked as you please, he strolled from the room. Serena hadn't meant to look, but gave up all pretense and merely gaped until she saw the last of him.

"My God," Lady Lucille whispered, the chicken leg dropping from her fingers. "Now there is a man. In more ways than one."

Serena strove for a gasp of air, her heart pounding unreasonably fast. "H-he's not a man. H-he's . . . er . . . the overseer."

"My dear, I had the better view," Lady Lucille said. "You but saw him from the back. From the front he is—"

"Lucille!" Serena cried, flushing scarlet. "I don't want to hear it."

"Very well," Lady Lucille said. "But I did have the better view."

Serena began to shake and discovered she was wringing her hands. "We cannot have him in the house. We cannot!"

"My dear, he *is* in the house," Lucille said, "and clearly doesn't mean to leave."

Serena paced across the room. "I'll not tolerate his presence, I will not! I'll . . . I'll have him arrested, that is what I'll do."

"Why? The man simply followed your orders," Lady Lucille said. "To the letter, in fact. You can't bring him up on charges for that."

"I . . ." Serena snapped her mouth shut.

"And he is not trespassing," Lady Lucille continued, far too sensibly for Serena's liking. "Robby hired him to be the overseer. You'll appear the silliest widgeon if you call in the authorities merely to make a man desert the very post your brother hired him to fill."

Serena halted, staring at Lady Lucille in complete frustration. "I will not remain under the same roof as that . . . that man."

"Then, my dear," Lady Lucille said, "I'd advise we decamp."

"You mean leave?" Serena asked, stunned.

She shrugged. "We can still rack up at the Grillons. Though if word gets out that it wasn't Darrel Applegate who routed you, but a hired overseer . . ."

"No," Serena said sharply. "I'll not leave my house. Not for some rude, impudent servant."

Something twinkled in Lucille's eyes. "That's my girl. Don't let that man beat you. Now, go to bed."

"I will," Serena said, lifting her chin. She stalked to the bed and then halted. "The beast left his pistol."

"Oh?" Lady Lucille said, her voice docile. "I'll take it to him."

Serena glared. "No. I'll keep it." Her eyes narrowed. "Surely you do not intend to have an affair with that man? He's a servant!"

"And I'd love him to serve me." Lady Lucille sighed. She then shook her head. "No, I'll leave him alone. Though 'tis a shame. He's quite magnificent. But I don't think he's the man for me." Her smile turned whimsical. "I've already had my Ivan."

With that odd remark, Lady Lucille stooped to pick up her chicken leg and then sauntered from the room. Serena stared after her a moment and then shook herself.

"The entire world has gone mad," she muttered, then stalked over to the bureau and drew out a nightgown. Unlike some people, she was not so indecent as to go to bed without proper attire. Still fuming and sputtering, she changed quickly and paced to her bed, scrabbling under the covers. She let out a shriek as she felt a cold, alien weight against her. Searching, she discovered the pistol. Holding it by two fingers, she laid it upon the bedside table.

"Utterly mad," she murmured and blew out the candle. She burrowed under the covers she had fought so fiercely to secure and drew in a deep breath. She immediately shivered. Her bed didn't smell like her bed. It had a different scent. Of shaving soap and man. Definitely of man.

A heat flashed through her and she closed her eyes tightly, trying to block out every thought. She'd have the sheets washed tomorrow, see if she didn't!

But before falling asleep she inhaled deeply again despite herself.

Two

Nicholas St. Irving, the Earl of Claremont, moved silently about the kitchen, putting on the tea to boil, slicing off a large piece of bread and then cheese. A dark frown marred his brow and his mood matched his scowl. His leg hurt as well as every other muscle in his body. He hadn't found one infernal bed in the servants' quarters which matched his length and size.

"Good morning, Tom," a bright, cheery voice said.

Nicholas looked up to discover Lady Lucille standing in the kitchen doorway. A smile came to his lips, despite himself. The lady was not only dressed most elegantly, but she also had the merriest of smiles. "Good morning, my lady."

"Do you mind if I join you?" Lady Lucille asked, walking to the kitchen table.

"Not at all. But if you wish, I will serve you in the dining room."

"Oh, no," Lady Lucille said, sitting down. She glanced around the kitchen. "This is quite cozy and unique. The rough and ready, as it were." She cast him a droll look. "Perhaps I could become a soldier."

Nicholas laughed, his eyes gleaming. "I would not advise it, my lady."

Lady Lucille's eyes gleamed back, with far more understanding than he expected from a lady of her standing. "No, you are right. Despite all the talk, there is no glory in war."

"No, there isn't," Nicholas agreed.

"Besides, from what I've heard, they'd not let me take more than a dress or two," Lady Lucille said lightly. "That would never do." Then she said, just as casually, "That is where you got that nasty scar, I assume. A ball to the hip, was it?"

"Yes," Nicholas said, stiffening. "But it is mending."

Lucille laughed. "So, I noticed." Her eyes turned teasing. "Among other things."

"You must forgive me for last night," Nicholas said. "What I did was atrocious."

"Don't apologize to me, dear boy," Lady Lucille said. "I was quite entertained and delighted, I assure you. I've never been one to demand strict formality between servants and employers."

Nicholas laughed, pouring the tea and handing it to Lady Lucille. "Unlike Lady Serena."

"Hmm, yes," Lady Lucille murmured, taking the cup. "You did shock poor Serena."

"I find that difficult to believe," Nicholas said, slicing off a few more pieces of bread. "She has had *five fiancés.*"

"All of them very proper," Lady Lucille commented softly before sipping from her tea. "And dead bores."

"Two words rarely applied to the lady Serena from what I've heard," Nicholas said dryly.

Lucille looked at him, an odd smile upon her lips. "Serena is not an easily understood woman. I've had the care of her since she turned sixteen, after her dear mother and father had that unfortunate carriage accident, and she still surprises me. She is far more innocent than many would believe."

"If you say so," Nicholas said, discounting her every word as he walked to the pantry and withdrew the last of the chicken. With Lady Lucille, anyone could seem innocent. He returned to the table, determined to be polite. "I'll strive not to shock her so. As I said, I know my behavior last night went beyond the pale. I fear I lost my temper."

"Yes," Lady Lucille agreed, her tone mild. "No doubt you got that from your father."

Nicholas tensed. "I beg your pardon?"

Lady Lucille smiled. "I'm sorry, but you do have the look of the late Earl of Claremont."

"Do I?" Nicholas asked cautiously.

"I knew him well when we were young," Lady Lucille said with a chuckle. Her fine brow arched. "As did many other ladies."

Relief washed over Nicholas. Thank heaven the woman had such a worldly mind. He forced a laugh. "My mother was one of the others, I fear. Though . . . she did not have the title of lady."

Lady Lucille nodded. "I see Adam did right by you. 'Tis clear you have had an education."

Nicholas grinned. "Only seamstress's son who did."

"I always liked Adam for that." Lady Lucille smiled even wider. "He was a wild rake in his younger days before he married Fanny Duval, but he never shirked his responsibilities."

"I was beholden to the man," Nicholas said.

"Does the family know about you?" Lady Lucille asked.

"No," Nicholas said quickly. "That is . . . the ladies don't. And I wouldn't want them to know."

"Of course not," Lady Lucille said. "Fanny is a dear, but she would never understand." She laughed. "Like all reformed rakes, Adam kept his own women quite protected and innocent."

"Indeed?" Nicholas asked, frowning.

"Though his son, his legitimate one that is, certainly followed in Adam's earlier footsteps."

A twinge of remorse passed through Nicholas. "Yes. I heard he was a bane to his mother."

"A bane to Fanny?" Lady Lucille asked. "Gracious, no. She adores her son, no matter what he did, or does, should I say. Though we in the ton haven't seen Rake St. Irving for years. He used to keep the gossip mill well turned, but then he up and joined the military and seemed to drop off the face of the planet."

"He grew tired of his wastrel life," Nicholas said, gritting his teeth.

Lady Lucille's eyes widened. "What?"

Nicholas started. He cast her one considering glance. The woman was far too perspicuous. He thought quickly. "You see, I met the earl when in the service."

"You did?" Lady Lucille grinned. "I'm sure that was an experience. He did not take exception to your existence?"

"No, not at all," Nicholas said.

"Stands to reason," Lady Lucille said with a nod. "I'm sure he has a few by-blows of his own. He certainly couldn't cast stones at his father."

Nicholas clenched his jaw. As far as he knew, he didn't have any by-blows. Many things could be said about his past, and had been said, but one thing he'd always made sure of was that he dallied with experienced women who knew how to take care of themselves. "No, of course not."

"So, tell me more?" Lady Lucille asked, her tone eager.

Nicholas shrugged. "There wasn't any more. We met, shared a drink or two, and left it at that." He forced a grin. "I must confess, we looked too damn much alike for it to be comfortable. It was like looking in a mirror."

"God forbid." Lady Lucille laughed. They then fell

companionably silent for a moment while they ate. Lady Lucille took a bite of chicken. "Did you cook this?"

"Yes, I did," Nicholas confirmed. " 'Tis simple fare, but I only know camp cooking."

"Don't worry. Serena has already gone to the employment agency. We shall have a full staff by this evening."

"What?" Nicholas roared, before he could stop himself.

Lady Lucille jumped. Then she raised her brow. "We should have a full staff by this evening. I thought you would be happy. You certainly won't want to be the only servant, especially when Serena starts entertaining."

"She intends to entertain?" Nicholas asked, this time more calmly. "I would think she'd wish to live quietly, all things considered."

"You mean because she's jilted Applegate?" Lady Lucille asked. "Heavens, no. Whyever would she want to do that? The best thing for her to do is to go right back into the thick of things. You've been a soldier. You know the best defense is attack." She rose with a smile. "Thank you for breakfast." She strolled toward the door. Then she stopped. "Oh, I forgot. Serena intends to be out for the day and I've decided to visit Lady Melton. Will you oversee the new servants and show them their places when they arrive?"

"Most certainly," Nicholas murmured.

"Thank you," Lady Lucille said with a smile and departed.

Nicholas stared after her, anger building within him. Damn and blast! He and Robby had set everything up flawlessly. He'd had a perfect hiding place, until now. A place where he could recuperate in peace without fear of discovery. No one knew he was in town. Not even his own mother and sister. Which was for the best. Not only for his sanity, since he never doubted they would have fussed and coddled him to death, but for their own safety as well.

Someday he would deal with the hotheaded Frenchman who lusted after his blood, but it would be upon his own terms in his own time. He'd not let his family become involved, nor would he fight until he had his full strength back.

Nicholas stifled a curse. Yes, everything had been perfect. Until the spoiled, capricious Lady Serena had decided to jilt her fiancé and return to London. He'd joined the military to escape women just like her. Now she was not only here, but expected to entertain society as well.

He chuckled. It was not a pleasant sound. Lady Lucille had said the best defense was attack. He'd plan his own attack. He'd not have the house overrun with servants and society. This was his bolt hold and Lady Serena would just have to go and find herself a different one.

Nicholas shook his stinging hand and looked down to the man sprawled upon the kitchen floor. "Do you still want to be in Lady Serena's employ?"

The man swiped the blood from his lip. "You bloody son of a bitch!"

"Do you?" Nicholas asked implacably. "Or do you wish to take my advice and find employment elsewhere?"

The man glared at him. "I'll find employment elsewhere."

Nicholas grinned. "Excellent. You would have found the lady Serena a difficult employer." He lowered his voice to a conspiratorial whisper. "She has a temper, you know."

The man crawled up from the floor and groaned. "Go to hell."

A knock sounded at the back kitchen door. Nicholas strolled over to it. "My good man, this is hell." He opened the door to discover a young man standing on the doorstep, paper in hand.

"Excuse me," he stammered. "But is this 'ere the lady Fairchild's 'ome?"

"It is," Nicholas nodded. "And I'm the overseer."

The boy beamed. "Yer the one I'm suppose ter see."

"Come in," Nicholas said. He looked to the other man. "This gentleman was just leaving."

The man glared through his bruises and limped toward the door, cursing up a fine stream. When he departed, the boy stared after him. "Gore, what happened to him?"

"We had a disagreement about terms of employment," Nicholas said. He looked at the boy, who goggled at him. "Now, if you take my advice, you will permit me to pay you your severance pay."

"Wh-whot?" the boy stammered. "B-but I ain't started working here yet."

"And you don't want to, my boy," Nicholas said firmly. "You must understand, the lady Serena is dangerous."

"Wh-whot?" squealed the boy.

"Dicked in the nob," Nicholas said, tapping his head. "She's been known to throw knives at disobliging servants."

"Blimy," the boy breathed, eyes bulging.

"Yes," Nicholas nodded. "Why last night, she stormed into my bedroom and screamed for me to get out of my bed."

"B-but why?" the boy asked.

"She claimed it was her own bed," Nicholas said. He

shook his head. "I tell you, lad, I consider myself a brave man, but I fled. Naked, mind you."

"Gawd." The boy blinked. "And she seemed such a perty and nice lady."

Nicholas leaned forward and whispered, "Her beauty hides madness. I suffer it, because I have nowhere else to go." He pulled out a few coins. "But you should save yourself when you can. Take the severance pay and run, my boy. Run!"

"That I will," the boy said, snatching it from him. He charged toward the door. "Be Jesus. I gots to warn Jake. He was coming ter work here."

"You do that," Nicholas said to the slamming of the door.

Whistling, he strolled over and sat down in the chair to await the next candidate's arrival.

"Mister Tom says he'll have the coach drawn round shortly," Tandy said as she fiddled with Serena's hair, jerking on a curl so sharply as to make Serena jump.

"Does he?" Serena tried to hold her temper as she quickly reached up and clamped Tandy's hand. Never had she had such a fiddle-fingered ladies' maid before in her life, nor so inexperienced a one. But then again, never had she had such a dirth of staff before.

For three days she'd been hiring and hiring. Yet, no servants ever showed up, except the green ones fresh from the country. That impertinent upstart, Tom, had intimated it was most likely because the London servants did not wish to work for a woman with a reputation like hers. A coil of indignation sprang up in Serena. How dare he act so sanctimonious, and how dare her lessers think to pass judgment upon her!

Her peers and the ton accepted her still and that was what mattered. Indeed, some had appeared cooler, but none of them dared to cut her. She tossed her head. Nor should they. She'd not marry some boor, simply for society's comfort. Deep in her heart, she would own to her mistake, as she had with all her other fiancés, but never would she admit it to the outside world. Nor would she permit them to stricture her. She fully believed in Lady Lucille's dictate that a woman was a fool if she ever let society rule her. She must rule society instead.

A feline grin curved her lips and she stared into the mirror. Tonight she would definitely rule society. Her raven-black hair was drawn back severely, except the two loose tendrils, one of which she was wresting from Tandy's hand. Her green eyes glittered, and looked all the larger from the proficient use of makeup. Her sapphire dress was the most risqué of the French fashion, with its clean, empire line; its stunning, low, sheer bodice. She had dampened her petticoats and they clung to her full, but lithe figure. It was not a dress of apology to the world, but one of demand and blatant pride.

"And Mister Tom says . . ." Tandy began.

"I do not care what Mister Tom says," Serena said, clenching her teeth. Faith, she was tired of hearing about the man. He clearly oversaw her meager staff with an iron hand. Except the maids, that was. The silly twits were all in love with him. An image of him, naked and walking proudly from her room, flashed through her mind and a faintness overtook her. She then shook herself sternly and lifted her chin. She was not some poor maid to fall in love with such a beast, nor was she the one ever to be ruled. "I am ready."

"Oh, yes, mum . . . I mean, my lady," Tandy said, and hurried to snatch up Serena's opera cloak and reticule.

"Thank you." Serena forced a smile. Inept Tandy was, but the child did try.

Serena nodded her head and walked from her room,

through the hall, and down the stairs. She stopped in midflight, however, and stared. Tom, who stood post at the front door as footman and butler, was dressed in the green of her livery, but the outfit had been altered, with fine lace at the neck and cuffs. He also wore paint and had powdered his blond hair. He looked like a Georgian gentleman, and an aristocratic one at that.

"Good God!" Serena cried, walking down the last few steps. "Why are you dressed like that?"

He walked up to her and bowed. "I am my lady's servant, am I not? As such, I did not wish to appear common. Though I see that my lady wishes to do so."

Serena stiffened. "What?"

"You look like an Orange Street trollop," he said, his voice low and stern.

"I beg your pardon!" Serena gasped.

"No, I take that back," he said, more calmly.

Serena nodded her head sharply. "You had better."

"You look like a paphian instead," Nicholas said. "On the hunt for a new protector to mount her."

"How dare you!" Serena gasped, enraged. Her hand automatically flew out to slap him. Pain, sharp and hot, speared through her wrist as he caught it tightly, mere inches from his face.

He stood looking down at her, his dark eyes glittering. "Don't you ever try that again."

Serena blinked back stinging tears, stunned. Never in her life had she struck a servant. Yet this man, this commoner, had dared to say things to her no one ever had before. Now his eyes were implacable, his voice the one which brooked no disobedience. A shiver ran down her, one close to fear, but she stood her ground, lifting her chin. A suspended moment passed, green eyes staring into brown, wills matched and neither turning back.

"What in heaven's name is going on here?" Lady Lucille's voice exclaimed.

Nicholas's hand gentled around Serena's wrist, and he released it as she slowly lowered it. Yet just before they withdrew their hands, they touched in the slightest clasp. There was no reasoning for it, but his fingers curved around hers and she returned the clasp for a moment, as if her hand had acted on its own accord.

Serena looked away quickly and toward Lady Lucille's voice. She stood on the steps, her hands upon her hips. Serena flushed. "H-he insulted me."

"She should change her dress," Nicholas said, his voice firm.

"I will not," Serena shot back. The safety of her ire returned, blurring the strange emotions of before. "You should change yours. I'll not have my footman looking like my grandfather!"

"Tsk, tsk," Lady Lucille said, walking down the stairs. Her gaze roamed over Nicholas for a moment and then lightened. "Most excellent, Tom, your innovation is astounding."

He nodded. "I strive to please."

"No," Serena said, her eyes narrowed. "You strive to infuriate."

"Serena, dear," Lady Lucille said. "Do come down out of the boughs. I think he looks famous. You shall set a trend with him. Every lady will want to dress her footmen like that." Then she studied Serena herself. "And you, my dear, have outdone yourself. You'll make the ton sit up and take notice for sure."

"As well as every rake, rouge and cad," Nicholas said.

"And what if I do?" Serena snapped back. "I shall . . ."

"Children," Lady Lucille scolded, a hint of laughter in her voice. "Do you wish to stand here and brangle all night, or are we going to the opera?"

Serena flushed, lifting her head. "I am going to the opera."

Nicholas's face darkened, even beneath his paint, and he bowed. "Of course, my lady."

Serena cast him a glittering, dangerous look and swept by him.

She cast him the same glittering look when he helped her down from the carriage before the opera, while everyone stared at them. She might have caught the men's attention, but many a lady whispered and pointed her fan at her footman.

Smiling coldly, Serena swept into the opera house and found her box. She stood looking about and waving to friends, all the while her anger building to a reckless height. She had forgotten she had planned to rule society tonight. Now she sought only to rule the strange wildness within her. She felt an unknown, rebellious passion. Formless, with no direction.

She found that direction, however, at intermission. Lord Andrews, a man she rarely held conversation with and who was considered not only a rake, but a dangerous one, entered her box. Normally Serena steered clear of men such as he. Not so, tonight. She felt dangerous herself. No man, especially a servant, would tell her what to do.

She flirted recklessly with Lord Andrews, feeling a triumph each time his wicked eyes sparked at her sallies. She also said yes when he asked in a liquid voice of sensuality if he could call upon her the next day. Serena totally ignored Lady Lucille's lifted brow and dry comment about flirting with danger.

"Are you sure you don't wish to come with me, dear?" Lady Lucille asked, drawing on her gloves and picking up her reticule from the table in the foyer.

"I'm sure," Serena laughed. "Lady Mortimar's gatherings generally leave me all at sea."

"Yes, they are excessively military," Lady Lucille murmured. Her eyes twinkled. "But Sir Alfred plans to attend."

"How is Sir Alfred? I hope he has survived his wife's passing."

Lady Lucille laughed. "He is on the road to recovery, I believe."

"How could he not be," Serena murmured. "With your kind assistance?"

"I am a charitable woman."

Serena laughed. "Do have fun, dear. But please, no scandals."

"I should say the same to you," Lady Lucille said pointedly.

Serena flushed. "No, of course not."

"Good," Lady Lucille said, walking toward the door. "Lord Andrews is not the man to play with."

"Goodbye," Serena said, making a face at Lucille. Lucille merely chuckled, waved her hand and closed the door. Serena sighed in relief. In truth, Lady Lucille hadn't needed to make a comment, for upon a night of sleep, and a cooler temper, Serena had realized she truly did not wish to begin anything with Lord Andrews. Now, without Lucille present, she could honestly deny his company if he called.

"What is this about Andrews?" an angry, male voice demanded.

Serena jumped and spun around. Nicholas, dressed in his ostentatious livery, was striding toward her. His face was not convivial. Serena frowned. "Where did you come from?"

"I was merely passing through the foyer when I heard Lord Andrews's name mentioned."

"Were you?" Serena asked coolly. "Are you sure you weren't spying? It seems to me you take your *overseeing* of this household a bit too far."

"What is this about Lord Andrews?" Nicholas asked bluntly.

Serena lifted her chin. "Nothing. We had a pleasant chat at the opera last night, 'tis all."

"Nothing is pleasant about Andrews," Nicholas said. "You shouldn't even be talking to a man like him. I told you that dress you wore last night would attract the worst kind of attention."

"You are wrong," Serena said, firing up. "Lord Andrews's attentions were all that were flattering. He is a very intriguing and cultured man, I hope you know!"

"He is a loose screw," Nicholas said. "And worse."

Serena lifted a taunting brow. "You do like to try and pass judgment upon your betters, don't you?"

"He's not my better," Nicholas said, clenching his fists. "Not by a long chalk."

"I certainly find him so," Serena said, smiling sweetly. "He is a gentleman."

Nicholas snorted. "Gentleman by title, perhaps, but nothing else."

"At least he has a title," Serena said angrily. "While you have neither the title of gentleman nor the behavior of one. And still you delude yourself in believing you have the right to criticize people so far above you—"

"Damn it," Nicholas said. "I am warning you. Andrews isn't above a garden slug. He is the lowest form on earth."

A rap at the door interrupted Nicholas's tirade.

Serena took advantage of it to lift a brow and say, "Do you mind? Or must I answer it?"

"I'll answer it," Nicholas said angrily and stalked over to the door and ripped it open. Lord Andrews, dressed to the nines and cane in hand, stood upon the stoop. "Speak of garden creatures," Nicholas said lowly. He looked directly at Lord Andrews and said in a cold voice, "Lady Serena is not at home."

Serena gasped in pure disbelief as Nicholas then slammed the door shut.

"What the devil are you doing?" she shouted. She bolted over to the door, slapped Nicholas's hand away, and grabbed the handle.

"Don't open it," Nicholas growled.

"I will, blast you," Serena cried, jerking the door open.

"I beg pardon?" Lord Andrews asked in a stunned voice as he stared at Serena.

Serena flushed and attempted to gain her breath. "Forgive me. My footman and I were having a . . . a discussion." Lord Andrews's brows rose. "Er, not a discussion. H-he misunderstood my . . . instructions." Serena smiled her most charming smile. "He gets confused easily."

"Does he?" Lord Andrews asked. "I could well understand his condition. Your beauty does that to a man, no matter his station."

Serena laughed lightly, even as she cast Nicholas a triumphant look. He merely crossed his arms and glowered. "You are too kind, my lord."

Lord Andrews bowed. "I only speak the truth." Then he smiled a devastating smile. "May I be so bold as to hope you will invite me in?"

"No, my lord," Nicholas said before Serena could even speak. "My lady is not receiving today."

"I beg your pardon?" Lord Andrews said, rightfully glaring at Nicholas as if he had spoken out of turn.

"She's not receiving," Nicholas said, performing a mere pretense of a bow. "That is what I meant to say before."

"But I *am* receiving," Serena said, leveling her own glare.

"I was trying to inform you," Nicholas said, his voice low, "that the lady Lucille is not present. You would not wish to receive a gentleman alone, would you? 'Twould not be proper."

"Gads!" Lord Andrews laughed. "Is this servant giving you lessons in etiquette, Lady Serena? I'd not thought to see the day."

Serena forced a smile. "You must forgive him, my lord. He is new to the job. Quite green, in fact."

Nicholas leaned close to her and whispered, "I'm not the one who's green."

"What did he say?" Lord Andrews's brow lowered.

"Nothing." Serena lifted her chin. "His confusion again. I fear he mistakes me for some young debutante straight out of the schoolroom who must need constant chaperonage. He also doesn't understand, since he is not of the upper classes, that you are a gentleman, and as such, would never do anything improper. Now, would you?" Serena asked, batting her lashes.

Lord Andrews laughed and bowed. "Of course not, my lady."

"See, Tom." Serena smiled at him. "Now do go and order us tea." Ignoring the spark in her servant's eye, she then said to Lord Andrews, "Please, come in, my lord."

Lord Andrews grinned. "Thank you, my lady." He entered and held out his hat and cane for Nicholas to take.

Nicholas didn't move one jot, but only stared at him obdurately.

"My hat and cane, old man," Lord Andrews said, his eyes narrowing.

Both men then glared at each other like two male dogs meeting for the first time.

"For goodness' sakes," Serena muttered. She grabbed hold of Lord Andrews's arm, and, regardless of ceremony, dragged him toward the parlor. Only when she had shoved Lord Andrews through the door did she discover that Nicholas still obstinately followed them.

"Tom, do go get the tea," Serena said. Fully irate, she slammed the parlor door shut in his face. Trying to shake off her anger, she turned with a forced smile to Lord Andrews. "New servants," Serena sighed, shaking her head. "They are so taxing."

"Never mind him," Lord Andrews said, laughing. "We're alone, at last."

Serena stiffened, and put on her most dignified expression. "Won't you please have a seat, my lord?"

Nicholas stood, rage shooting through him. Damn the woman. She was either a jade of the first water or the most stupid of women. Lord Andrews was one of the worst rakes ever known. Not only were Lord Andrews's cruel and unusual appetites well known in the bawdyhouses of London, but he was also known to have ruined two girls of good standing. He was a leech, which clung to society's back, and now Serena had sequestered herself with him. And had ordered, him, Nicholas St. Irving, to serve them tea.

Cursing long and fluidly, Nicholas strode through the house and into the kitchen. He all but gnashed his teeth as he told the new French chef, Louis, to prepare tea.

"Oui," Louis said with a nod and smile. Humming, the little Frenchman set about putting the pot on to boil and setting out the silver tea service.

Ignoring Louis's good humor, Nicholas paced the kitchen. He swore he didn't care. Whatever was transpiring within the parlor at this moment wasn't his concern after all. Serena had asked for whatever happened. She'd just said she wasn't some debutante from the schoolroom. She knew what she was doing. He halted. But then again, Lord Andrews had said he was a perfect gentleman as well. That Nicholas knew was a complete lie.

"Damn it," Nicholas muttered. He wasn't going to let Serena be either seduced or raped by Lord Andrews. Not when he was in the house. He owed that much to Robby. "Is the tea ready?"

Louis jumped at Nicholas's fierce tone. "But, no. The water, it is not boiling."

"Forget it," Nicholas said. Stalking over, he snatched the kettle from the fire.

"What are you doing?" Louis asked, wide-eyed.

"I'll make the tea," Nicholas growled. He carried the kettle over and poured the water into the silver pot.

"But it is not even warm!" Louis cried.

"It might be warmer than you think," Nicholas muttered, and ruthlessly tossed the tea into the pot and shut the lid. He lifted the tray. "I'm going to serve the tea now."

"Y-you cannot serve it that way," Louis cried, rushing over.

"Watch me," Nicholas countered and headed toward the door.

"But the cream and sugar!" Louis implored, aghast. He snatched up the crockery and scurried to slam it onto Nicholas's tray.

"Thank you," Nicholas gritted. He charged through the house and reached the parlor in record time. He swore at the closed door, shifted the tray, and opened it. Once again securing the tray with both hands, he entered. Then he froze. Red washed his vision. Serena and Lord Andrews rolled upon the sofa in a blatant display of passion, he atop her.

Nicholas bit back a curse and turned to leave, but a hand movement of Serena's caught his attention. He turned back. Her one hand was outstretched and scrabbling upon the table beside the sofa. It grasped a letter opener and lifted it high over Lord Andrews's shoulder.

Nicholas's eyes widened as she started to bring it down. He barked loudly, "No, Serena!"

Serena's hand froze. Lord Andrew, unaware of his impending death by letter opener, lifted his head only slightly and muttered, "What?"

"Tea is served," Nicholas said, stalking over to the sofa with the tray.

Lord Andrews lifted his head higher, his face dark with lust. "Leave us."

"I said, tea is served," Nicholas growled. With a swiftness, he upended the tray, crockery, teapot, and all, on top of Lord Andrews. Lord Andrews roared, while Serena shrieked beneath him.

"Damn you!" Lord Andrews exclaimed, scrabbling up from the couch, his face enraged.

"More, my lord?" Nicholas asked, and swung the tray up to crash it over Lord Andrews's head. Andrews stumbled to the ground.

"G-good service," Serena said. Her voice was shaky as she sat up.

"Are you all right?" Nicholas asked, sidestepping the stunned Andrews and going to her.

"Of course," Serena said. She stood up unsteadily. "S-see."

"I see," Nicholas growled and hauled her to him, holding her close. Serena didn't fight him, but only gave him a wan smile. Her eyes were hollow, and her lip had blood upon it. "You're bleeding."

"No," Serena said. "It's his blood."

"Is it?" Nicholas asked, breaking into a grin.

"Damn you," Lord Andrews said hoarsely from the floor. "I'll have you horsewhipped for this."

"No, you won't," Serena said. The vitality flared back

into her eyes. She pulled from Nicholas's arms and rounded upon Andrews. "You'll not lift a hand to my servant, is that understood?"

"That's her job," Nicholas murmured, both amazed and amused at the woman's fighting spirit.

Some of Serena's stiffness disappeared and she chuckled. "Yes, that's my job."

Lord Andrews glared up at her. "You laugh at me?"

"No," Serena said. "I wouldn't even waste that much on you. You are pathetic." She walked around Andrews, stumbling slightly over the scattered tea items, and went to the chair which held Andrews's hat and cane. She picked them up and literally tossed them at the man. "Now, get out. Or I'll have Tom throw you out!"

"It would be my pleasure," Nicholas said, grinning. Serena definitely did have style in casting men out. It was even more enjoyable, since it wasn't he on the receiving end this time. "A real pleasure."

"Will it?" Andrews snarled. He snatched up his cane and sprung to his feet. Nicholas stepped back, prepared for attack. Andrews didn't swing the cane, however, but twisted its head, drawing out a thin blade from it. He flourished it, taking up the perfect dueling stance. "I don't think you will."

Nicholas cursed and lowered himself into a fighting crouch. He should have known Andrews would carry such a weapon.

"Not so proud now, are you?" Andrews asked, stalking Nicholas.

"I'm just a humble servant," Nicholas murmured, circling carefully.

"Lord Andrews, I want your attention!" Serena called.

Andrews ignored her call, keeping his eyes glued to Nicholas. Nicholas watched Andrews closely, though he fully recognized the tone of Serena's voice and what it would portend. He felt no surprise as a gilt clock winged its way into his vision and knocked the sword dead on straight.

Andrews was not as prepared. He cursed as the sword flew from his grasp. Nicholas, grinning evilly, sprung on him, tackling him to the ground. He wrapped his hands around Andrews's throat with deep satisfaction.

"No, Tom!" Serena cried. "Don't kill him. He's not worth it!"

Nicholas shook with rage, but her words brought him to his senses. Growling, he pulled his hands away from the stunned Andrews. He rose, looking down at him in disgust. "Get out."

"Crawl if you must," Serena said, coming to stand beside Nicholas. She held the thin blade within her hand.

Andrews sat up slowly. He swiped the blood from his lip. His eyes held a feral gleam as he looked at them. "Y-you'll both be sorry for this, that I swear."

Nicholas stepped menacingly forward at the same time Serena lifted the blade in a vicious manner. The feral look quickly vanished from Andrews's eyes, a look of fear replacing it. He crab-crawled backward away from the double threat. Then he rolled to his feet and stumbled from the room.

A moment passed, and then Serena broke out into a peal of laughter. "You serve a punishing tea, Tom."

Nicholas looked at her. Her hair was disheveled, her green eyes glittered, and she dangled the sword in her hand. He broke into a laugh himself. "Better than what you intended to serve him with. A letter opener, for God's sakes?"

Her lips curved into a wry smile. " 'Twas the best I had at hand." She cast a considering look to the blade. "Now, if only I had known about this. I believe I'll have one commissioned for myself."

The humor drained from Nicholas. The woman was outrageous. "You don't need a damn sword. What you need is some common sense and proper decorum. None of this would have happened if you had listened to me."

Serena started back, her eyes widening. Then they flared. "No, none of this would have happened if you hadn't all but forced me to receive him."

"I forced you!" Nicholas roared.

"Yes," Serena snapped. "You were so rude to him, that there was nothing else I could do." Nicholas blinked, shaking his head at the insanity of the woman. "And then you had to challenge him as well. I declare, you both would have brawled right there in the foyer if I hadn't separated you and taken him to the parlor."

"So you did it for my sake now?" Nicholas asked hotly.

"Yes." Serena tossed her hair. "And if you hadn't treated me with so much disrespect, I'm sure he wouldn't have either. I mean, if a servant can be so impertinent, I'm sure he thought he could do the same."

"Don't," Nicholas said lowly. "Don't you dare try and place the blame on me. The fault is all yours, and you know it. If you hadn't worn that dress last night, you would never have attracted his attention. If you had acted as a lady should, he wouldn't have gotten near you. You were asking to be raped!"

"I was not!" Serena shouted. She suddenly shivered, and her eyes darkened. She turned swiftly from him. "No woman asks for that."

Remorse shot through Nicholas. What kind of villain was he? Serena had almost been raped, and had suffered more than most women could handle. Faith, if it had been any other woman they'd be fainting and hysterical by now. They would not have stood Andrews off one wit.

He reached out his arms toward her, and then

dropped them. Confusion whirled within him. Serena's strength and spirit awed him. Yet it was that very spirit which had thrown her into such a dangerous situation as this. He wanted to comfort her and praise her. At the same time he wanted to shake her and break her until she cried and promised never to put herself at risk again.

It was the thought of her at Andrews's mercy that finally won out. It made Nicholas's voice rough and cruel as he said, "Try and stay out of trouble, if you can. I may not always be around to save you."

He heard her gasp, but didn't wait. He stalked from the room. Then he stalked from the townhouse, his words still clear within his own head. No matter what he said, Serena would not be able to stay out of trouble when it came to Andrews. She had made a true enemy. He growled. If he weren't in masquerade, he could call the man out and send him to hell personally. Yet, there were other avenues, and other ways to send a man to hell.

In his travels, Nicholas had come across many different people. He knew more of the dark side of London than most. Lord Andrews, the leech on society's back, would soon be plucked, and thrown in with a society more fitting to his own nature.

Serena walked slowly up the stairs. What she needed was a bath, to wash away the horror of Lord Andrews's touch. She might be able to do that, but she knew she wouldn't be able to wash Tom's words away. It had been her fault, all her fault. His last words stung the most. "I may not be around to save you."

She shivered. With Lord Andrews hating Tom as much as he did, those words might be prophetic. Her own safety didn't concern her. Lord Andrews was a beast, but with her power and position in society, he wouldn't dare to move against her. Tom was different. He was but a servant, without rights or protection. He *had* lifted his hand against an aristocrat, and she never doubted Lord Andrews would demand his revenge.

She thought long and hard, thinking of every source available to her. Then she smiled. This was war, wasn't it? Maybe Lord Andrews would be better off if he got a taste of it himself, firsthand, as it were. Lady Lucille was seeing Sir Alfred and the naval set, wasn't she?

Lord Andrews stumbled out of the flophouse, and walked along the back streets. That greedy Francesca had charged him double, whining that he had ruined her girl for the next two months. He shrugged. It didn't matter to him. It had felt good, so very good.

Then he frowned as he turned down an alley. It hadn't felt good enough, though. It was the lady Serena he had wanted sobbing and whimpering with pain beneath him. She had humiliated him. She and that damn servant of hers. He'd still get that bitch, and that servant would rue the day he lifted his hand to a lord of the realm.

So deep was he in his dark thoughts that it surprised him when a gruff voice said, "Hello, mate."

Lord Andrews looked up to discover a band of five large and roughened sailors before him. His lip curled. "Don't call me mate. I am Lord Andrews to you."

The man grinned. "Not for long, mate. His Majesty's service is looking for a man like you."

"I'm a nobleman," Lord Andrews said, though the first qualm entered him. None of the men seemed terribly amazed by his title. "You can't press me into service."

The man grinned. "I got orders that says I can."

Andrews started. He swiftly drew out his pistol, and began retreating. "I'll shoot whoever comes near. And then I'll see you all hanged for your effrontery."

None of the men moved, and Lord Andrews continued to back off. The leader of the band cursed, but his gaze was directed somewhere past Andrews's shoulders. "Here now, what are you blokes doing here?"

Andrews snorted. He'd not be taken in by that ruse. He managed but one sharp cry when he felt a stunning blow to his neck. He dropped his pistol as he caved to the ground. Dazed, he watched as a huge Indian snatched up the pistol.

"Who are you?" he muttered, stumbling up.

The large man who held the pistol was flanked by a cortège of men. Some were clearly English, while the others wore Mideastern dress.

"He's coming with us," one of the English men in the group said, forging to the front.

"No, he ain't," the leader of the sailors growled. His band all withdrew clubs and knives, crouching for a fight. "He's going into His Majesty's service, he is."

"I've got the Sultan's mother who likes her Englishmen," the other man grinned.

"Do your slaving somewhere else, man," the sailor said. "We've got us a healthy purse coming for this one. And our employer is mighty powerful."

"We've got the same," the slaver said, spreading his legs apart. "I bet my employer's more powerful."

Lord Andrews began to tremble. He was surrounded. There was no escape.

The sailor's look turned challenging. "Who's yours?"

The slaver narrowed his eyes. "Who's yours?"

"I works for the lady Serena Fairchild," the sailor said. "She's one of the richest women in all of England. She hobnobs with old Prinny himself."

The slaver cracked a grin. "Well, I works for the Earl

of Claremont. He hobnobs with Prinny, too, and he's a war hero."

Lord Andrew shook his head. "Wait. I don't know the Earl of Claremont. I swear I don't."

"Well, he knows you," the slaver said. "And I ain't going to go back empty-handed. Not to Lord Claremont or the sultan's mother."

"Neither are we," the sailor growled.

Fear, cold and numbing, seeped through Andrews. He slowly sunk to his knees. "No, don't. Please don't." His voice cracked. "I—I'll pay you b-both. Just leave me be."

The slaver looked at him and snorted. Then he looked at the sailor. "What's it going to be? I don't want bloodshed over this here yellow crawler, but I ain't going back without him."

The sailor rubbed his chin. "Well, now, I feels the same. Mean, no reason for any of us to break our bones. Seems like our 're-spective' employers," he said, with a grin, "want this here swabby put in one kind of service or another. We both deserve a purse if either of us takes care of him." His look turned cagey. "What you say we roll the dice for it?"

"No!" Lord Andrews cried out. "No, don't!"

"Sounds all right by me," the slaver said.

The sailor withdrew his dice and Andrews felt the press of men about him as the sailor rolled them. He heard them all mutter and exclaim.

"What is happening?" he cried, trying to struggle through to see.

"My turn," the slaver called. Lord Andrews, renewed by his fear, fought through the group to finally see the dice the slaver had rolled. A strangled sob escaped him as he stared at the betraying dice that lay in the alley's dirt and refuse.

"I win!" the slaver cried.

"So ye do," the sailor said. He shrugged. "Don't think His Majesty needs him anyhows."

"No," Lord Andrews pleaded to the sailor, crumbling to his knees again. "Please take me. Take me."

"The sultan's mother will like him," the slaver said as his men grabbed hold of the sagging Andrews.

"But . . . but I don't know the Earl of Claremont," Lord Andrews whimpered. "I don't!"

Three

"Ouch," Serena gasped as her partner's foot ground her slippered one into the dance floor.

"What's the matter, my lovely?" The man, dressed very ineptly as a courtier of Louis the XIV's court, grinned down into her face, pulling her indecently close. Close enough for her to get a good whiff of wine from his breath.

"Nothing, nothing at all," Serena said, making a pretense of adjusting her mask when in truth she was covering her nose. She wished to God she hadn't permitted Lady Swafford to tease her into attending the Cyprian's masquerade ball. Lady Swafford had claimed it was delicious fun to masquerade and observe as the courtesans of the day danced the night away and changed partners and protectors all at one time. Of course, Lady Swafford hadn't told her it was also her excuse to behave as bad, if not worse, than the beau monde. Serena wouldn't have been dancing with her foxed partner now if it hadn't seemed a better choice than remaining to watch Lady Swafford and her "gallant" put the professionals to shame.

Serena cursed to herself. She should have known better when Lady Lucille had said she'd have none of it. Then Tom had overheard their conversation while he served them breakfast. The man had actually possessed the brass to *order* her not to attend. It simply had been the outside of enough.

Ever since the incident with Lord Andrews, Tom had been watching her like a hawk, lifting a brow at any dress he deemed improper and commenting upon the suitability of every invitation she received. She had tolerated it for two weeks, but when he ordered her point blank not to attend the Cyprian's ball, she had decided the situation was no longer tolerable.

She was a woman full grown and she'd not be treated like some young miss at a boarding school for wayward girls. Faith, the man was worse than any headmistress she'd ever known. Guilt made her strive to listen to him with good will, but it had only gained her more frowns and more strictures. Then he had pushed it to the limits by outright ordering her. No matter what, he was still the servant and she the employer. She ignored the fact she had stooped to conniving and deceiving to ensure Tom didn't get wind of her attendance. She told herself it was merely because she didn't wish to be taxed with his snobbery.

"You're a beauty," her partner breathed again. "Sure you don't want to give old Neddy a little peek beneath the mask." He lifted his hand toward the strings of her mask.

"No," Serena said, instantly slapping his hand away. If she were discovered here, it would be scandal broth for a year.

Neddy actually hee-hawed. He picked Serena up and swung her around.

"Stop!" Serena gasped, through ribs she was sure were cracking. She pounded him on the shoulder. "Stop!"

Neddy lowered her to her feet, but still hugged her close, like a marauding bear. "You're a sp-spirited filly. Just what I've been looking for." He grinned sloppily.

"Old Neddy's mighty good to his mistresses, I'll have ye know. Now, let me see your pretty face." He reached once more for her mask.

"Excuse me," a deep voice said from behind Serena. "But I have prior claim with this woman and ask you to release her."

Neddy's eyes widened and his hand fell from Serena's mask. "Wh-what?"

"Release her," the deep voice repeated.

"Yes, do," Serena said, struggling away from Neddy. She turned with a grateful smile upon her lips for whichever merciful man had come to rescue her. She looked up the imposing height of a man in a black domino with black mask. Her heart began to pound. Then it stopped completely when she met the man's dark eyes. "You! What are you doing here?"

Nicholas's smile beneath his mask was wide. "Coming to retrieve you, sweetheart. How could you think of leaving me?"

"Here now," Neddy said. "What's he talking about?"

Serena looked at the drunken Neddy and found herself at a loss for words. She certainly wasn't about to confess she was a peer, and that her disapproving servant had come to take her home.

Nicholas laughed, as if divining her dilemma. "Sorry Neddy, but my . . . mistress and I had a disagreement." He held out his hand. "Come back to me, sweetings. I'll give you that carriage you've been holding out for, but you've got to promise to be a good girl for Daddy." His eyes turned positively wicked. "A very good girl."

"Throw him over," Neddy said, suddenly excited. "Take me instead. W-will give you a carriage . . . and a necklace, bedamn."

"I've already given her one, old man," Nicholas said, his voice rife with amusement. "Diamonds and emeralds, mind you."

"Oh," Neddy said, looking crestfallen. "Both?"

"Both," Nicholas confirmed and sighed. "She's a greedy mistress. As well as a willful piece."

"I am not!" Serena cried, shocked and outraged. "Don't listen to him. He lies."

"All right," Neddy said, clearly not one to argue. He beamed. "Will give you diamonds and rubies instead. Would you like that?"

"What?" Serena gasped.

He leaned forward and winked. "You must be something like if he's givin' you all that." He puffed out his chest. "Old Neddy can do just as good."

Nicholas chuckled. "Doubt it, old man, doubt it." He cast Serena an all too confident look. "Make up your mind, sweeting." Serena clenched her hands, her nails digging into her palms. He was enjoying using those overly familiar terms upon her all too much. "Are you going to stay under my protection? Or are you going to go with old Neddy?"

"It's not much of a choice," Serena said. "But I'll go with you."

Nicholas slapped a hand to his chest. "Ah, she still loves me." He grabbed up Serena's hand and hauled her to him. "Excuse me, Neddy. My little love and I wish to dance."

"Let me go." Serena's words were muffled against Nicholas's chest.

"Come, don't be a cruel mistress," Nicholas murmured, swinging her into the dance and ruthlessly steering her away from the objecting Neddy. "You should be kind to your protector."

"You are not my protector," Serena hissed, finally gaining a decent inch away from the man. "And I would never be your mistress . . . that is, if I were ever going to be anyone's mistress."

"No?" Nicholas asked, a thread of laughter in his voice. "That sounds like a challenge to me."

"A challenge?" Serena asked, her gaze flying to his. His eyes were light and warm and . . . and teasing. An odd shiver raced down her spine. She looked away quickly. "Don't be ridiculous. There is no challenge. You are my servant, for goodness' sake."

"Too far below your exalted heights, am I?" Nicholas asked. He actually sounded amused more than anything else. "The great lady of the house would never stoop to have a tendre for her lowly overseer?"

"Of course I wouldn't," Serena snapped.

"It has happened before," Nicholas said, his voice lowering to velvet. "In the finest households, in fact."

"Well, it wouldn't in mine," Serena said quickly. His lips quirked into the slightest of smiles. Serena found herself gazing at those lips. They were truly well sculptured and amazingly sensuous. She flushed. "Why, I—I don't even like you."

"You wound me, my lady," Nicholas murmured.

"Well, I don't," Serena said with more force. "When you are not being odiously rude, you . . . you are forever nagging at me."

"Nagging?" Nicholas's brows suddenly snapped down and disappeared beneath his mask.

"Yes," Serena said. "You remind me nothing more than of a headmistress. This is not proper. You cannot do this. You should do this." Serena shook her head. "Faith, you are the most priggish man I've ever met."

"Priggish! Me?" Nicholas asked. He looked totally astounded. "Good God!"

"I don't know why you look so surprised." Serena frowned. "Surely other women have told you that already?"

"No," Nicholas said, shaking his head. "They haven't."

"Truly?" Serena asked. She thought a moment and said without consideration, "The women of your class must be very unusual."

"Not *that* unusual," Nicholas said, stiffening. "In fact, many women find me charming."

"Impossible!" Serena said, her own eyes widening. Then she bit her lip. "Forgive me."

"No, 'tis clear I've lost my . . . touch," Nicholas murmured. He grinned and pulled her close. "Too long out of practice evidently."

"Stop that!" Serena gasped. " 'Tis not proper."

Nicholas laughed. "Now who is being priggish? You are at the Cyprian's ball. What did you expect?"

"I—I . . ." Serena began and then stopped. A surprised laugh escaped her. "I don't know. But I didn't expect to be dancing with my overseer, I assure you."

Nicholas chuckled. "And I didn't come here expecting to dance with you, either."

Serena made a face. "How did you know I was here? Who told you?"

"No one did," Nicholas said. He shrugged. "I just knew you would come. No matter the evidence to the contrary. Poor Tandy was totally flabbergasted to discover your green domino and mask were gone."

"I see," Serena said. She looked away. "I suppose you'll want me to leave now."

"No, since we are here, let us stay," Nicholas said. His voice softened. "And since this is a masquerade, let us merely pretend we are two people who don't know each other and have just met." He twirled her about. "I am not your servant and you are not the lady Fairchild. I am merely a man who thinks you are a beautiful woman, and you are a woman who thinks . . ."

"Yes?" Serena lifted her brow, though her heart began to beat an odd rhythm.

He smiled. "That I'm one of the best dancers you've ever met."

Serena stared and then she laughed. "You are. Where ever did you learn to dance this way?"

Nicholas's eyes grew dark. "Remember, you don't know me."

Serena looked up at him, a breathlessness overtaking her. "No. I don't believe I do know you."

He nodded his head. "I am pleased to meet you, madame."

"And I you, sir," Serena said, laughing. It was absolutely crazy, but she suddenly didn't care.

"They will have the unmasking soon, madame," Nicholas said softly, as he twirled Serena around in another waltz.

Serena's green eyes turned dark. "Is it already that time, sir?"

"Yes, I am afraid it is," Nicholas said, pulling her close. He didn't know who the woman he held in his arms was, but she wasn't the lady Serena Fairchild. At least, not the one he knew, or thought he knew. This woman was intriguing, quicksilver in flirtation, yet with an elusive part of her always hidden, a promised depth always tantalizing from beneath her laughter and banter. It was that hidden depth which made a man desperate to know her, and to own her. No wonder so many men had asked for her hand. And why so many had lost it.

"I—I wish this night didn't have to end," Serena said softly.

"Neither do I," Nicholas said. "But we must go."

He stopped dancing and took up her hand, as easily as if it had always belonged in his grasp. Silently they walked from the dance floor and slipped out of the ballroom into the night air. Nicholas paused a moment and then started laughing.

"What is so amusing?" Serena asked.

He smiled wryly. "Madame, I would that I had a white steed awaiting us, or a grand carriage, but I only brought the coach . . . without the coachman."

Serena's eyes glittered behind her mask, brightened to cut emeralds by the moonlight. "Indeed? You travel this way often, sir?"

"Not normally," Nicholas said. "But you see, I came for . . . a different lady, and I wanted to make sure none of her servants, not even her coachman, knew that she was here."

"I see," Serena said, her tone solemn. "Well, that poor lady must be out, for you are taking me home, are you not?"

"Yes, madame. I would be honored. And though not a coachman by trade, I promise not to overturn you."

"Very well." Serena's smile turned mischievous. "But if you get to be the coachman, I get to be your partner."

Nicholas laughed. His original intent was to have discovered the lady Serena, throw her into the coach and drive her home. Yet this woman he wanted by his side. "Let us go then. The night is still young."

Together they slipped out to the coach which awaited them and Nicholas paid the boy he had commissioned to hold the team. The boy's eyes lighted at the exorbitant amount of coins he tossed him, and then shuttered wide to pure shock as Nicholas swung Serena up to the coach box and climbed up behind her.

Nicholas whipped up the team and directed them out onto the street. He heard Serena's low laugh beside him and smiled down at her.

Her gaze was approving. "You handle the ribbons well, sir. I'd like to see what you really can do with this team."

Nicholas started. Every well-bred woman he knew would have been either frightened or complaining over his rapid departure. Yet this woman only laughed and challenged him all the more. He laughed himself, not only from the challenge, but from the pure devilment and delight that showed in her eyes. He slowed slightly, but changed direction, heading out of town, rather than into town. Serena only smiled and lifted her face to the night breeze, as if reveling in it. Nicholas knew that heady feeling, had felt it many times, but never had he expected a woman to feel it as well.

The moment they cleared town, Nicholas gave the team their head. The horses sped down the road, a course Nicholas knew well and had raced upon when he was young and reckless. Serena only laughed and Nicholas could literally feel her enjoyment of the speed and the wind. Suddenly he slowed the team, bringing them to a halt.

"What is the matter?" Serena asked.

Nicholas didn't say anything. He wanted to kiss that wind and speed in Serena. He pulled her into his arms and lowered his lips to hers. She stiffened. One moment of stillness. Then she melted into him, and it was the wind and speed he sought. And a passion like he'd never felt. He tasted and held the very depth of what had tantalized him beneath Serena's flirtation, beneath her capriciousness, beneath her obstinacy.

Her lips clung to his, sweet and fierce. Her body strove against his, pliant and soft, wild and strong. Nicholas lost control. Never in his life had he done so, but he lost control of both his passion and hers. It didn't matter.

"Hey, Zack, now ain't this a scene," Nicholas heard a rough voice say.

The passion didn't stop in Nicholas, yet an instinct not only of survival but protection, too, took control.

He tore his lips from Serena's. For a moment he gazed into her eyes, saw desire mixed with moonbeams there, and then he turned his gaze away.

Two men, both with pistols, had positioned their mounts to either side of the coach.

"Lud!" Serena exclaimed. "Highwaymen." She looked with disdain toward the man upon her side. "I suppose you want my money and jewels. I am sorry I do not have very much with me tonight."

"Here now," the man said, his voice indignant. "I ain't no bridle cull!"

"I beg your pardon?"

"Be quiet, my dear," Nicholas said to Serena under his breath.

Serena looked at him. "What is a bridle cull?"

"He's not a highwayman," Nicholas said, gritting his teeth.

"Not a highwayman?" Serena asked. "Then whatever does he want?"

"Try whoever," Nicholas muttered, more to himself than her.

"Oh," she said softly.

"Take off yer masks," the man on Nicholas's side ordered, sidling closer.

"Yeh, take off yer masks," the second man said.

"No," Serena said, lifting her chin. "No. I shall not."

Nicholas glanced quickly at Serena. Leave it to her to take the high and dangerous road. However, since he himself couldn't risk unmasking, he crossed his arms and said, "I won't, either."

"Whot?" the one on Serena's side exclaimed. "Hear that, Jack?"

"I hear, Zack," his partner said testily. He glared at Nicholas. "Are ye cracked? It's us that have the poppers."

"Indeed you do, Jack," Serena said in a kindly tone.

"But what a waste it would be to kill us if we aren't the people you are looking for."

"We's knows who you are," Jack retorted. He waved his pistol. "Now take off yer mask, my lord and lady!"

"Well, see there," Serena said with a laugh, which sounded totally frivolous. "You have it all wrong. He certainly is no lord, but just a coachman. And, really! If I were a lady, would I be riding up here with him? I suppose you want the lady Serena Fairchild whose coach this is, but I am not her."

"No, we want . . ." the man began.

Nicholas tensed. He couldn't afford such chatter. Coiling all his strength, he sprung at Jack. Stunned, Jack discharged his pistol. The shot must have went wide, for Nicholas felt no extra pain as he rammed into the man, unseating him from his horse. They both tumbled to the ground, Jack's mount taking off. Nicholas heard the screech of other horses even as he untangled himself from the man and jumped to his feet.

For a moment he stood frozen. The coach's team was screaming in terror, the lead horse rearing up in anger. Serena had seized the reins, and stood, sawing on them and calling out to the horses to stop.

The lead horse came down.

"Bloody hell!" Serena cried out.

Then the team bolted away and Nicholas received a crashing blow to his chin. It brought his attention back to hand abruptly. Cursing, he focused a furious gaze upon his attacker and returned a punishing left.

The two men dodged and feinted, delivering blows. Nicholas realized he had the advantage, and pressed it heavily.

"Lay orf, Jack, or I'll shoot!" Zack's voice interrupted Nicholas in a healthy swing.

Nicholas unhappily stayed his fist, turning slowly toward Zack's voice. Zack had dismounted his horse and was standing within good firing range, legs spread and pistol pointed.

"Put your h-hands in the air," Zack ordered, glaring at Nicholas. Nicholas did so, not so much because of Zack's glare, but because that man's hand shook. A nervous man was always more dangerous. "N-now, Jack, take the bloke's mask orf."

"Don't try any funny business," Jack said, approaching Nicholas slowly. His left eye was swelling shut and he squinted with the other one. He slowly untied the mask and let it fall. Then he peered into Nicholas's face. Nicholas coughed, the man's breath upon him strong with garlic and onions. "It's him, Zack."

"Yer sure?" Zack asked, his voice excited.

"Course," Jack said. His tone lacked conviction, however, and he moved closer.

Nicholas saw his chance. Lady Lucille had already shown him the way. "Good God. Now I understand. I bet you think I'm Claremont!"

"Of course we think you're Claremont," Jack said. His voice lowered. "Ain't ye?"

Nicholas forced a laugh. "Well, I'm the old earl's son, if that's what you mean. One of them."

"What?" Zack yelped.

"But from the wrong side of the blanket," Nicholas said, grinning.

"Go on with you," Jack growled.

"Sorry, old man," Nicholas sighed, shaking his head. "You've got the wrong side of the blanket, as it were, and the wrong man."

"Awe, you're lying," Jack said. "Trying to throw us orf, but you ain't going to. We's got the description. Got information you were hiding out at that Fairchild's place."

"As a servant?" Nicholas asked.

Jack snorted. "You nobs are all queer anyhow. Always

playing orf tricks. Zack, it's him. Go ahead and shoot him."

"Are you sure?" Nicholas retorted. "You can barely see."

Jack reared back, his face outraged. "Shoot him, Jack. Just for that if nothin' else."

"Don't want to s-shoot the wrong man," Zack said, his hand still shaking. "Won't get paid fer it."

"Listen, the man looks like him. It *is* him," Jack growled, stepping back out of range. "We'll get paid if you just shoot the blighter."

"But Jack . . ." Zack said.

"Aw, for God's sake," Jack muttered, and strode over to Zack. "I'll shoot him, if'n you won't." He grabbed the pistol from Zack's shaking hand and pointed it at Nicholas, cocking it.

"Huzzah!" a loud voice called out. There was the sound of thundering hooves, as if God's chariots were approaching, and then out of the darkness a coach appeared. Serena stood abrace, whipping the wild team forward. Her black hair flew, her green domino billowed about her, and with her green mask on, she looked like a witch flying from hell.

"Gor!" Zack breathed.

"Bejesus!" Jack shouted as Serena drove the team directly at them. He pointed the pistol at the coach. Still they came. He fired. Still the team raced down upon them.

"The Devil!" Jack shrieked, and tossed the pistol aside. "Run!"

Jack and Zack skittered and scrambled away as the lead horse came into breathing length of them. Nicholas himself was forced to jump back as the steaming team crashed by him.

"She'll k-kill us!" Zack cried. He spun and took off

down the road from whence Serena and her mad team had come.

"Zack!" Jack called. "Come back."

"By God, she's doing it," Nicholas said in pure amazement. Serena had slowed the horses and was performing a hairpin turn.

"What?" Jack stammered.

"Isn't she magnificent," Nicholas murmured, truly appreciative. Serena had accomplished the turn without overturning and was whipping up her team again.

"Magnificent?" Jack cried. He muttered something else, which didn't sound as appreciative, but it was sent to the breeze, for Jack had taken off down the road after Zack.

Grinning, Nicholas stepped from the road and saluted as Serena and coach rocketed by him. Both men and the coach disappeared into the darkness.

Nicholas then doubled over and roared with outright laughter. He had only just brought himself under control, when once again he heard the sound of horses. The coach approached at a much slower pace this time.

"I'm sorry, I lost them," Serena called, bringing the team to a halt before Nicholas. She tied off the reins and Nicholas walked over, lifting his arms up to assist her. "They bolted into the woods," Serena said, and tumbled into his arms. Her voice was breathless and her green eyes glittered behind her mask.

"And you didn't follow?" Nicholas asked, holding her close.

"I consider myself a fine whip," Serena said, her voice indignant. "But not that fine."

"No, of course not," Nicholas said, his voice teasing.

Serena looked at him and then she burst into laughter. She hit him slightly upon the chest. "Beast."

"Ouch." Nicholas laughed. "Beating your servant again, are you?"

Serena's eyes darkened suddenly and she lifted her hand to his cheek. "I'm sorry, Tom."

Nicholas grinned, and held her even more firmly. "You didn't hurt me that much."

"No." Serena shook her head. "I mean about all this. This is the second time you've been endangered because of me."

Nicholas frowned. "Because of you?"

"Yes," Serena said simply. "They were after me."

"After you?" Nicholas asked, stiffening.

"It must have been Darrel," Serena said thoughtfully.

"Darrel?" Nicholas asked. A nasty emotion passed through him. He was not accustomed to holding women in his arms and having them speak of other men.

"I know he said he would do anything to get me back," Serena said. "But I never thought he'd send someone to abduct me."

"It wasn't Darrel," Nicholas said, quickly dropping his arms from about her.

"It had to be," Serena said. She studied him. "Oh, I see. You think it was Lord Andrews."

"No, I don't," Nicholas said. He'd taken care of that matter.

"Good," Serena said, her tone far, far too positive. "Because it wasn't him."

"How would you know that?" Nicholas asked.

"I—I just do," Serena said, flushing. She waved a hand. "It was Darrel. I thought since it's been a few weeks, he had gotten over me, but . . ."

"It wasn't Darrel," Nicholas said, having heard more than enough. "They were after me!"

"After you?" Serena's brows rose. "Don't be silly. You're just a servant."

Intelligence should have kept Nicholas's mouth shut,

but jealousy and ire didn't. "Servant or not, they were after me."

"It's your delusions again," Serena said, laughing lightly. Then she frowned. "I did think I'd escape all these dramatics with Darrel, but he's just like the others after all."

"The others?" Nicholas growled.

"Yes." Serena sighed. "Men just act so insanely when you jilt them. Lord Valentine said he would kill me." Her eyes widened. "Perhaps it was Lord Valentine instead of Darrel."

"It wasn't! They were after me," Nicholas repeated.

"Why do you keep saying that?" Serena asked, frowning. "It's simply ridiculous."

"Not as ridiculous as you thinking every man you've jilted is still after you," Nicholas said curtly. He stepped past her and climbed up to the coach's seat. "As if they all pine for you. Ha! They probably are thanking their lucky stars for their escape."

Serena glared up at him. "You, sir, are rude and odious. And arrogant!"

"Arrogant?" Nicholas snorted.

"Yes, arrogant," Serena confirmed. "You always think the world revolves around you."

"I do not," Nicholas said testily.

"You do," Serena insisted. "You are forever telling everyone what they should do and not do, but then you yourself do whatever you wish. Why, you are more arrogant than the highest nobleman I know. Now, despite the most obvious of facts, you think those men were after you!"

"They were," Nicholas ground out.

"Oh, they were?" Serena asked, setting her hands upon her hips. "Then do tell me why?"

Nicholas glared at her, wishing nothing more than

to tell her the truth and put her in her place. He clenched his jaw. "They just were."

"See!" Serena exclaimed. "You don't have a reason!"

Nicholas narrowed his eyes. "Perhaps I've jilted five women, and one of them wants me abducted because she can't live without me."

Serena stiffened, her eyes shooting sparks. "You are impossible, just simply impossible." She paced around the coach and clambered up to the seat beside him. She looked straight ahead and tilted her chin to an imperious angle. "I wish I hadn't saved you. I wish that man had killed you."

"You did not save me," Nicholas said angrily. "I would have taken care of it myself."

"Oh, yes," Serena said, her tone sarcastic. " 'Twas clear you had it under control."

"I would have," Nicholas said, eyes narrowed and voice fierce.

Serena did not seem quelled by him, but only shrugged a shoulder. "Indeed."

"Indeed," Nicholas said, gritting his teeth. "And you can take off your mask now, my lady. Nobody, but nobody could make a mistake and think you anyone but the lady Serena Fairchild."

"And nobody could make a mistake and think you anything but a boor," Serena shot back. "An arrogant boor."

Nicholas cursed and whipped up the team. The horses sped through the night, but Serena didn't laugh and neither did he.

Four

Serena entered the modiste's shop, her maid, Tandy, trailing behind. She attempted to focus her mind upon whether she would buy the blue silk or the red. Unfortunately, Serena had reached no conclusion, her mind straying continually to the night before. Just what kind of madness had overtaken her she couldn't say. No matter what people said about her, she did hold to her own sense of right and wrong. Dancing all night with one's servant was wrong. Kissing one's servant was wrong. The wild feelings she had felt when in her servant's arms were most definitely wrong.

The problem was, last night she hadn't seen Tom as a servant. Granted, he rarely acted like a servant, no matter how she tried to remind him of his proper place. But last night the rightful distance that should lie between them had totally disappeared. She had only been able to see him as a man, and a man like none other she had met. Worse, his kiss had been like none other she had experienced before, either.

She flushed. It had been madness, pure and simple madness. Thank heaven they had been interrupted, no matter if the interruption had been fraught with danger. Indeed, those two men had been far less dangerous than what might have happened otherwise. Never would she become one of those ladies who lowered themselves to dallying with the servants. Worse, as a rule, she detested Tom. The man overstepped his bounds far too often. What would he think he could do now, since she had permitted such a breach of propriety? The man would truly think her a low creature.

Serena sniffed and tossed her head. She was sure she didn't care. Insanity it had been, and she would make certain it never happened again. He'd soon find out that he wouldn't be able to overstep the bounds again. She would demand correct behavior from him if it killed her, or him. He'd also find out she didn't give one jot for his opinion.

"But, Mama," a charming, vibrant girl's voice cut into Serena's thoughts. "This dress is so dull."

"Dearest," a woman's voice said, "you look lovely. You will charm all the young men."

"Yes," the girl's voice said, laughter in it. "But will I cut a dash?"

Serena looked up at this. A handsome, mature woman stood but a short distance away, and beside her was a petite girl with a pixie face. The girl turned, as if she could detect Serena's gaze upon her. Her blue eyes lighted as they met Serena's, and with an impish smile she plucked at one of the many pink bows which festooned the white skirt of the dress she wore. "What do you think, madame? Is this charming or dull?"

"Alvie!" her mother exclaimed. "Behave yourself."

"Sorry, Mama," Alvie said, without taking her eyes from Serena. "But don't you think it dull?"

Serena looked at the pink-and-white dress. It was the most common of debutante affairs and seemed completely wrong for the girl who wore it.

"I think," Serena said, her lips twitching, "the pink bows are a bit much."

Alvie grinned. "I myself want a dress in red, deep red."

Serena laughed. "I have no doubt but that is definitely out."

"I know," Alvie said with a sigh, though her eyes twinkled. "It is so very hard to walk the line between propriety and doing what one wishes, isn't it?"

"Believe me, I understand," Serena said. "Yet I fear red will never be a wise color for you. It is far too strong for your fair complexion. Propriety might be ignored, but never good fashion."

Alvie's eyes widened and then she chortled. "I am so glad I've met you."

"Alvie, you haven't met her," her mother said, clicking her tongue. "You merely started talking to her. 'Tis not the same thing."

"But I feel like I have met her," Alvie said, her gaze turning quizzically upon Serena's. "Haven't I?"

"Of course you have." Serena walked forward with a smile. "But do let us perform the proper introductions. I am Serena Fairchild."

"I'm Alvie St. Irving," the girl said, quickly holding out her hand. "And this is my mother, Lady Claremont."

"Alvie," Lady Claremont said, her voice low.

Serena took Alvie's proffered hand and shook it. "It is a pleasure to meet you."

"Isn't it?" Alvie said. Then she laughed. "What I mean is, it is always nice to meet someone you immediately take to." She paused a moment and her eyes widened. "Are you the lady Serena Fairchild who's jilted five fiancés?"

"Alvie!" Lady Claremont shrieked.

"Yes, I fear I am," Serena said, laughing.

"Then I am doubly pleased to meet you," Alvie said, her eyes sparkling. "I do hope you will share your secret of success with me. You see, I am just up from the country for my first Season, and though I tell myself not to fret, I do wonder if I'll manage to even make one poor gentleman come up to scratch, let alone five."

"Alvie," Lady Claremont said. "I have told you not to use such vulgar expressions as 'come up to scratch.' And how dare you ask Lady Fairchild to share the secrets of her success. It's much too forward and pushy." Then she blinked. "Come to think of it, it simply isn't a proper question. It sounds as if you are . . . are asking for a recipe for baking a cake, or perhaps a pudding."

"But I am," Alvie said, grinning. Lady Claremont blinked again and clearly became flustered. Alvie, in the most natural manner, ran over and hugged her. "I'm sorry, Mama. I promise not to tease so, and you know I'll behave when I must." She looked at Serena. "But I don't think Serena is one who will demand I stand upon ceremony."

"No," Serena said. "Indeed, not. However, it still does not mean I think you should buy a red dress."

"I suppose not," Alvie sighed and batted at her skirts. "But this will definitely not do. I feel like a tart!"

"Alvie!" Lady Claremont cried out. "How can you say that? 'Tis a very proper dress."

Alvie giggled. "I meant a strawberry tart, Mama."

Serena only laughed. "Well, pink is not your color, either."

Alvie's gaze turned innocent. "Really? As my mentor, what do you think I should wear?"

Serena's own eyes sparkled. "You only say mentor because you hope I'll tell you the secret of my success."

Alvie laughed. "Too true."

"Alvie," Lady Claremont warned. "A lady is not so . . . so persistent and nagging."

Serena and Alvie's eyes met. The younger woman giggled. *"We* are."

Then, with Lady Claremont clucking and dithering, Serena and Alvie proceeded to run the poor modiste off her legs, all the while conversing in an open and forthright manner. Within two hours they had arranged a sumptuous wardrobe, one which followed the lines of convention, but with enough judicious alterations as to ensure Alvie would "cut a dash" upon the marriage mart.

At the end of such exhilarating and exhausting business, Serena invited Alvie and Lady Claremont for tea. Alvie exclaimed with delight, whispering how she had already heard of Serena's footman. Serena laughed, finding herself in a much better mood, and, other than telling Alvie she knew far more gossip than any young debutante fresh up from the country should, said not another word.

Nicholas lounged at the kitchen table, playing a friendly game of cards with Louis. He was just raking in his winnings when Serena entered the kitchen. He cast her a discerning glance. She wore her cold "lady of the house look" upon her face. 'Twas clear she intended to ignore the events of last night. It nettled him unaccountably.

"Now I see why no one was present to open the door for us," Serena said, lifting a brow. "Cards are ever so much more important."

"My lady," Louis exclaimed, dropping his cards and rising. "Do forgive us."

Nicholas did not rise, but only grinned in the most insolent of manners. "I'm sorry, my lady, but this was a very fine hand."

"I have no doubt," Serena said, her eyes narrowed and her tone wonderfully sarcastic. "However, we have company and I thought it might be nice to offer them tea. If the card game can be interrupted, that is."

"Well, I don't know," Nicholas drawled, and leaned back in his chair.

"Of course, my lady," Louis interrupted quickly, frowning at Nicholas darkly. "Of course. And I have made some special cakes. They are magnificent, I promise you."

Some of the rigidness left Serena and she smiled warmly. "We look forward to them, Louis. Thank you." She then looked at Nicholas. Once again her gaze turned arctic. "I do hope you can manage to serve?"

Nicholas smiled lazily. "You know I can."

Serena glared at him as if she contemplated murder, but then spun and walked from the kitchen.

"Mon Dieu," Louis muttered, tromping over to the fire. He shook his head. "I do not see how you can behave that way to my lady. You should be . . . what is the word? Eh, zacked, yes?"

"No," Nicholas said. He grinned. "Besides, she cannot sack me. I'm in her brother's employ."

"No matter. You do not treat her in a good manner," Louis said. "You do not show the r-respect. She is a grand lady, you should show her r-respect!"

"I am not impressed with her title or station," Nicholas said dryly.

Louis halted, and looked at him closely. He laughed. *"Non.* That is not what I speak of." He shrugged his shoulders. "Many aristocrats, pha, they are nothing. Nothing! The women . . . they are *putas."*

Nicholas cracked a laugh. "For shame, Louis. Now that is definitely not respectful."

"And the men!" Louis said, waving his hands about. "They are not men. They put their boot to our necks, yes, but they are not men. They are the vultures in the sky. They feed off us."

Nicholas controlled his smile. "I never knew you held such strong politics, *mon ami."*

Louis grinned a wide grin. "I do not talk of them, but to you. You! You think the same, *non?*"

"Well, I wouldn't say that," Nicholas said in a neutral tone.

"You do. You show respect to no one. A title? It does not mean that to you!" He snapped his fingers. Then he sighed. "But, *mon ami,* you should listen to me. Politics, they are fine. Yes, very fine. But they can kill a man." He shrugged. "Me, I wish to live. I wish to cook. I must create. So I cook my sauces and special cakes for the *putas* and vultures."

"I'm sure Serena, I mean my lady, would be pleased to hear this," Nicholas said, grinning.

Louis shook his head vehemently. *"Non. Non.* She is different. I cook for her because . . . because she is a grand lady!"

"A grand lady?" Nicholas asked, raising a brow.

Louis laughed, still scurrying to prepare the tea. "You are a good man, but you are so very English."

"Insults, insults," Nicholas said, shaking his head.

"No," Louis said. "It's true. You Englishmen are strong. So strong, yes. But your women? Heh! Your women you want to be weak and puling. What you say, 'milk and water misses,' yes? You do not want them with the fire." He shrugged. "You do not love women."

Nicholas laughed. "I have loved many women, *mon ami.*"

Louis's dark eyes twinkled. "Milk and water misses, yes? But women? *Non.* I do not think so." He looked at the tea service he had so diligently prepared and sighed. "Now, this is fine, a beautiful thing." He looked to Nicholas, a severe frown upon his face. "This time you will present it well, *non?* You will not . . . throw it about the way you did before?"

Nicholas laughed. "I promise, I won't." He rose,

shook out his cuffs and smoothed down his green
jacket. "How do I look?"

"Bien, bien," Louis nodded. Then he waved a hand.
"But the powder in the hair, it is stupid, yes? A man
with your politics should not put the powder in the
hair."

"Forgive me," Nicholas said meekly and took up the
tray. Smiling, he left Louis and the kitchen. His smile
lessened, however, as he walked through the house.
Louis simply did not know what he talked about. Nicholas had had numerous affairs, and none of them had
been with milk and water misses. He was not afraid of
"the fire" in a woman. Suddenly he remembered
Serena's kisses. A heat flashed through him. In truth,
he had never felt the fire like that with any other
woman, but he would not do that again. Not because
he was afraid of that fire, certainly not. It was because
he knew better than to play with a capricious, jaded
woman. He'd left those games behind years ago. He
shook his head. Louis could worship Serena Fairchild
all he wanted, but Nicholas knew better.

Nicholas reached the parlor door and halted a moment. He smiled wickedly. Louis had commanded him
to present the tea well. Straightening, he assumed the
studied dignity mixed with obsesquience, which was pe-
culiar to a well-trained servant, and entered the parlor.
He intoned in a portentous voice, "Your tea, my lady."

Then he froze as he fully recognized the inhabitants
of the room. He was serving tea to his very own mother
and sister!

Alvie's eyes lighted as she gazed at him. "Oh, Serena,
so this is your footman. He is simply divine."

"Now, Alvie," Lady Claremont said, clucking. "One
does not talk of servants in that fashion. 'Tis rude and
improper."

Nicholas stood rooted to the floor, totally stunned.

His little sister was studying him with an admiring eye, as if he were nothing more than a handsome fixture. His dear mother clearly did not even recognize her own son, but was rather prosing on about the proper chasm between servant and aristocrat.

"You may put the tray over here, Tom," Serena said. Only she looked at him as if he were a human, her eyes showing narrowed warning. "Tom, do you hear me?"

"What?" Nicholas muttered.

"You may put the tray down," Serena said, her tone sharp.

Alvie giggled. Nicholas's stunned gaze turned to hers. She winked at him. Actually winked at him!

"Damn and blast!" he exclaimed. Louis may have claimed him a strong man, but even Nicholas knew his own limits. Serving tea while his sister winked at him was not one of them. He promptly dropped the tray, special cakes and all, and turned smartly on his heel.

"Tom!" Serena cried. "What are you doing?"

Nicholas didn't bother to answer, so quickly was he out the door.

"Good heavens, what an odd servant," Lady Claremont's voice drifted to him as he bolted across the foyer.

"God," muttered Nicholas. Just how odd a servant he was she'd never know. Not if he had his way.

"But he is handsome," Alvie's voice said with a giggle. "Even if he is a slow top."

Nicholas skidded to a halt, stiffening as if he had been shot in the back. He clenched his fists. His younger sister needed a stern talking to, confound it. Speaking about men in that manner! He spun around, determined to go back and ring a peal over her head. Then he stopped. What the devil did he think he was doing? Going insane was what he was doing. Muttering deep and dire curses, he once again spun around. This time he did not halt, but stalked across the foyer, ripped open the door, and charged down the steps and into the street. He hailed the first hack he came across and demanded the driver to take him to the very first pub they found.

It wasn't until Nicholas had shot down his first bumper of blue ruin that he unclenched his jaw. God! No man should ever be forced into such an infernal situation as serving tea to his mother and sister. He shuddered. He could only imagine their reaction if they had recognized him. He didn't even dare try and contemplate what Serena's reactions would have been. That path would lead to madness.

Over the second bumper, Nicholas relaxed a little, even enough to laugh bitterly to himself. Faith, the situation was not only infernal, but also asinine. He was honestly on the run from his own family. He did it for their own good and protection, but still, the whole event had been asinine. Ridiculous. Humiliating!

With his third bumper, Nicholas began to scowl darkly. The situation should never have occurred. His mother and sister shouldn't even know Serena Fairchild, let alone come to her house to take tea with her. He'd not seen his sister often over the past four years, but she was a young girl, too innocent to know what she was doing. She shouldn't be in the company of the capricious and worldly Serena. She shouldn't be in the company of the woman he had kissed with such wild passion just the night before! Heat flashed through him again, and want rose within him.

He cursed. By God, Serena and his sister simply could not be permitted to know each other. Serena would only lead his dear sister astray. He was a strong man, and she led even him astray! A sudden vision arose before Nicholas, vivid and well painted with blue ruin. He could see Alvie, four Seasons from now, wild and head strong, kissing men the way Serena had kissed him, and having a string of jilted beaux. Beaux he would have to protect her from and send to India when they grew out of hand!

Nicholas ordered up his fourth bumper, almost sweating. He'd not permit it. Serena would not be allowed to lead Alvie down that path. He had enough trouble dealing with that siren, let alone having Alvie become like her. One woman like Serena was enough for the planet!

He all but snatched the blue ruin from the barmaid when she brought it to him. He took a heavy gulp of it. His courage rose strong and mighty. He might have retreated under fire this afternoon, but he'd return and settle it with Serena. He might have to live in her toils for the moment, but never would his family. Never would his sweet sister!

Yes, he was going to return and set Serena straight upon that head. That was, after he finished his blue ruin . . . and perhaps had another one.

"I cannot believe the man," Serena said, seething, as Tandy handed her a sheer dressing gown, which Serena jerked on over her corset and petticoats.

"Careful, my lady," Tandy breathed as the sheer fabric groaned from the rough handling.

"He dropped the entire tray!" Serena exclaimed, stalking over to the vanity table and sitting down to grab up her hairbrush. "Right in front of Lady Claremont and Alvie. Tossed it up and left, without a by your leave! I swear he did it just to embarrass me."

"Oh, no, he wouldn't have I'm sure," Tandy said, drawing out the emerald ball gown Serena intended to wear for the evening. She shook her head. "I am that bumfuddled though. It just ain't like Mister Tom."

"Not like him?" Serena snorted. "The man does

whatever he pleases, without regard to the feelings of others. He's been gone the entire day. Just where is the confounded man?"

"Here I am, my lady," Nicholas's voice suddenly boomed. Both ladies jumped. Stunned, Serena turned in her chair. Nicholas stood within the bedroom doorway. She hadn't even heard the door open. She narrowed her gaze. She knew full well she hadn't heard a knock upon it, either.

"Eeks, Mister Tom!" Tandy cried. "You can't be here. My lady is dressing. You must get out!"

"But my lady wished to know my whereabouts," Nicholas drawled, strolling into the room. He wore a surly and dark expression. "Did you want my services tonight, my lady?"

Serena's eyes widened even as Tandy squeaked in shock. Then anger ripped through her. "I most certainly do not want your services. Not as clumsy and oafish as they are. You cannot even handle a tea service tray."

"Oh, no," Tandy said, wringing her hands. "Everyone has accidents once in a while."

"Accidents!" Serena exclaimed. "The man threw the tray down on purpose, I tell you. I was never so embarrassed in my entire life."

"Considering the things you do," Nicholas said with a snort, "I'm amazed."

Serena gripped her hairbrush. "Don't you dare talk to me of my behavior. I'll not take lessons from a low, common servant."

"Won't you?" Nicholas growled, lurching closer.

"Mister Tom!" Tandy cried, rushing to him and grabbing hold of his arm. "Ye must get out."

" 'Tis you who were derelict in your duties," Serena flared. "Just where in blazes have you been?"

Tandy suddenly coughed and waved a hand over her

nose. "I know where's he's been, my lady." Her voice lowered to a whisper. "He's been drinking."

"Drinking!" Serena gasped, enraged all the more. "How dare you come before me sotted! Get out! And that's an order!"

"You heard her, Mister Tom," Tandy said, actually leaning her shoulder against his broad chest and shoving at him. She appeared to be striving against a granite wall. "Ye got to go. This ain't proper."

"I'll leave," Nicholas said, his jaw clearly clenched. "Once my lady understands she's to stay away from my . . . from Alvie St. Irving." He glowered at Serena. "And that's an order."

"Oh, Mister Tom," Tandy gasped, her face now all but scrunched against his chest as she attempted to move him. "Y-you can't order my lady."

"Stay away from Alvie St. Irving?" Serena's mouth dropped open. His lightning change of subject was dumbfounding. "What do you mean?"

"Alvie's a sweet, innocent girl," Nicholas said. "I'll not have you leading her astray. Teaching her to be like you."

"Master Tom!" Tandy yelped. "Whot are ye saying?"

A shocking, unbearable pain ripped through Serena. The insult cut through her very heart. At the moment she couldn't even fathom how he would know Alvie St. Irving, but clearly he knew her, and loved her, and thought she, Serena Fairchild, an unhealthy influence upon her. Suddenly, for no earthly reason, tears burned at her eyes. She sprung from her chair, clenching her hairbrush, determined, no matter what, never to let him see he had wounded her. "I will do what I want, and you'll not order me about, do you hear? Now get out."

"You will not see her," Nicholas roared.

"Get out, I say!" Serena yelled. The mortifying tears

threatened to fall. Wildly, Serena flung the hairbrush at him.

"Move!" Nicholas ordered, and quickly shoved a squealing Tandy aside. He received the spinning hairbrush smack in his chest. He didn't flinch one lick as it bounced off him. He only glared all the more. "You will promise me."

"I shan't!" Serena cried. Twirling, she snatched up the powder box and hefted it high. "Now get out!"

"Oh, no, miss," Tandy breathed, though she stepped farther away from Nicholas.

Serena let the box fly. The powder dusted Nicholas even before the box nabbed him on the shoulder.

Nicholas laughed. "Stop throwing things, you shrew."

"Ooh, yes, my lady," Tandy breathed, wringing her hands. "Please do."

Tom's laughter only salted Serena's raw wound. The cur would not laugh at her! She turned and grabbed up the rouge pot.

"Stop it, I say!" Nicholas said, stalking toward her.

"Get out," Serena ordered, her voice strangled. She flung the pot. It went wide of the mark, and Nicholas reached her, snatching up her arm. He shook it and growled, "Stop it!"

"Oh, Mister Tom," Tandy cried and rushed forward. "You can't touch my lady!" She flapped her hands, even as both Serena and Nicholas stood frozen, staring at each other. Serena's tears suddenly escaped and slid down her cheek.

"Serena," Nicholas said, his voice rough. He dropped her arm and reached to place both hands on her shoulders.

"Oh, no, Mister Tom," Tandy screeched, attempting to squeeze herself between them as a buffer. "Ye can't be touching her."

Serena couldn't move, her tears suddenly incapacitating her. Inexorably, Nicholas drew her to him, forcing the dithering Tandy out from between them.

"Now yer hugging her!" Tandy gasped. "Ye can't be huggin' my lady!" She threw up her hands and fled the room, crying out for Lady Lucille to come quick 'cause Mister Tom "was a doing what he oughtn't."

"Don't cry." Nicholas's voice lowered. "I didn't mean to make you cry."

Serena hid her face against his chest. She knew she should force him away, but she couldn't seem to find the strength. "I'm not crying, you p-peasant lout." She heard him chuckle, but it was low and odd. "And don't touch me. Y-you smell like a gin house."

"Serena," he said again, only enfolding her closer.

"What is going on in here?" Lady Lucille's voice said with authority. "Tom, release Serena."

"I tried to stop him, Lady Lucille," Tandy's voice wailed. "I did. He . . . he shouldn't be hugging my lady! He shouldn't!"

Serena felt Tom's arms fall from about her. He stepped back. Serena quickly dashed the tears away and glanced toward the door. Lady Lucille stood, hands upon her hips and amusement upon her face. Tandy stood behind her, wringing her hands.

Nicholas straightened. "Forgive me, Lady Lucille. I will leave." With that, he walked from the room.

Lady Lucille watched him go. She shook her head. "At least he's leaving with his clothes on this time."

"Whot!" Tandy cried.

Lady Lucille ignored her, looking closely at Serena. "Fighting with the servants again, Serena?" She asked in a mild tone.

Serena lifted her head and strove for some dignity. "I wasn't fighting with the servants."

The other two women merely looked at her and then at the room. The hairbrush lay close to the overturned powder box, a large splotch of white surrounding the circumference. The rouge pot was spilling out a fine circle of red upon the carpet as well.

"I see," Lady Lucille said, with only the slightest trace of amusement in her voice.

"Nor will I ever again," Serena said.

"Of course not," Lady Lucille murmured, clearly biting her lip.

Serena quickly turned toward the vanity. She forced a calmness to her voice. "We must hurry, or I will be late for the ball."

"Yes, my lady," Tandy said in a hushed tone and moved quickly toward her.

"Very well." Lady Lucille shook her head and then left the room.

Tandy wisely did not say a word to Serena as she finished her toilette. Serena found she herself could say nothing as well.

It was noted that evening that the lady Serena did not appear her normal self. Her hair was loosely arranged. She clearly had natural beauty that night, for her face was void of any hint of powder or rouge. Nor did she act in her usual manner. She neither flirted nor danced with her normal vivacity. It seemed she moved through the evening like a sleepwalker, her mind totally someplace else.

Nicholas walked through the crowded fish market, studying the catches the fishmongers all shouted about. He had his instructions from Louis upon exactly what fish he required. Firm. Pink. Fresh. Smell it to be certain. Nicholas laughed. The Earl of Claremont had sunk to smelling fish for their freshness. Then the haggling would start, of course. Louis had explained the entire procedure, and Nicholas daren't spend one copper too much. Once again he shook his head. Sitting in the House of Lords seemed easier by far.

Being a proper servant was more difficult than one would imagine. A darkness settled within him. Or perhaps it was regret. He had finally succeeded in becoming a proper servant, for an entire week now, in fact. And his employer had been a proper lady. It seemed as if the fire had gone out of Serena. She was completely cool toward him. Not a feigned coolness, but a true coolness. Of course, that was whenever she was at home. However, she was rarely at home. Nor, in truth, could Nicholas blame her. As drunk as he was that night, he doubted he would ever forget the tears in Serena's eyes. He had never intended to bring her to such.

"Here ye are, mate," a voice suddenly said from behind. Nicholas felt the sharp jab of a pistol muzzle in his right side.

"Yeh, here ye are," another voice gruffed, and Nicholas felt another pistol on his left side.

He sighed. "Hello, Zack and Jack. What are you two doing here?"

"We've come fer ye," Jack said.

"What took you so long?" Nicholas asked, walking forward at the double prodding of their pistols.

"We had to think things over," Jack responded.

"I have no doubt," Nicholas said. "So, do you really think you'll get to kill me this time?"

"We're not going to kill you," Zack said. Nicholas glanced back to see a pleased grin upon his face.

"We're going to take you to the Frenchie," Jack said on the other side. Nicholas looked at him. He was smiling evilly.

"We'll let him decide if yer a bastard or not," Zack said. "Then we'll kill ye."

It was obvious both men were extremely proud of themselves and their clever thinking. Nicholas sighed.

He had no intention of traveling anywhere with these two idiots. He looked narrowly about and his focus settled upon a man walking in front of him, who carried on his back a wooden cage with two geese in it.

"But I am a bastard," Nicholas said. Bolting forward, he grabbed the cage, jerking it from the man's unsuspecting hold. The birds squawked loudly. So did Jack and Zack as Nicholas twisted with the cage, flinging it at them. Jack, apparently the quicker wit, lifted his pistol and fired. One of the feathered friends loudly honked its last goodbye.

"What the devil!" the large, decaged man roared, spinning. His broad face mottled to purple as he saw the foul deed, with Jack standing over it, his pistol still smoking. "You shot me goose, you bloody ass!"

Jack paled, as if he'd cooked his goose, rather than shot it. Zack, obviously dumb but loyal, took his stance beside his partner, waving his gun like an ineffectual wand, first toward Nicholas and then toward the enraged, menacing goose owner.

Nicholas took advantage of Zack's dilemma, and sidled to the nearest stall, which vaunted a fine catch of fish for the day. He snatched up the nearest halibut, a dandy one at that, and, taking aim, threw it. The winging fish smacked Zack's pistol clean out of his hand.

The fishmonger unfortunately took even more offense over the use of his halibut than did the goose man. He roared and jumped at Nicholas, heedless of the fish stand between them. It toppled. Suddenly Nicholas was swamped by both fish and fishmonger and knocked to the ground. The goose man, apparently emboldened by such action, charged into the fray. Actually, since he skidded upon a cod and flew forward, one should say he dove into the fray. Jack and Zack, two chaps not to be left out, followed suit with even less grace.

Then all hell broke loose. If hell included shouts about birds and fish and bastards and lords. Nicholas only knew there was a tangle of bodies and the smell of fish. A lone goose honking rose over the sound of heavy blows and the grunts of men. Nicholas didn't care which body he struck, knowing full well it was each man for himself. From the hefty blows he received in return, he couldn't doubt his strategy. Unfortunately, he feared he struck as many fish as men.

Soon, over the other sounds, a new one arose. That of the watch approaching. Nicholas had expected it. Nay, even depended upon it. He kicked out viciously at the man who had grappled his leg. He thought it was the goose man, but wasn't sure. He heard a responding curse and rolled away, scrambling to his feet. He almost slipped on a white fish. He could see the authorities breaking through the now surrounding crowd. He noticed Zack crawling to his feet as well. Jack was well buried under the fishmonger, and the goose man was howling and rocking amongst the fish all by himself. Nicholas realized that not only had he kicked the goose man, but he must have kicked him in a very vulnerable spot.

Wasting no time on remorse, Nicholas looked quickly about. He spied a sizable salmon and snatched it up. Then he waded over and snagged Zack by the shirt. "Come on, man!"

He jerked the stunned Zack forward. They both heard the renewed shouts of the authorities and broke into a run. Nicholas dragged the panting Zack into an alley and then ruthlessly slammed him up against the one wall. Zack choked, and then stared at the large salmon Nicholas held in the other hand. "Wh-whot you going to do with that?"

"I'd like to beat you over the head with it," Nicholas growled.

"Oh, God," Zack gurgled.

"But I can't," Nicholas said. "It's dinner."

"D-dinner?" Zack stammered.

"Yes, dinner," Nicholas said. "Now listen to me, Zack." Zack's gaze remained upon the dangling salmon. He seemed fascinated by it. Nicholas shook him. "Forget the fish and listen to me."

"Whot?" Zack asked, his frightened gaze finally rising to Nicholas's.

"You go to Randolf Dorvelle and tell him to come after me himself," Nicholas said. "Tell him I'll have no more of this. Is that understood?"

"Yes," Zack said vehemently. Apparently he wanted no more of it, either.

"He's a nobleman and I'm a nobleman," Nicholas said.

Zack's eyes lighted. "So you are him?"

"Of course I'm him," Nicholas said in exasperation. Then he glared. "You tell Dorvelle that I'll be glad to have it out with him in a duel like two noblemen should."

"Yes," Zack said, nodding. "Duel. Yes."

"Tell him I'll be waiting for him. He can find me at my country estate." He rattled Zack. "Tell him the fight is between him and me. No one else. If he is a man of honor, he'll abide by it."

"Y-yes, m-my lord," Zack said.

"Very well," Nicholas said. "And if he doesn't pay you for the information, come back to me and I'll pay you."

"Yes, my lord," Zack said.

Nicholas heard the tramp of heavy feet. He glanced down the alley and saw the authorities coming. "Run, man."

Nicholas unleashed Zack and darted down the alley to the sound of the following authorities. White-hot pain shot through his injured hip. Nicholas merely gripped the salmon harder and kept running.

"I am so very pleased you came for a visit," Serena said with a forced smile to Lady Standout and Lady Treat. She all but herded them toward the door. Serving them tea had been horrendous. Tom was once again nowhere to be found and she had commandeered Tandy into serving. Tandy had kept up a running commentary all the while she served the ladies their tea, even offering to read their tea leaves in the end, if they wished. Needless to say, Lady Standout and Lady Treat had declined, but Serena had no doubt they would be telling the story to their friends soon enough. Serena couldn't believe it, but, for once, she was anxious for Tom to return.

"Indeed, it was a delight," Lady Lucille said, her eyes twinkling.

Serena glared at her. Even if Lady Lucille did not care for the two ladies, who were admittedly the worst sticklers in the ton, not to mention two of the worst gossips, she should have sympathy for Serena's feelings.

"Yes," Serena said. "And Lady Lucille and I, both of us, would be delighted to attend your drum."

This time Lady Lucille glared at *her.* "Indeed."

"It shall be an intimate do," Lady Standout said, stopping in the middle of the foyer.

"Yes," Lady Treat said with a regal nod. "We've invited only the best of the ton." Her thin nose quivered. " 'Tis shocking, how even the best of the ton have lowered their standards these days."

"Shocking," Lady Standout said.

Suddenly the outside door flew open, and Nicholas burst through the portal. He entered so abruptly that all the ladies started. Then Lady Standout let out a small shriek, her eyes widening. "Oh, my stars!"

Nicholas stood swaying before them. His hair had lost its powder and was loose from its quay. His ornate livery was rent and dampened to dark green in patches. That, however, was not the worst of it. The torn lace of his left cuff dripped over a huge, but clearly dead, salmon.

"Rather, oh my nose!" Lady Lucille cried, coughing and covering that offended member.

"Blast!" Nicholas cursed, starting back and staring at the women as if it were they who were out of place and reeking. The women stared back. It was a decided stand-off.

Nicholas finally straightened into a dignified pose. "Good afternoon, ladies." He offered them a low, courtly bow. The movement only wafted his seafaring cologne more strongly to them. The ladies in unison skittered farther away from him. When he straightened, he smiled a rather stupid smile and lurched toward Serena. "Tonight's dinner, my lady. Fresh."

"I can see," Serena said, her words muffled as she stepped back.

"Large sized," Nicholas said, lurching even closer. He was like an unwanted puppy determined to follow.

"Indeed," Serena murmured, stifling a cough.

"And I didn't pay a copper too . . ." He stumbled up to her. ". . . much."

His left leg wobbled in an odd way and then he toppled forward. Serena's arms were suddenly full of foot-man and dead fish. She was not prepared for the weight. She cursed as Tom and she, salmon well sand-wiched between them, went down, Tom on top of her. She heard the good ladies shriek, and irately wondered what they had to cry about, since it was she who had a salmon pressed into her chest, and a far too large and heavy man anchored atop her, to boot. Her temper flared.

"Fiend seize it, Tom," she cried. "You're drunk again. Get off me."

"I'm not drunk," Nicholas said, in an odd, pained voiced. "Just run off my legs. Or . . . leg, that is."

"You're drunk," Serena insisted, and shoved at him. He felt like a dead weight.

"Am not," Nicholas said. He lifted his head slightly toward her. "You can smell my breath."

"All I can smell is fish," Serena exclaimed. Frustrated, she punched at him.

"Damn it, woman," Nicholas groaned, his face twisting in agony. "I've already been hit there."

Serena froze. She looked closely at Tom, who'd closed his eyes. Only then did she notice the blue of a bruise on his cheek, and a bleeding cut on his forehead, hidden by his falling hair. He groaned once more and merely lowered his head to her shoulder.

Serena, stunned and truly frightened, wrapped her arms about him. Turning her head at an angle, she was able to get a view of the other ladies. They all stood, gaping at her. They were rather cockeyed in her vision, but they were definitely gaping. She forced a cool, polite smile to her lips. "Please forgive me if I don't see you to your carriage, ladies."

"Er, I shall," Lady Lucille said, apparently coming to life again. She turned, and, grabbing both ladies by the arm, dragged them away.

"Tom?" Serena's voice came out embarrassingly soft in concern. "Can you move?"

"I don't think so," Nicholas said, his voice low.

"Well, we can't remain here," Serena said, forcing a prosaic tone. "My . . . my backside is becoming quite cold on this marble."

She gained a chuckle from him. "Forgive me."

"You don't have to really move," she said in an encouraging tone. "Just help a little. I want to roll you over."

"G-good proposal," Nicholas said, with an actual hint of humor. "Improper perhaps . . ."

"Oh, be quiet," Serena said, flushing. "I want to roll to the right. Ready?"

"Yes, my lady," Nicholas said.

"Roll," Serena said. She put all her strength and energy into the action. Apparently more than she intended, or else Tom was regaining his strength, for roll they did. Twice. At least, when they finished, Tom was the one beneath her.

He grinned. "Always have to be on top, don't you, Serena?"

"Shut up," Serena said, and scrabbled off him none too gracefully or carefully.

Nicholas groaned and merely closed his eyes. Serena grew frightened as she stared down at him, the salmon flattened to his chest. "Tom?"

He opened his eyes. There was just a glimmer in them. "More, sweeting?"

Serena's mouth fell open. Then she put her hands upon her hips. "You are the most odious of men. This is not humorous, one wit. I . . ."

"Serena," Lady Lucille said, returning from the outside. "What is the matter now?"

"Nothing," Serena responded, gritting her teeth. "I'm going to assist Tom to his room. Could you please take the fish."

"What?" Lady Lucille asked, her brows rising.

"Take the blasted fish," Serena said. "And order up a bath for him. Also a doctor."

No," Nicholas said. "I don't need a doctor. It's just my leg. I overtaxed it."

"You certainly did," Serena said tartly. She looked pointedly at Lucille. "Lucille?"

"Oh, very well," Lucille said. She walked over and, leaning down gingerly, picked up the fish from Tom's chest.

"Take good care of it," Nicholas said. "I did a lot to get it."

Lucille looked once at the fish, and then at Nicholas, who still lay flat on the floor. "Fought like the devil, did it?"

"You could say that," Nicholas said, chuckling.

Lady Lucille, holding the fish out with one hand and pinching the other one to her nose, left the foyer.

"Now," Serena said, drawing in a deep breath, "for you."

"Yes, for me," Nicholas murmured. Serena bent down and offered him a hand. Wincing, he sat up and waved her hand away. "I can do it myself."

"Let me help you, for goodness' sakes," Serena said, fear sharpening her tone. "You are in no condition—"

"I can do it," Nicholas grunted, and slowly, precariously, rose to his feet. He swayed. "Damn!"

"Tom!" Serena exclaimed, and quickly grabbed hold of him. "Just let me help you, or we'll be all day at it."

Nicholas muttered a curse under his breath, one Serena was sure she was glad she didn't understand, and without another word between them, Nicholas limped, with Serena half carrying him, through the house and to the servants' quarters. She sighed in relief when they found his room and she had deposited him upon the bed.

"The bath should help your leg," she murmured as Nicholas sucked in his breath, clearly in pain. Concerned, and without thought, she reached for his jacket. "I'll send some brandy up as well. I still think you should have a doctor. You may have done permanent damage to it this time."

"I don't need a doct—Blast it, woman," Nicholas exclaimed as Serena jerked a little too forcefully upon the jacket's lapels. "What are you trying to do?"

Serena blinked. "You need to get out of those clothes."

An odd look flashed through his eyes. "No, I don't."

"Yes, you do," Serena said, frowning. "They smell. You can't be comfortable in them, I'm sure."

"I am comfortable," Nicholas insisted.

"But . . ." Serena persisted.

"Confound it," Nicholas growled. "I don't need your fussing and cosseting. I'm not a damn charity case."

Serena lifted her chin. "I was not treating you like a charity case."

"No, just like a bloody baby," Nicholas said, glaring. "What? Were you going to bathe me as well?"

Serena paled, and jerked her hands back. "Of course not."

"Thank God for small mercies," Nicholas said, sneering.

Serena sprung up, indignant. "You need not take that tone with me. I was only trying to be kind."

"Well, I don't need your kindness," Nicholas shot back. "Crippled I may be—"

"I didn't say that," Serena exclaimed.

"No?" Nicholas asked. He mimicked her tone. "You may have damaged it permanently this time."

"Well," Serena said angrily. "It might be a consideration."

"It's not," Nicholas gritted out. "I don't want your damn doctor or your infernal help. Now, would you just leave."

"Gladly," Serena said angrily. "I'm sure I don't care what happens to you. You brought it upon yourself, after all." With that, she spun on her heel and stormed from the room.

Serena paced her room in her nightgown. The man was rude and odious. No doubt the stubborn beast was still sitting in his stinking, filthy clothes merely because he wouldn't accept her assistance. Or perhaps he'd made it to the tub but drowned in it. She tossed her head. It would serve him right if he had. She wouldn't care a fig, to be sure.

Serena halted, another indignant thought blazing through her already tumultuous conscience. Faith, she had not only permitted the man to be rude and officious to her, but she had actually permitted him to dismiss her from his room as if she were a lacky. It had been rank insubordination. She was the mistress of the house, and, as such, had the full right to determine what was required for her servants. Not the other way around!

Without thinking, Serena grabbed up her robe and rammed her arms into it. Muttering under her breath, she slammed out of her room and chased through the darkened house toward the servants' quarters. She rapped on Tom's door but once, and then without waiting, shoved it open and stalked into the room. She came to an abrupt standstill.

Tom lay upon the bed, bolstered by pillows. He wore britches and a shirt, loose and opened. She had grown accustomed to seeing him in her livery, with powder and paint. His long, flaxen hair rested clean about his shoulders. He was a stunning man.

Tom looked at her, his brown eyes darkening. Serena couldn't find her voice. He lifted a brow. "A social call, my lady, at this time of night?"

"No," Serena said, pulling herself together. "Of course not."

"Ah, then you came to see if the cripple still lived," Nicholas said, his lip curling.

Serena stiffened. Unfortunately, the man had the right of it. No matter what she had told herself, she had wanted to see for herself that he was all right. Forcing a coolness to her eyes, she stalked toward him. "No, I came to see if you were dead instead. But since you are not, to my disappointment, then I wish to tell you I will not tolerate your behavior any longer."

Nicholas snorted. "You will not need to do so."

"What do you mean by that?" Serena asked, placing her hands to her hips.

"Never mind," he said, shifting in apparent irritation. As he moved, his shirt fell open.

Serena gasped. His ribs showed a bruise the size of a fist upon them. "My God!" Forgetting her pose, forgetting everything, Serena sat down upon the bed, her knees almost giving out. She stared at the cruel mark. "You must have a salve or ointment put upon that." She gently reached out her hand to the bruise, as if by touching it she could draw the pain from it.

"Don't," Nicholas said, drawing in his breath. "I told you . . ."

"I know, you don't need my charity," Serena said, jerking her hand back. She flushed, truly shaken. Just what in heaven's name was the matter with her? She had come to ring a peal over his head, not to . . . to touch him!

Her gaze flitted to his in embarrassment, and then froze. Tom's eyes were dark, and something unknown, compelling, flickered within them. Serena caught her breath, unable to turn away. He slowly reached out his hand and twined it in her hair. A shiver coursed through Serena.

"Perhaps I do," he said, his voice low.

"D-do what?" Serena asked. She licked her lips nervously. She should move. She knew it, but couldn't.

"Need your charity," he whispered. He pulled on her hair. Gently. It wasn't a tug, it didn't hurt. Yet Serena leaned forward, in answer to the sound of his voice, the command of his hand. His mouth hovered close to hers. "Just one kiss."

"One kiss," Serena murmured. Their lips met, warm and soft. Nicholas drew back. Serena sighed, the warmth still glowing through her. "One kiss."

Nicholas growled, and then his lips covered hers again, fierce and demanding. The warmth in Serena ignited, ignited into passion and need. She could feel its very texture and fiber. Just as she could feel the fire of Tom's lips, inhale the scent of him, feel his strength as he released her hair and wrapped his arms about her.

Nicholas shifted her, laying her down upon the bed. Serena willingly moved with him, shivering when his strong body covered hers. She gasped and moaned at the same time, shocked by his intimate touch, captured by the sensations that reverberated to the very core of her. Nicholas groaned, and she drew in the very breath of his desire in their kiss.

His lips left hers, and she felt wild and lost without them. New sensations filled the void swiftly, as Tom's lips trailed a sensual, drugging path along her neck to the valley of her breasts. Serena heard another low moan. She didn't know if it came from her. She didn't care. Her body arched of its own desire, rising in demand to meet his lips. It trembled with hot chills, as his freed hand smoothed down her rib cage, caressed the curve of her hip.

Then his hand slid to caress between her legs. Serena's legs suddenly clenched tight, catching his hand as they instinctively drew together and her knees came up. It could have been from modesty. Should have been from modesty. But it was an instinctual fear, fear of that final intimacy and fear of the man who had driven her so incessantly to the moment.

Nicholas lifted his head. "Serena?" He attempted to withdraw his hand. Serena remained frozen. "Serena! You're breaking my hand." Still Serena didn't move, as reality, passion, and fear warred within her. "Serena, stop it. You are acting like a virgin."

Tom's words cut through the fog. Outrage blasted out all the other battling emotions. Serena indeed released his hand. She slapped at it, and then fiercely shoved him away.

"Of course I'm acting like a virgin," she said. Shaking, she sat up. "I am one."

"What?" Nicholas asked, falling back.

Serena glanced over at him, even as she attempted to ignore the hot flush burning her as she adjusted her clothing. The expression on Tom's face was one of stunned confusion. The look riled Serena's slowly returning propriety. "How could you not think I'm a virgin? I am not married."

"But you've been engaged five times," Nicholas said, his eyes narrowing.

Serena stiffened. A numbing pain engulfed her, effectively killing any desire and passion. She shook her head, trying to survive the hurt settling into her very soul. Desperately, her mind attempted to place matters in an acceptable light. "Maybe—m-maybe in your class that would mean that I . . ." She flushed hot. "Well, it would mean . . ."

"I know what it would mean," Nicholas said, rising to settle on his elbow. His eyes shot fire. "You can't mean out of all those men you've been betrothed to that this didn't happen. That you didn't—"

"No!" Serena shouted. Suddenly a lonesome, bitter wind whipped through her. She'd never done anything like this with her fiancés. She'd never even felt the desire to do so. A cruel, honest voice whispered that neither had her fiancés felt the need to do so with her. Her mind strove to ignore that voice, drawing around itself a cloak of comfort. "Th-they were honorable men. Of course they wouldn't have . . . have made such advances."

She sprung from the bed, attempting a dignity. "People in our class d-do not do this unless they are married. In fact, they have to marry if they . . ." She halted abruptly, turning pale as Tom gazed at her with a steady, unreadable look. "Please, don't think I—I was suggesting we . . ." She waved her hand feebly, totally mortified. "I was only attempting to explain the differences between our c-classes. I understand how you could think . . . you were merely behaving in a manner common to . . . to your order. And I . . ."

Serena clamped her mouth shut, realizing she was digging a hole the width and breadth of Christendom for herself. Choking back a ridiculous sob, she spun and fled from the room.

Five

" 'Twas a sad crush at Lady Arrowroot's last night, wouldn't you say?" Lady Lucille murmured as she scooped a goodly amount of marmalade upon her toast. "Lord Fullen seemed excessively enamored of you, but then in that new ensemble you wore, who would not be?"

"Yes," Serena said absently as Nobles, their new butler, poured tea into her cup. She nodded. "Thank you, Nobles, that will be all."

"Yes, my lady," Nobles said, bowing. He walked with a stately tread from the breakfast room.

Lady Lucille sighed, staring after him. "I do miss Tom."

Serena's hand froze as she lifted her teacup. Realizing it trembled, she set it down carefully. "I assure you, I—I do not."

"Don't you?" Lady Lucille murmured.

"Of course not." Serena lifted her chin. "Not one whit. And you most certainly cannot complain about Nobles, he is an excellent butler. He is managing our new staff to perfection."

"Yes," Lady Lucille said, grimacing. "But it is so dull now without Tom."

"Dull?" Serena asked. She felt a flush rising within her, as well as the odd ache she'd felt ever since they'd discovered Tom missing the morning after—Serena ruthlessly cut her thoughts short. " 'Tis peaceful, as it should be."

Lady Lucille shook her head. "I must own it. I didn't think you would manage to run Tom off."

Serena's hand clenched around the coffee cup handle. "I didn't run him off."

"I do wish you would tell me what you finally said to make him decamp," Lady Lucille said, her eyes inquisitive.

Serena's mouth turned dry. "I did not say anything."

"Then you did something?" Lady Lucille persisted.

"No!" Serena answered quickly, far too quickly. It was, unfortunately, the same argument she'd had with herself for the past week. She'd had nothing to do with Tom disappearing. The man had already shown signs of dereliction to his duty long before his leaving. Clearly he'd intended to leave, and that night had merely thought to have a dalliance with the mistress of the house before doing so, knowing he'd have his pleasure and be gone in the morning. Self-loathing rose within Serena. The man had almost succeeded with her. She had almost given herself to a servant!

Serena glanced up. Lady Lucille was watching her with a deep intensity. She flushed. "I did nothing, I tell you."

At that moment, Nobles entered again. He bowed. "My lady, there is a person who claims—"

"Don't bother, old man, I'll introduce myself!" a well-known voice called out.

"Robby!" Serena cried, and sprung from her chair.

By that time, a young gentleman with the same dark hair and green eyes of Serena entered the room. Nobles was well nigh run down and shoved aside as brother and sister rushed toward each other.

"Hello, sweetheart," Robby said, wrapping strong

arms about her and lifting her off the ground to swing her around in the circle.

"What are you doing here?" Serena asked in pleasure as he set her down.

"Got leave," Robby said, grinning down at her with his wide, crooked grin. "Heard you tossed old Applebee over and came back here."

"Oh," Serena said, flushing.

"Was glad to hear it," Robby said, his eyes warm and supportive. "Thought he was a dull dog. Didn't want him for a brother-in-law anyway."

Serena smiled in relief. Regardless of their offhand manners, both were close, very close. "Thank you."

"Don't bother about the popinjay," Robby said, his arms tightening about her again. Then he grinned. "You're looking as fine as five pence, my dear."

"Palaverer," Serena laughed, her heart warming nevertheless. "You know I don't. One of these days that silver tongue of yours . . ." Serena halted as she noticed a tiny, dark-haired woman who stood quietly within the entrance. She drew back from her brother. "Robby, who . . . who is this?"

Robby started and then he turned. "Oh, sorry." He held out his hand and the woman stepped forward and took it without a word. "Serena, this is Sparrow. Sparrow, meet my sister, Serena."

"How do you do?" Serena said, studying the woman, who merely smiled and nodded. She had the largest brown eyes, eyes deeply vulnerable, but also with a sad, wise look in them. Serena forced a smile. "Sparrow, 'tis an uncommon name."

"I gave it to her," Robby said cheerfully. "I don't know her true name. Sparrow can't speak, you see."

"I . . . see," Serena said, blinking.

"Found her after . . . well, you know what old Bony is up to now he's off the island. And the federalist troops ain't doing anything. But, anyway, not saying I was involved. Mean, we English ain't at war with him yet . . ."

Serena felt a shiver and waved her hand. "Let us not talk about it."

Robby grinned. "You're a trump." He glanced at the woman he called Sparrow. "My sister can bedevil you most times, but other times, she's the most knowing woman I've ever encountered."

Without missing a breath, he looked back to Serena. "Well, anyhow, I found Sparrow. Just wandering, mind you." His voice lowered, even as Sparrow's eyes lowered. "She was in a bad way, I can tell you. Didn't think she'd make it there for a few days. She's a tiny thing, but she's got spunk for all that. Regular Trojan. Still don't eat enough." Sparrow's eyes rose at that and she made a face. Robby laughed. "But if she wants to be a rack of bones, guess I can't stop her from that."

"Men," Lady Lucille said, finally rising from the table and crossing over and holding her hand out. "Ignore him. We are pleased to have you here, my dear."

Sparrow's eyes darkened and she nodded, taking up Lucille's hands.

"See," Robby said to Sparrow. "Told you they'd be glad to have you come." A flush covered Sparrow's cheeks. Robby smiled to Serena. "She thought you might not want her. Told her it was rot, but you know women."

Serena started back slightly. Since Sparrow did not speak, it was difficult to understand her brother's ability to communicate with her, but clearly there was communication indeed. Which was strange, for Robby, though a dear, was the carefree sort, who generally needed a brick thrown at him for him to understand any subtlety. She smiled at Sparrow. "Of course we are glad to have you here."

"Thought you might want her to be your dresser," Robby said, his voice changing slightly.

"My dresser?"

"Yes," Robby said. "I'll lay odds she'll be a dandy dresser. She's French after all. can't help but know about all that, don't you think."

Serena started to laugh. She stopped quickly, however, when she realized both Sparrow and Robby were watching her intently. Evidently this was important. "Of course she can be my dresser," Serena said, thinking that after Tandy's talkative ways, a silent dresser might be perfect. She doubted if she would be turned out properly, but these days it didn't seem to matter. "But only if she truly wishes it."

"She does," Robby said quickly. "My Sparrow can make her own way."

He said it in such an odd way, with both pride and protectiveness, that Serena shook her head to clear it. "No, of course not. But please, do come over to the breakfast table. Nobles, we'll require two more place settings."

"Yes, my lady," Nobles said, bowing. He departed quickly.

"Starchy fellow, ain't he?" Robby said, striding over to the breakfast table.

"That's what I say," Lady Lucille laughed as she took up her place. "I far preferred Tom."

"Who's Tom?" Robby asked. He pulled out a chair. "Here, Sparrow." Sparrow quickly moved to take up the chair. He grinned down at her. "Now be a good girl and eat it up when it comes." He plopped down in the chair next to her and sighed. "Gads, I'm famished."

"What do you mean who's Tom?" Serena asked, striding quickly over to take up her seat. "You're the one who hired him, and why you ever did, I cannot fathom."

Robby's eyes widened. "I hired this Tom?"

Serena tensed and her eyes narrowed. "The man said you hired him as an overseer for the house."

"Indeed," Lady Lucille chuckled. "Serena attempted to try and throw him out upon our arrival. But he said you'd hired him and he'd not desert his post."

Robby stared at her a moment, and then the confusion left his face. "Oh, I see. You mean *that* Tom. Yes, I did hire him. Of course I hired him," he said more firmly. "In fact, that was going to be my next question. How is old . . . er, Tom?"

"I wouldn't know," Serena said coolly. "He took French leave of us a week ago."

Robby started back. "What do you mean he took French leave?"

"I mean he took off," Serena said. "Deserted us."

"Yes," Lady Lucille said, her tone dry. "Serena drove him away."

"I did not!" Serena exclaimed, glaring at her.

"She couldn't have." Robby shook his head. "He ain't the kind to run, unless he had to." He frowned. "Did he leave a note or anything?"

"No," Serena said in frigid tones. "He just disappeared."

Robby's face turned pale. "Oh, Lord, don't say so."

"I do," Serena said. "And good riddance to him."

"Damn it," Robby muttered, running his hand through his hair.

"What is the matter?" Lady Lucille asked.

"He's got to be in trouble."

"He will be if I ever see him again," Serena said, with far more bluster than she cared to admit.

Robby sprung from his chair. "Blast it. I've got to find him."

"No!" Serena exclaimed, standing. "Don't you dare go after that man!"

Robby dashed toward the door. "You don't understand. I've got to!"

"Robby, no," Serena called, picking up her skirts and

chasing after Robby. "I'll not have that man in my house again, do you hear me!" She caught up with him in the foyer, all but skidding into him. "You mustn't go after him. There is no need to!"

Robby caught her by the shoulders. "You don't understand, Serena. I don't have time to explain now, but I've got to find him. Make sure he's safe."

"Please, Robby . . ." Serena gripped the lapel of his jacket. Her voice, despite her best efforts, turned pleading. "Don't go after him."

Robby stilled, and his eyes narrowed upon her. "Why? What happened?"

"Nothing," Serena said quickly "I—I just don't want you to go after him. I—I don't want to ever see that man again."

"Why?" Robby asked, his grip tightening on her shoulders. "Why?"

"Because he made advances toward me," Serena said, goaded. "That's why!"

"What?" Robby's eyes widened in shock.

Serena flushed hot. "He . . . he made advances."

"I can't believe it. He'd not . . ." Robby stopped, and his face darkened. "Damn and blast him! I thought he'd reformed."

Serena stared, aghast. "Do you mean he's done this with other employers?"

"No . . . yes," Robby said, looking totally confused. "In a sense, he has."

"And you hired him!" Serena exclaimed, enraged.

"You weren't supposed to be here," Robby said, his voice tormented. "And even if you were, I'd never thought he'd . . . I thought he had more honor than that."

"Honor?" Serena snorted. "No, of course he doesn't have any honor. He's a low-born, common . . . lout."

Robby's gaze darkened. "Just how far . . . ?"

Serena flushed as much. "I stopped him before . . .

I stopped him in time." She looked down. "I—I don't know how it happened . . ."

"Well, I do," Robby said. He hugged her quickly. "It wasn't your fault. He's . . . well, he's just too experienced for you, the damn rake. But don't you worry, I'll find him, and if he's not already dead, I'll make him pay."

"No." Serena shook her head. "I don't want you to. I just want this matter to . . . be left as it is."

"I can't do that," Robby said, his voice strangled.

"Yes, you can," Serena said desperately. She drew in a ragged breath. "I—I don't want anyone to know I was so indiscreet with a servant. He's left and we'll never see him again. Can't we just leave it at that?"

Robby's complexion turned rather green. " 'Fraid that ain't possible." He set Serena away from him. "Now, don't you worry. I'll find him, and when I do, he'll be sorry. Damn philanderer. Thought he was my friend." He strode to the door and jerked it open. "Take care of Sparrow for me, will you?"

With that, Robby was out the door, the resounding slam of it echoing through the foyer. Serena stood, stunned and confused. Her only consolation was the dependence that Robby wouldn't be able to find Tom.

Nicholas gave his horse one more brush. He heard a sound at the stable door and looked up.

"Robby!" Nicholas broke into a grin. "What are you doing in England?"

"What am I doing in England?" Robby said, stalking toward him. "This is what I'm doing in England." He drew back a fist and plowed it into Nicholas's jaw.

Nicholas had but a moment to shake the pain away before Robby was upon him. Nicholas didn't even hesitate to question why Robby was attacking him, but only returned the fight with equal ferocity. He knew he must. Though few would think it, Robby was a bruising and dangerous fighter. They'd stood beside each other in too many battles for Nicholas not to know.

The two men fell and tumbled to the stable floor, rolling and pummeling each other. Their grunts of pain were far quieter than the sound of fist against bone. They fought across the stable, causing the horses to whinny in fright, ramming against the tackle and causing it to fall. Soon they tumbled out of the very stable itself, scuffling in the already trampled dirt of the entrance.

Neither man noticed their surroundings. Nicholas grabbed Robby around the neck. Spying the water trough directly behind Robby, Nicholas gathered his strength and shoved Robby backward. Robby's knees hit the wood. He let out a shocked yelp and toppled back, dragging Nicholas with him. Both men splashed into the trough. Nicholas felt Robby's grip slip from him, and he quickly released his own, rolling from the trough.

He stood dripping, watching with narrow eyes as Robby, spurting and sputtering, surfaced.

"Are you cooled off now?" Nicholas asked.

"Yes, damn it," Robby said, dirty ripples of water running down his face. He grabbed hold of the trough's sides and attempted to pull himself out. His fingers slipped, and he fell back, water sloshing over the sides.

Nicholas, unable to help himself, broke into laughter. He sloshed over and extended his hand as Robby surfaced once more, cursing and spitting. "Come on, hot-head."

Robby glared at him a moment, but then took the proffered hand. Nicholas groaned as he hauled Robby from the trough. Then both men, bloodied, wet, and panting, fell to the ground.

"Mind telling me the purpose of your greeting?" Nicholas asked, swiping both water and straw from his face.

"Serena," Robby said, coughing.

Nicholas froze. The ache in his bones settled in deeper. His face stiffened and he nodded. "She told you then."

"Yes," Robby said. His face twisted. "Meant to call you out, but er . . . lost my head."

Nicholas laughed. "Good. This was better."

Robby grinned. "Yes. You're too good with the pistols anyway." He touched his swelling lip. "Too damn handy with the fives also."

"Sorry," Nicholas said. "Been in bad skin lately."

Robby looked at him with understanding. "Serena?"

"Serena," Nicholas nodded. He looked away. "I'm sorry for what I did."

"I hadn't thought you'd . . . you'd dally with her."

"I thought she wasn't as innocent as she was," Nicholas said. Deep in his heart he knew he lied. He'd had his growing suspicions, but that evening he'd refused to believe them. He'd wanted her too badly to consider any of the consequences.

"I should hit you for that," Robby said. He sighed. "But I'm too tired." He grimaced. "And too bloody wet." He frowned, and his green eyes, so very like his sister's, darkened. "I know what the world thinks, because Serena is different. I thought you of all people would see through her."

Nicholas's laugh was bitter. "No, I didn't."

This time Robby looked away. "It's a devil of a fix."

"No," Nicholas said. "I dishonored her. I'll marry her."

"You will?" Robby asked, his eyes widening.

Nicholas nodded. "Yes, I will."

Suddenly Robby looked enraged. "You mean you let

us almost kill each other, when all along, you'd already planned to marry her?"

"You didn't give me a chance to tell you," Nicholas said, shaking his head wryly.

"No. I didn't. Sorry, old man," Robby said. His look turned sheepish. "I knew you were a man of honor."

"No," Nicholas said, his tone stern. "I wasn't a man of honor. But I am prepared to make restitution."

A boyish grin crossed Robby's lips. "Gads, you'll be my brother-in-law. Never expected to be so lucky. Not with all the addlepates Serena's been engaged to before."

"Don't send out the invitations yet," Nicholas said with a bitter laugh. "Serena has to accept first."

"Zeus," Robby said, his eyes widening. "You think she'll object?"

"She just might," Nicholas responded dryly.

Robby worried his lip and then winced. "Damn. But she has to marry you. And so I will tell her."

"No you won't," Nicholas said sharply. "I'll tell her myself. This is one battle you need to leave to me."

"Battle?" Robby asked, his eyes widening.

"Yes, battle," Nicholas said grimly. "I don't think Serena will be pleased to discover our deception."

"Gads, no." Robby's eyes darkened in concern. "What are you going to do?"

"I'm not sure," Nicholas said. "But it's going to have to be a surprise attack. If you tell Serena who I am and that she has to marry me, the odds are she'll take off, and I have no intention of chasing her across the Continent. Courting her will be difficult enough."

"Courting her?" Robby said, choking slightly. "It don't sound like that's what you intend to me."

Nicholas looked steadily at Robby. "No, but she'll marry me."

Robby blinked, and then a hesitancy crossed his face.

"Maybe you two don't have to marry each other after all."

Nicholas barked a laugh. "Turning faint of heart?"

"Well," Robby said, frowning. "I mean, no one knows that you and she did . . . well, whatever you did."

"But I do," Nicholas said curtly. The now familiar self-disgust rose within him again. Not only because of the fact he had almost taken Serena under false pretenses, but that he still desired to take her. He'd not sit back and pretend anymore; neither would he step back and let some other man have Serena. Nicholas rose and forced a smile. "Serena will come around."

"All right." Robby sighed.

Nicholas grinned. "Trust me. But I'm going to have to do it my way."

"Very well." Robby nodded. He crawled to his feet and held out his hand. "I'll let you do it your way. That's a promise."

"Thank you," Nicholas said, and grasped his hand. Their handshake was firm.

"I know I shouldn't be talking to you in this way," Robby said, running his hand through his hair, and leaning back into the large winged-back chair. Sparrow sat upon the ottoman, close to his feet. She reached out a hand and lightly touched him on his sleeve. "But I can't help it. It's the devil's own coil."

He sprung up and paced across the floor. "I promised Nicholas not to say anything to Serena. But Lord, I don't know how Serena will react when she discovers Nicholas is an earl, and not just a servant." Sparrow raised her brows. Robby waved his hand. "Nicholas was Tom, the servant."

He flushed. "I—I don't want to sully your ears, and I don't want you to think the worst of Serena, but . . .

but St. Irving and she . . . well, he's dishonored her."
Sparrow's eyes turned into dark pools of sadness. "No,"
Robby rushed on to say, pacing back to her and touching her upon the shoulder. "It ain't that bad . . . I
hope," he muttered under his breath. "The devil of it
is, they didn't behave properly. I don't know if you understand, but they have to get married now."

Sparrow cocked her head to one side and then
shrugged her shoulder in a very Gaelic way.

"Yes, yes," Robby said, returning to his pacing. "But
when Serena finds out that St. Irving is St. Irving and
not a servant . . ." He let out a long sigh. "Well, I don't
know. I mean, he deceived her for a good purpose. It
wasn't as if he did it out of malice or anything." Sparrow
looked curious. "Nicholas was wounded in an er . . .
encounter in Paris. Well, there was a young Frenchman
involved in it and he got killed. Now his brother, who's
very powerful, is after Nicholas's blood. I sent Nicholas
here to recuperate and hide out. It was a fine notion,
but then Serena came back. Nicholas pretended to be
a servant so as not to ruin his story." He suddenly
chuckled, despite himself. "Gads, just the thought of
Nicholas playing a servant is humorous. Ain't no one
more born and bred to give orders than Nicholas." He
sighed and ran his hand through his hair. "Except
Serena, that is."

Sparrow rose and walked over to Robby who had
halted a moment, frowning and chewing on his lip.
She reached out, took his hand and led him back to
the chair. Robby absently sat back down in it. Then he
sighed. "What am I worrying about? There ain't nothing to be done. Serena must marry Nicholas." He
glanced up and flashed a smile. "I'm glad I talked to
you. You're a sweet Sparrow."

Then his eyes fell and Robby went back to mulling it

over. "It will work out," he muttered once more, staring off into space. "It's just got to work out."

Sparrow sat silently, gazing upon Robby, with a soft, hopeless look in her brown eyes.

Serena sat in a gilt chair, waving her fan against the heat in the Tarringtons' ballroom. She had danced every dance, and was grateful for the one moment of respite. Indeed, her courtier surrounded her, but she was talented at listening with half an ear to the talk and responding, while the other part of her remained distant. She could not say why, but balls had somehow lost their appeal, and flirting its delight.

Serena saw Alvie St. Irving winding her way quickly through the crowd toward her, and she smiled despite herself. Alvie's enthusiasm for life was contagious, and Serena needed that these days. She refused to think about Tom and how he had warned her away from Alvie. Then again, she refused to think about Tom at all.

"Serena," Alvie said, cutting through the men about her with a careless ruthlessness. "My brother will be coming tonight."

"Your brother again," Serena laughed. "Alvie, you have threatened his arrival for two weeks now."

"St. Irving," rumbled Baron Henson, one of the oldest of Serena's admirers. "Ain't glad to see him back in town."

"I beg your pardon?" Alvie drew herself up to her full and short height. She could become imposing when she wished.

"He meant no offense, Miss Alvie," Lord Doring said. "Only thing is, he's such a devil with the ladies. Cuts all of us men out."

Alvie giggled. "He is wonderful, isn't he? I think he's one of the handsomest men around. And . . ."

"Enough," Serena said with a laugh. "You have sung his praises more than enough."

Not that every other woman hadn't been doing the same thing for the last week. Alvie had outrun the town crier in announcing her brother had returned from the fight, and would soon take his place once again in society. For those who had remembered when he had been on the town, that was enough. Stories of his skills on the sporting field, as well as those in the boudoir, circulated, setting the ladies all atwitter. In truth, Serena was heartily bored with the subject at hand. Alvie's brother was clearly a premier rake, and Serena was done with rakes, highborn or commoner.

"Then you'll not let St. Irving sweep you off your feet, my lady?" Lord Thomas, the youngest of her admirers, asked, his voice squeaking. He immediately flushed a deep red.

"I believe I can restrain myself," Serena said, laughing again.

"Serena," Alvie said in a hurt voice, appearing wounded.

Serena knew better. Alvie, as a would-be matchmaker, lacked any form of subtlety. "I may be your friend, Alvie, but that does not mean I must fall in love with your brother as well."

"But I think it would do nicely," Alvie said. "I would like you for a sister."

Serena rolled her eyes and all the men laughed. Alvie performed a perfect pout. "Serena, truly, you and Nicholas would be perfect . . ."

"Alvie, dearest," Lady St. Irving's voice called out.

"Yes, Mama?" Alvie said. "I'm here."

The men parted as Lady St. Irving marshaled her way through them in very much the manner as Alvie had before. Serena's laughter suddenly choked in her throat. A man followed behind her. It was Tom! Tom dressed as a lord.

"Nicholas!" Alvie screeched and rushed toward the man.

"Nicholas?" Serena gasped. Dazed, she rose slowly. It couldn't be. He couldn't be!

"You came!" Alvie cried, hugging him. "I was worried you might not."

"Behave yourself, brat," Tom-Nicholas murmured, even as his eyes met Serena's over Alvie's head. "And introduce me to your friend . . . properly."

"Yes, yes," Alvie said in excitement. "I've been dying for you two to meet." She turned to Serena, her eyes bright and without any glimmer of deceit within them. "Serena, this is my brother."

"Oh, my God," Serena whispered. She swayed. The man she had known as Tom was indeed Nicholas St. Irving. He was of her class and an earl! Everything fell into place—his autocratic behavior, his manners and uncommon knowledge. Then something else fell into place. She had done things with a man of her station that only married people did. She had dallied with Rake St. Irving!

"Are you all right, my lady?" Lord Doring asked. "Do you feel faint?"

"Y-yes, I do," Serena answered. In contradiction to her words, however, she picked up her skirts and bolted with amazing vigor through the throng of men, her flight instinct in full force. She would not, could not, remain. God only knew what the man might do or say.

She heard Tom-Nicholas call out her name. She increased her speed, darting through the dancers and bystanders. Unfortunately, like Lot's wife, she couldn't resist glancing back, and like Lot's wife, it was her undoing. She slammed into a servant, carrying a tray of champagne. It clattered to the ground resoundingly, glasses shattering and champagne splashing.

Tom-Nicholas shortened the distance while Serena was involved in untangling herself from the cursing waiter. He grasped up her wrist in a tight grip. "Pleased to meet you, my lady!"

"No!" Serena exclaimed. She attempted to jerk away. She pulled so hard she lost her footing on the champagne-christened floor. She would have crashed to the ground, but Nicholas caught her. He abruptly swung her up into his arms.

"Let me go!" Serena cried, pushing at his chest. It felt like iron.

"No, you've swooned," Nicholas said in a firm voice, even as his arms crushed the wind out of her.

"I have not . . ." Serena refuted and then gurgled to a halt. She flushed hotly. Everyone stood staring at them, eyebrows and quizzing glasses raised.

"Er, I've swooned," Serena said in a weak voice. She laid her head down upon Tom-Nicholas's shoulder quickly.

"It must be the heat," Nicholas announced loudly. He began to carry her through the stunned crowd. "Pardon me, I must take Lady Serena to a retiring room."

"What!" Serena's head popped up. She most certainly wouldn't be alone with this man again. "No! I feel better now."

"No, she doesn't," Nicholas said in a conspiratorial voice to a shy debutante they passed. "She's still faint."

"I am not!" Serena exclaimed, glaring at him indignantly.

"Yes, you are," Nicholas countered. A ripple of laughter went through the crowd.

Alvie rushed up to them, her eyes sparkling. "Serena, he did sweep you off your feet after all!"

"No," Serena said in a waspish tone. "I merely felt faint."

"See, I told you," Nicholas said. "Excuse us, Alvie. Serena needs peace and quiet."

"No, I don't," Serena objected, and received such a squeeze she finally fell silent. Especially since people were no longer staring at them in shock, as much as they were pointing and laughing. Silently seething, but with no other obvious option open, Serena permitted Nicholas to carry her out of the ballroom, down the hall, and into a deserted anteroom.

"Now we are going to talk," Nicholas said, his tone dangerous. He walked over and dropped her unceremoniously upon a settee.

"No," Serena objected, bouncing hard upon the cushion. She gained a semblance of dignity and glared at him. "I need peace and quiet!" She smiled quite maliciously. "You said so yourself. So if you would please leave me to rest."

Nicholas stared at her and barked a laugh. "Sorry, Serena, but as you've noticed, I am not your servant."

Serena lifted her head, though a tremble went through her. "Sir, that was a request of a lady to a gentleman. Now, would you please leave me?"

His gaze darkened. "But as you know, I am no gentleman."

"I can see that," Serena said in cold tones.

"Neither are you a lady," Nicholas said. "You made a complete spectacle out of yourself out there."

Serena flushed. "I would not have, if you had let me go."

Nicholas shook his head ruefully. "But I should have expected it. The lady Serena does what she wants, and let the world be hanged."

"You are one to talk," Serena said, her rage breaking its leash. "From what I've heard sirrah, you have just as much of a reputation for that as I have. Lud, the stories I have heard! You are nothing but a rake and a bounder." She sprung up. "And a liar and deceiver."

He stiffened and his face took on rigid lines. "Then we shall make a perfect pair."

"What?" Serena gasped.

"I had never thought to have a wife like you," Nicholas said, his tone bitter. "But I warn you, no matter my reputation, I will not tolerate such displays when we are married."

"Married?" The blood in Serena's veins turned to ice. "W-we are not going to be married."

"Yes, we are," Nicholas said, his dark eyes implacable. "I may not be a gentleman, but I am a nobleman. If I play, I will pay."

"What a disgusting phrase," Serena said, her voice weaker than she wished.

"No matter," Nicholas said. "I dishonored you and I will marry you."

"No," Serena said, shaking her head. "No!"

"Don't act so surprised," Nicholas said, stalking up to her, his face fierce. "You know we must marry. That's why you ran, isn't it?"

"I ran," Serena said, lifting her chin, "because I did not wish to talk to a man who deceived me in such a manner."

"Now who lies?" Nicholas asked. His laugh was mirthless. "God, I always thought when I finally proposed I might receive some maidenly reserve and hesitancy, but certainly not this. Especially after what has gone between us."

Serena flushed hot and began to shake. "We are not going to marry. Whatever we did, it was when y-you were a servant. I—I wouldn't have . . . if I'd known that you were . . ."

"I know," Nicholas said angrily, cutting her off. "You

would dally with a servant, because you knew you'd be safe from the consequences. You'd not be caught." He leaned into her, his eyes blazing. "But you are caught, Serena."

"No, you deceived me!" Serena cried. Her eyes widened. "Is that why y-you pretended to be a servant?"

He started back, and then laughed. "Faith, but you are conceited. No, my lady, I did not act as your servant in order to seduce you or gain a wife." His eyes narrowed. "I don't give a damn about your fortune, or anything else. And I assure you, I could have found a wife far more easily than playing servant to you. Far more easily!"

"Then why?" Serena asked, bewildered.

"Because I needed a place to recuperate and hide," Nicholas said. "There is a man who wishes me dead."

"Then those men on the road were—" Serena stopped short.

"Yes," he said, nodding. "I'm sorry if it is a blow to your consequence, but they were after me, not you."

"I see," Serena said. She gritted her teeth. "I wish to God I had let them take you."

"Yes, I have no doubt," Nicholas said, laughing. Then his face darkened. "But that doesn't change anything. It doesn't change the fact of what we have done."

"Yes, it does!" Serena exclaimed. "I did not do anything with you. It was with Tom."

"We are one and the same," Nicholas said.

"Not to me you aren't."

"We are," Nicholas said, his tone low. "Like it or not, we are. You dallied with the wrong man, Serena, and you are caught."

Serena lifted her chin. "Not yet, I'm not."

Nicholas smiled. "As I said, we will make a fine pair." He reached out and ran one gentle finger down her cheek. Serena stiffened, even as heat burned her just from that touch. "Say what you will, do what you will, my lady, you will be my wife."

Then, without another word, Nicholas walked out of the room. Serena stood stiff, even as an odd tension and frizzier shot through her. She said lowly, "Like it or not, whatever you say, whatever you do, my lord, I will not be your wife."

Six

"Do hurry," Lady Cecile said as she skipped up the steps to the Carstairs' home. "We are already late, Dorinda."

"You know I hate mornings," Lady Dorinda said, yawning delicately. "I never can understand these breakfasts."

Lady Cecile giggled. "Yes, but Serena Fairchild and Nicholas St. Irving are attending. Lady Carstairs assured me."

"Really?" Lady Dorinda's face brightened and its sleepiness vanished. "How famous! I declare, 'tis better than going to Drury Lane."

"Yes, isn't it?" Lady Cecile said, her tone eager. She shook her head as she pounded upon the door for entrance. "I think Serena Fairchild is a positive noddy. If St. Irving were but to look my way, I'd not be acting in such a manner."

"She acts as if he's a villain," Lady Dorinda laughed. "Faith, would that I had the villain paying me such insidious court."

Lady Cecile laughed. "Were you at the Cranstons' ball?"

"No," Dorinda said with a sigh. "Mother was determined we attend the Wetherfords' musical."

"My dear, it was incredible!" Lady Cecile enthused.

"Apparently St. Irving had sent her a corsage to wear of wild orchids. The lady Serena chose to wear another gentleman's. St. Irving appears, and declares that the roses she wears do not suit her outfit. Indeed they didn't. Red roses with purple satin? Then he snaps his fingers, and one of the servants appears carrying a burlap bag, mind you. St. Irving pulls out another corsage of wild orchids and hands it to her. The lady Serena, as cool as you please, takes it and throws it to the floor."

"She didn't!" Dorinda exclaimed.

"She did," Lady Cecile confirmed, nodding. "Oh, why haven't they let us in yet? Then St. Irving reaches into the burlap bag and draws out yet another corsage. This one of daisies."

"Never say so," Lady Dorinda gasped.

"Yes," Lady Cecile said, laughing. "Well, Lady Serena declares she's allergic to daisies, and tosses that corsage down as well."

"Fool," snorted Lady Dorinda.

"That's what I say," Lady Cecile said. "St. Irving proceeded to present her with six more corsages, each and every one different. Lady Serena found fault with each and every one and dropped them. The floor was strewn with flowers. It looked like May Day."

"Oh, my!"

"But you haven't heard the best," Lady Cecile said, giggling, to her friend. "The very last corsage St. Irving offered her was one made of thistles and thorns."

"Never say so!"

"Yes." Lady Cecile began to laugh. "It was as if he had known exactly how Lady Serena would act and had it planned to the last."

The Carstairs' butler opened the door at that moment. The poor fellow was milled down as Lady Cecile and Lady Dorinda rushed in and legged it into the courtyard in fear that they might have already missed something.

"Here's a good vantage point," Lord Farrel said, strolling to lean against a tree. "We've got a clear shot."

"Might not have any action today." Lord Thomas shook his head. "Looks like they are just sitting together."

"The morning's still young," Lord Farrel said, pulling out his timepiece to glance at it. "Got to give them time to wake up, don't you know?"

Lord Thomas chuckled. "You should have seen them at the park last week."

"Was out of town," Lord Farrel grumbled. "Pity. Had a dying aunt, else I would have been here, sure as check."

"Seems they both got into a race," Lord Thomas said. "Lady Serena's a fine horsewoman, but St. Irving with that black beast of his overtook her in no time flat."

Lord Farrel nodded. "Damn fine sporting man."

"Lady Serena made her comeback that evening though. Evened the score," Lord Thomas said, chuckling. "She knocked St. Irving into the Pendletons' ornamental pond. You know the one with the statue of that naked gel? The one old Pendleton swears is from Greece?"

"Yes," Lord Farrel snickered. "Don't care if she's from Greece or not, she's a bit of something like."

"Well, St. Irving took her arm right off when he toppled in," Lord Thomas said. "Had full dress on, of course."

"Gads! What did he do then?" Lord Farrel asked.

Lord Thomas chuckled. "Well, he took off his wet coat and wrapped it around that Grecian lady, then he picked up her arm and sloshed through the ballroom, making all his proper goodbyes. When he reached old Pendleton, he apologized for the accident, gave him the arm, and promised him he'd get a Grecian man to match the Grecian lady in the garden."

"What!" Lord Farrel exclaimed. "Can't have a Grecian man undressed. What about the ladies?"

"Well, none was too sure which lady he meant," Lord Thomas said. "Since he'd left Lady Serena there as well." He shook his head. "Can't understand why he's still chasing after her."

Lord Farrel snorted. "You were hot-footing it after her yourself until a few weeks ago."

"True, true," Lord Thomas said. "But couldn't stand the pace. St. Irving's let it known that the lady is his and his alone. Threatened to call anyone else out who thinks to interfere."

"Wouldn't want that," Lord Farrel said. "He's too fine a shot."

"Besides," Lord Thomas said, "don't think I'd want a wife like Lady Serena after all. She's a damn beautiful woman. Always knew she was spirited, but I didn't know she was *this* spirited."

"Bit of a shrew, ain't she?" Lord Farrel nodded. "No wonder she's jilted so many. Always thought it was because they couldn't come up to the mark. But now I know differently."

Lord Thomas snorted. "Funny, ain't it? St. Irving always was such a devil with the ladies. All of them just swooning for him. He's come a cropper setting his sights on Lady Serena."

Lord Farrel glanced at his timepiece and then at the couple they watched. "Lay you a monkey there will be action within the next fifteen minutes."

"No," Lord Thomas said, growing serious. "You're right. They ain't awake yet. I say it will be within an hour."

* * *

"Beautiful morning, isn't it?" Nicholas said, leaning back in his chair. "We shall have many of these when we are married."

"No, we won't," Serena sniped, picking up her glass of punch. She realized her hand was shaking. It must be because she was exhausted. "We are not going to get married."

"Yes, we are," Nicholas said, grinning.

Serena set her punch down quickly. "Why can't you just leave me alone? Surely after these past weeks, you must see we shall never suit. Ever."

"I don't know," Nicholas said, shaking his head. "If our marriage is like our courting . . ."

"Courting! This is not courting. This is fighting!"

Nicholas smiled. "I tailor my style to suit the lady."

"You are making us both laughingstocks," Serena said lowly.

"You would not be a laughingstock," Nicholas said, shrugging, "if you chose to behave differently."

"Behave differently?" Serena sputtered. "I suppose you mean I should meekly wed you, merely because we . . . we . . ."

"Yes." Nicholas's eyes darkened. "Because we did."

" 'Tis not a good enough reason," Serena said, looking away. "And it is not as if we . . ." She halted and blushed. "I am not totally dishonored."

"Yes, that will be for the wedding night." St. Irving's eyes sparkled. "Aren't you glad we waited?"

"No, I'm not!" Serena snapped.

St. Irving grinned. "You must be patient, my dear."

"I did not mean that!" Serena said, rattled. "What I meant is, I wish we had never done anything. Anything which would give you reason to believe you have a right to pursue me like this."

"You mean *court* you, my dear," St. Irving said. "You say we shall not suit each other, but in that regards we shall, Serena. You lie if you say we don't."

Serena looked away. "A marriage is not based on . . . on such."

"For a woman like you, it will be," St. Irving said, his tone far too positive.

Serena willingly disregarded his statement. "It must have compatibility and—and respect." She looked narrowly at him. " 'Tis clear you do not respect me."

"You mean I will not permit you to ride roughshod over me," Nicholas said, his tone dry "And no, I will not."

" 'Tis you who wishes to ride roughshod over me," Serena said angrily.

"If that is what it takes," St. Irving said, grinning. "You've thrown off every other rider, Serena, but you won't throw me. I believe I've shown you my horsemanship before. And on our wedding night I'll gladly show you it much better."

"Why, you . . . you low, despicable beast!" Serena gasped. Enraged, and embarrassed to her toes, Serena snatched up her glass of punch. She meant only to take a cooling drought, but then Nicholas laughed at her, with such an intimate, insulting look in his eyes, that before she knew it, she had dashed its contents directly into his face.

The red punch dripped down Nicholas's cravat and shirt, staining it pink. He sat perfectly still, not flinching a muscle. He only said in a low, mild tone, " 'Tis the second outfit of mine you've ruined, Serena."

Someone shouted out, amidst the laughter surrounding them, "Damn, fifteen minutes to the mark! Pay up, Thomas. Pay up!"

Nicholas stood. Serena tried not to cringe as he

looked down at her, his eyes glittering. "The man has
it right. Pay up, Serena."

He reached down, grabbed her wrist, and hauled her
from her chair. Serena didn't have a moment to object,
for he jerked her to him and kissed her ruthlessly. It
was as if she were a lightning rod, and a bolt of lightning, white hot, came out of the morning skies and
shot straight through her. Nicholas prolonged the kiss,
and the sound of laughter faded from Serena's ears,
replaced by a rushing wind.

Nicholas tore his lips from hers, and Serena, limp
from both the lightning and wind, clutched rather
hopelessly and limply to him.

"I wish I had thought of this before," Nicholas said,
his voice rough as he gazed at her. "Each time you behave like this, I'll take my toll."

Serena could only stare dumbfounded at him. He
grinned and gently pushed her back, lowering her into
the chair. "Now, I'm going home and change my
clothes." He leaned closer and whispered, "Don't miss
me too much while I'm gone."

Serena blinked, but Nicholas was gone. Then in a
daze she looked about her. She noted that everyone
watched her. The ladies were wide-eyed and fanning
themselves, as if they were as faint as she. She flushed,
trembling. They may have seen the lightning, but she
had felt it.

Alvie threw down the fashion magazine and sighed.
She had thought a morning at home resting would put
her in better spirits, but it was not so. She had told her
mother that she was feeling under the weather, but in
truth, she was suffering a fit of the blue migraines. She
had come to London with cherished dreams of finding
a husband. She had worried she'd not be able to attract

a man, but with Serena's counseling and her own native intelligence, she had discovered she was gaining quite a court. The only thing was, none of the men made her feel the least bit giddy, as a man who had captured a girl's heart should do. They all seemed so dull. No spirit or romance amongst the lot of them.

She suddenly heard a commotion from outside the parlor, and a male voice shouted, "You lie. He is here, I know it!" Suddenly the parlor door burst open. "I shall find the coward!"

Alvie's heart caught in her throat as a tall, thin, black-haired man stalked into the room, dark eyes flashing beneath flaring black brows. Though he was dressed to ultimate perfection in coat and pantaloons, Alvie thought he looked the dashing picture of a marauding corsair. Suddenly odd, little effervescent bubbles rose within Alvie.

The man stopped abruptly at the sight of her. He straightened and said, "I am sorry, mademoiselle, I—I did not mean to intrude."

His accent was French, divinely French. A giddy laugh escaped Alvie. "I hope I am not the coward you look for?"

"*Non,*" the man said, vehemently shaking his head. An appealing dark lock fell over his forehead as he bowed. "I would never call a lady so. Forgive me. I would not wish to frighten you."

"*Non,*" Alvie said breathlessly. She was anything but frightened, though her heart did race madly. "But then whom do you seek?"

The man came to a formal stance, almost clicking his heels he was so rigid. "I seek one Nicholas St. Irving."

"Do you?" Alvie exclaimed, springing up. "How famous. I am Alvie St. Irving, Nicholas's sister." She rushed across the room, her hand stretched out. "How do you do?"

The man stepped back, his eyes astonished. "You are h-his sister? Impossible!"

"No, not impossible," Alvie said, still holding out her hand pointedly. She batted her lashes. "What do you want with Nicholas?"

"I am sorry, mademoiselle," he said, and true to a gentleman, took up her hand and kissed it in the most courtly manner. "But I have come to call your brother out in the duel."

"How delightful," Alvie murmured as he released her hand. It tingled in the most delicious way.

"Excuse me?" he asked, frowning.

"I mean, oh, dear," Alvie said, blinking. She drew in a deep breath. "W-would you like some tea?"

"Tea?" the Frenchman asked, his face turning darkly fierce. "I fear you do not understand. I am here to call your brother out. I shall run him through."

"Yes, of course," Alvie said. The man had the longest eyelashes, longer than a girl's, in fact. She smiled and waved her hand airily. "But we here in England have tea no matter what. It is our custom." She lowered her gaze. "I am sure Nicholas will return shortly, and then we can settle this matter, don't you think?"

"Nothing can be settled, but by blood," the Frenchman said sternly.

Alvie sighed. He was so very forceful. Such passion and fire. A thrill went down her spine. What a challenge it would be to calm this man down. She wasn't sure how she'd manage it, but of course, since she adored Nicholas, she most certainly would have to make a push to do so. She dimpled and gave him her most sincere look. "No, of course not. But certainly tea could not harm you while you wait. I am sure you are very thirsty after your travels."

The Frenchman looked mollified. "I believe I am."

"There, you see." Alvie clapped her hands together.

Then she frowned. "Wherever is Hobson? He should have been here to introduce you."

A dull flush covered his face. "I am sorry, mademoiselle, but if you mean your butler, I fear I, er, hit him."

Alvie's eyes widened. "You floored him, did you?"

"What?" the Frenchman asked, frowning.

Alvie flushed. "Oh, nothing, nothing at all. But do let us find him."

"H-he may still be within the hall," the Frenchman said, rather shamefaced.

"Oh, yes, of course," Alvie said, and rushed past him. She discovered Hobson, their longtime butler, sitting sprawled in the middle of the hall, rubbing his head, his eyes rather crossed.

"Hobson, are you all right?" Alvie exclaimed.

"Yes, Miss Alvie," Hobson said, blinking rapidly.

"Can you stand?" Alvie asked.

"I believe I can." Hobson nodded. He crawled, groaning from the floor, and stood swaying.

"You are doing well, Hobson," Alvie said approvingly. "Do go to the kitchen and have Mrs. Hobson look to your wounds."

"But, Miss Alvie . . ." Hobson protested.

"And while you are there, do tell her to prepare tea for our guest," Alvie added blithely.

Hobson's eyes widened, and then they skittered to the man who Alvie knew now stood behind her. "But Miss Alvie, y-you cannot entertain this . . . this gentleman. H-he is dangerous!"

"I would never harm a lady, monsieur," the Frenchman said, his tone indignant. "Never!"

"See," Alvie said, well pleased. "He is not dangerous."

"But, Miss Alvie," Hobson said, lowering his voice, "y-you have no chaperone. A lady does not entertain a gentleman alone."

"This is true," the Frenchman said, nodding with a sincere look. "I should leave you."

"Oh, pooh," Alvie said, waving a hand. "You have not come here to court me, but to kill my brother."

"My lady!" Hobson exclaimed. "Never say so."

"In a duel," Alvie said quickly. "It will all be very proper. But you see, we are enemies, so therefore he couldn't have any designs upon me." She looked at the man and asked in a hopeful voice, "You don't, do you?"

He stiffened. "No, mademoiselle. I am an honorable man."

"See," Alvie said to Hobson, though she was slightly disappointed. "Now, do go and order up tea."

"Yes, Miss Alvie," Hobson said. It appeared he wished to argue, but then sighed heavily, and turning, stumbled away. No doubt the knock to his head had aided in his docility.

Alvie turned with her widest smile to the Frenchman. "I fear he left again without announcing who you are."

The Frenchman, looking as bemused as Hobson had before his departure, bowed. "I am Randolf Dorvelle, mademoiselle, the Marquise de Beaucamp."

"Randolf." Alvie sighed. It was a lovely name. She noted he appeared shocked, and flushed. "We need not stand upon ceremony, do we? After all, you intend to kill my brother, which is a rather personal affair."

"Er, yes, mademoiselle," Randolf said.

"Do come with me," Alvie said eagerly, and led him back to the parlor. "Do take this seat next to the fire," she said in a calming tone. The moment he did, she settled quickly upon the ottoman next to it, almost at his feet. "Now tell me, why do you wish to kill Nicholas?"

"Mademoiselle," Randolf said, his tone stiff, "a man does not speak to a lady of things most evil and sad. I would not wish to upset you."

"Evil? Nicholas?" Alvie asked, intrigued. "I knew he is the very devil with the ladies, but evil? Are you sure you have the right of it?"

Randolf's face turned brooding, so romantically brooding. "He . . . no, I cannot tell you. You are the innocent. But your brother . . . he . . . he is—"

"He is what?" Nicholas's voice asked from the parlor door.

Alvie squeaked and jumped up. She turned in dismay to view her brother. "Nicholas, what are you doing here? You're not supposed to be home this early."

"Nicholas!" Randolf exclaimed. He stood quickly, his dark eyes flashing. "So! You are Nicholas St. Irving!"

"I believe I am," Nicholas said, smiling slightly. His eyes narrowed. "You must be Randolf Dorvelle."

"I am, monsieur," Randolf said, pacing over to him in a menacing stride. "And I have come to challenge you . . ." He halted a moment, and blinked. "Monsieur, you are . . . are wet . . . and pink!"

"Yes," Nicholas said, his tone mild. "Someone tossed a drink in my face."

"*Sacrebleu,*" Randolf exclaimed, frowning direly. "Someone has challenged you to the duel before me?"

"Yes," Nicholas said dryly. "A lady did."

Randolf started, his face astonished. "Ladies, they duel with the men here in England? I have never heard of this."

"Well," Nicholas said, "this particular lady does."

"I do not care," Randolf said, showing great upset. "Me, I have the prior claim. You shall duel with me first." He stepped forward, and with the back of his hand, slapped Nicholas upon the cheek. Nicholas growled and balled his fist.

"No!" Alvie cried in alarm. She rushed forward and squeezed herself between the gentlemen. "Do not. I am sure it is a mistake."

"It is not!" Randolf said, lifting his chin. "He is evil and I shall run him through."

"It will be my pleasure to meet you," Nicholas said, his stance tense, his tone dangerous. "I've had more than enough of this!"

"Oh . . ." Alvie's heart pounded. Her brother, despite his earlier sang froid, was indeed in the mood to be difficult. He was the finest swordsman in all of England, and very possibly in France. She thought quickly. Hitting upon the easiest solution, Alvie let out a weak cry, raised her hand to her forehead and swayed. "Oh, my, I feel faint, so very faint!"

"Mademoiselle!" Randolf cried.

"Oh, dear," Alvie said, and flung herself toward Randolf.

"Mademoiselle!" Randolf breathed. Gratefully he caught her. Alvie sighed. He was a man of action! His arms were strong, and he smelt so very good. She closed her eyes and let all the tension drain from her body, so that Randolf was forced to clutch her to him all the more. "She has fainted!"

"Ignore her," Nicholas said in a cool tone. "In fact, you can drop her if you wish."

Alvie almost squeaked in indignation, but managed to turn it into a moan.

"Drop her?" Randolf asked. Alvie peeked her eyes open. His face was appropriately outraged. *"Sacrebleu!* but you are evil." She snapped her eyes shut as he lifted her up into his arms. "Mademoiselle," he soothed as he carried her over to the sofa and laid her gently upon it, "forgive me." He patted her cheek. "Open your eyes, mademoiselle. Where . . . where are the . . . the salts, *non?*"

"We don't have any," Nicholas said, strolling over. "The women in our family don't faint. Not unless they wish to do so."

Alvie knew by his tone that Nicholas was not amused. She moaned slightly, and fluttered her eyes open to gaze at Randolf with what she hoped was confusion. "Wh-what happened?"

"You fainted, mademoiselle," Randolf said, his face agonized. "Forgive me. I—I should never . . . have lost my temper so . . . to challenge your brother in front of you. Can you forgive me?"

"Yes," Alvie sighed, reaching her hand out to touch his clasped one.

"Very touching," Nicholas said, laughing. Both Alvie and Randolf glared at him. "No," Nicholas said, raising up his hands. " 'Tis clear we'll not progress any further in this." He lifted a brow. "Dorvelle, where are you racking up?"

"I stay at the Hotel Carlaise," Randolf said.

"Very well," Nicholas said. "I will meet you there tomorrow morning and we can make the arrangements." He looked pointedly at Alvie. "Where there are no tender sensibilities to wound."

"Yes, of course," Randolf said, nodding. "Of course."

At that moment Hobson entered with a tea tray. His eye was turning a decided black and blue. "Tea, my lady." Then he halted, taking in the scene. "What happened?"

"Alvie fainted," Nicholas said.

Hobson's face showed surprise. "Fainted?"

"Yes," Alvie said, quickly sitting up. "But the tea will revive me." She looked quickly to Randolf. "You will stay for tea?"

"Mademoiselle," Randolf said, his eyes widening. "It would not be . . . be proper."

"It is the least you can do," Alvie sighed, and fluttered her lashes. "After you made me faint."

"*Non, non,*" Randolf said, coloring. "I should not."

"That's right," Nicholas said. "It wouldn't do." He

smiled when he looked at Randolf. "Run, old man, if you wish to fight another day."

Randolf drew in a breath. "I—I shall see you tomorrow." Then he looked at Alvie, his eyes dark and contrite. "Forgive me, mademoiselle, forgive me. I—I hope you will recover from this terrible, terrible thing I have done."

"She will," Nicholas said cheerfully. He waved toward the door. "I'll see you tomorrow, Dorvelle."

"Yes," Randolf nodded, clearly torn. He bowed quickly and departed.

Alvie stared after him and sighed. "Isn't he divine?"

"Indubitably," Nicholas said, his tone dry. "Hobson put that tray down before you fall down."

Hobson promptly set it down on the nearest table.

Alvie looked quickly at Nicholas. "Nicky, you aren't going to . . ."

"Forget it, dear," Nicholas said, strolling toward the door. "You can play off your tricks with that poor man, but not with me."

"Poor man!" Alvie exclaimed. "Then you do mean to kill him?"

Nicholas stopped. His smile was whimsical. "I wonder if I'll need to. Now that he has you after him, it might be the most merciful thing to do."

"Nicky!" Alvie shrieked, indignant and frightened at the same time.

"If you will excuse me," Nicholas said. "I have a prior . . . duel to attend." With that, he strolled from the room.

"Tea, Miss Alvie?" Hobson asked in a kindly tone.

"Yes," Alvie agreed, upon another sigh. She sat in deep contemplation while Hobson served her. Her brother was such a tease. She frowned. Then again, perhaps he wasn't. All she knew was she wouldn't permit him to kill Randolf Dorvelle. She had a totally different future in mind for that Frenchman.

She sipped her tea and sighed yet once more. It was a tangle which would require great delicacy, great delicacy indeed.

Nicholas strolled down the corridor of the hotel toward Dorvelle's room. He halted a moment. Pretending to study the painting upon the wall, he glanced back. A maid, carrying a mop, which was as large as she and well nigh covered her entire face, was the only one to be seen. She had stopped and was knocking upon one of the doors. Nicholas smiled grimly.

The little widgeon. She should have worn something other than the St. Irving livery if she wished to play cloak and dagger. He shook his head and continued to Dorvelle's room, knocking upon the door. It opened, and Dorvelle met him, his demeanor extremely formal and grave.

"Good morning, Dorvelle," Nicholas said in a cheery voice, and shoved his way in, closing the door.

"Good morning," Randolf said, his eyes widening.

Nicholas walked over and sat in a chair, though he shifted it in order for the door to be within his sights. "Let's settle this business post haste."

Dorvelle stiffened. "Of course." He walked stiffly toward another chair. "Since 'twas I who challenged you, it is your choice of weapons."

Nicholas saw the door handle turn and the door creak open. He stood abruptly and stretched. "I think I feel like fresh air."

"What?" Dorvelle asked, falling back into his chair in astonishment.

"That's it," Nicholas said. "Fresh air and exercise."

"Exercise?" Randolf glared. "You will have the exercise when we duel."

"Indeed," Nicholas said, and smiled. "But it's always good to keep fit. We can discuss matters while we walk." He strode toward the door and jerked it open. At least Alvie had possessed enough sense to be gone before he'd opened the door. "Come, Dorvelle, don't be a laggard." Nicholas strode out the door, not waiting for Randolf.

Randolf finally caught up with him at the end of the corridor, panting slightly. "What is this? Do you run from me, monsieur?"

"No, no," Nicholas said, chuckling. "Not from you, old man."

"Stop!" Randolf said, lengthening his strides.

"Outside, Dorvelle," Nicholas said with determination. He could see a flash of petticoats farther behind them both. Randolf, muttering about the insanity of the English, followed Nicholas out of the hotel and onto the street.

Nicholas glanced back. He didn't see Alvie anywhere. "All right!" he said, slowing his pace.

"Sacrebleu!" Randolf said, falling into step beside him. "I wish to duel with you, not run a race!"

"And duel you will," Nicholas said. "I am tired of your hounding me for your brother's death. The fight was not of my choosing, but your brother's."

"You shot him in the back," Randolf accused. " 'Twas murder."

Nicholas halted and looked the red-faced Randolf squarely in the eye. "Yes, it was murder, but I did not do it."

"You lie," Randolf said hotly.

Nicholas clenched his fist and then relaxed it. "It's good we meet tomorrow, or I would not permit the insult. I do not lie. I did not shoot your brother. The man I was with did."

"*Non,*" Randolf said, his tone fierce. "Sabastian's man was there, he saw it."

"I don't care what he saw," Nicholas said. "I was not the one who shot your brother." He glanced back and cursed. He took Randolf by the arm. "Come on, man, keep walking."

Randolf shook his hand off. "What is this forever walking? You tell me you did not shoot my brother and then you say walk. You are crazed."

"No," Nicholas said, forcing a brisk pace. "Only bedeviled." He glanced at Randolf, who, despite his protests, matched his steps. "I'm sorry, Dorvelle. Your brother should not have died in such a fashion. I understand that in your eyes it was ignoble."

Randolf's face showed torment. "Sabastian chose to fight for . . . for Bonaparte. A disgrace to our family, yes. We chose the king." He lifted his chin. "But he was a soldier. He should have died upon the field, yes. Not in an . . . an alley, shot in the back is if he were *canaille.*"

Nicholas sighed. "Your brother was not a soldier, Dorvelle. He was a spy, just as I have been. Death in that profession is never glorious, but it is still noble."

"To be shot in the back," Randolf said, his tone furious, "is never noble."

"No," Nicholas said softly. "And I regret that it happened so. Your brother fought well, and honorably. No matter the results, the fight between him and me would have ended fairly. But Hampton would not wait, and shot your brother in the back." He shook his head. "I don't know why your brother's man lied to you. Or if in the dark, he truly believed that was the way of it, but I did not kill your brother."

"You lie," Randolf said, his voice strangled.

"No, I do not," Nicholas retorted. Then he softened

his tone. "But if it is any consolation, Hampton is dead. He himself was killed in a drunken brawl two evenings later. Stabbed in the back, in fact."

"Very convenable," Randolf said, his eyes flashing.

"Not for Hampton, it wasn't," Nicholas shot back. He sighed. "I am sorry, Dorvelle. I know you feel cheated. Therefore I will meet you."

"You will meet me?" Randolf asked, frowning. "Even though you say it was this Hampton who murdered Sabastian?"

"Yes," Nicholas said curtly. "The man was my partner. And for that, I will accept responsibility."

"I do not understand you," Randolf said, shaking his head.

"No," Nicholas said. "But I understand you. You will not rest until we duel." He smiled grimly. "Besides, I did not care for the two buffoons you sent after me. You truly insulted me there, Dorvelle."

Randolf's face reddened. "I—I did not think you were a man of honor, prepared to meet me as a man of honor."

"Yes," Nicholas said. "But Jack and Zack? For God's sake, they were nuisances, not assassins, and that I cannot forgive."

"They . . . they fooled me," Randolf said, his face showing even more consternation.

"I didn't think they could fool anyone," Nicholas murmured. He glanced back and shook his head. His sister was indeed a game one. She lagged quite a few paces behind, still clutching her mop, and hitting not a few passing pedestrians with it as she came. Later he must give her lessons on how to properly trail someone.

"I believe I will choose foils," Nicholas said absently.

"Foils?" Randolf asked. He frowned. "I must warn you, monsieur. I am most excellent with foils. One of the finest in France. If you wish to reconsider," he said, even as Nicholas picked up his pace, "I will permit you to choose the pistols."

"No," Nicholas said. "Foils will be fine."

"But I tell you," Randolf said. "I am the best with the foil."

"I am not too paltry myself."

"You should choose the pistols," Randolf said obstinately.

"Foils," Nicholas reiterated. "And let us meet tomorrow at dawn on the Commons."

"The Commons?" Randolf asked. "Where is this?"

"No," Nicholas said quickly. "The Commons is too common. She will guess that, the minx."

"The minx?" Randolf asked. His brows snapped down. "What is this minx? Who is this she?"

Nicholas thought a moment. "Why don't I just have my man come round and take you up. I know a place where we can fight without interruption."

"Very well," Randolf said, nodding.

"I'll also make arrangements to bring the surgeon and a few seconds." He glanced at Randolf. "Or do you have your own chosen?"

Randolf flushed. "*Non.* I did not think. All my friends are in France."

Nicholas glanced over his shoulder and smiled. "Not all of them, I believe." He shook his head. "I'll take care of it, but you must promise me that you won't tell anyone the particulars about this affair. Especially my sister."

"Never," Randolf gasped. "I—I was not . . . not thinking yesterday. It was unforgivable. But I promise, never will I tell your sister."

"No matter how she coaxes you?" Nicholas asked.

Randolf frowned. "Monsieur, I fight the duel with you. T-to see your sister would be dishonorable. Already I have caused her great distress. I cannot not forgive myself. But *non,* I will not cause her more pain. I promise."

"Good," Nicholas said. He halted and smiled. "It is settled then. Let us shake upon it." He held out his hand. He frowned. Randolf had come to a standstill, his face white, his gaze directed across the street.

"Mon Dieu! Angelica!" Randolf suddenly cried out. He then dashed out into the middle of the street.

"Blast and damn," Nicholas swore, and charged after the Frenchman. He knocked Dorvelle away just as a carriage rushed down upon them. Nicholas dragged the stunned Frenchman to the walk. "What in blazes were you doing?"

"Did you see her?" Randolf asked, his voice hollow, his gaze wild.

Nicholas frowned. The street was vacant at the moment. "See who?"

Randolf blinked and then blinked again. "Nobody."

"Nobody?" Nicholas asked. "You almost got yourself killed. And you call me crazy?"

"Forgive me," Randolf said. "I—I thought I saw a lady. A lady who . . . who I once knew . . . I once loved."

Nicholas frowned. "Who?"

Randolf sighed and shook his head, his eyes dark agony. *"Non.* I only . . . only imagined. My beautiful Angelica. She is dead."

Nicholas studied Randolf a moment. He said quietly, "I am sorry."

The Frenchman nodded, clearly unable to speak. Both men turned and walked back toward the hotel in silence. Nicholas kept looking for a sight of Alvie. Apparently she had realized she had failed and returned home. Heaven only knew what fresh start she'd try next.

He glanced at Randolf. The man's gaze still scanned the crowds, his dark eyes haunted and searching. Poor devil, Nicholas thought. He looked for the ghost of a woman he had once loved, never realizing he'd best beware of the live woman who had followed them instead.

Seven

Two women rushed toward the steps of the Fairchilds' town house, both from the same direction. They collided at the front door, the one dropping her mop.

"Oh, excuse me," Alvie breathed. She glanced at the tiny woman, whose brown eyes were dark pools of what seemed to be fear. "Are you all right?" The little woman nodded. "Are you sure?" The lady flushed, but nodded again. Then she cocked her head to the side and looked at Alvie in concern.

This time Alvie flushed, and her hand flew to her hair to straighten its wild strands. "Forgive me. I must look a fright. Do . . . do you know if Lady Serena is home? I must see her." The lady nodded quickly. She opened the door, and led Alvie into the townhouse without a word. Alvie, confused and worried, permitted the lady to lead her through the house, both women peering into rooms. It wasn't until they entered the conservatory that they found success. Serena and Robby were there, sitting at a charming wrought-iron table.

"Thank you," Alvie said to the lady, and blinked. The woman was gone, and disappearing through the foliage. Alvie frowned, drew in a deep breath. "Serena?"

Serena jumped slightly and looked up. Her brows rose. "Alvie, what are you doing here?"

"I'm sorry," Alvie said, rushing forward. "But I must

speak to you. A lady let me in," she continued, blushing as they stared at her. "She . . . she disappeared, but I promise, she did let me in."

"A lady?" Robby asked, frowning.

"Yes," Alvie said, frowning as well. "She didn't speak to me. She seemed terribly upset about something."

"It must be Sparrow," Robby said, standing abruptly. "I'll go and see what is the matter."

"Sparrow?" Alvie asked Serena, quickly taking up the vacated chair and setting her mop down.

"Yes, she is my dresser," Serena said. "Don't worry about her not speaking. She is mute."

"I see," Alvie said, nodding.

Serena studied her. "What is the matter, Alvie?"

Alvie flushed. "I suppose you wonder why I am dressed as a maid . . ."

"No," Serena said, her tone dry. "I am accustomed to the ways of your family."

"What?"

Serena waved a hand. "Nothing. I assume you have a reason for dressing so, is all I meant."

"Yes," Alvie said. She leaned forward. "You may find it hard to believe, but there is this Frenchman, Randolf Dorvelle, who has come to England and intends to duel with Nicholas."

Serena stiffened.

"Serena, he will kill him," Alvie said, turning slightly teary eyed. "I just know it."

Serena paled. "Perhaps not."

"Yes, he will," Alvie said. "Nicholas is a devil with the foils, as well as the pistols. Randolf will not have a chance."

"What?" Serena exclaimed. "I thought you meant Randolf would kill Nicholas."

"No." Alvie shook her head. "I really don't think that could happen." Then she gasped. "But Lord, what if it did happen? No!" She sprung up. "We cannot permit it to happen."

"We?" Serena asked, her brows rising.

"We must find out where they intend to fight," Alvie said, pacing around the large potted palm. "If we know that, we can warn the authorities."

"You would inform upon them?" Serena asked.

"Yes," Alvie replied with determination. " 'Tis better than one of them killing the other. And if Nicholas kills Randolf, he would be forced to flee the country."

"Hmm," Serena murmured. "I don't think I'm going to interfere."

"You can't mean that, Serena," Alvie cried, rushing over to her. "Nicholas has just returned home. Please, you don't want him hurt, do you?"

"I'm sure I don't care a rap," Serena said in a light tone.

"But I do," Alvie said. She looked down. "I think I love Randolf."

"What?" Serena asked. "How long have you known him?"

"I just met him yesterday," Alvie said. She sighed. "Oh, Serena, I never thought it would happen. But it did. I saw him, and suddenly I just knew. I felt positively giddy."

"Giddy?" Serena asked. She shook her head. "I'm sorry, Alvie. But love is not a laughing matter."

"No," Alvie said, growing serious. "That is why I don't want either man hurt. I tried to discover where they were going to duel." She frowned. "I tried to follow them and hear what they were saying, but I think Nicholas caught on to me. He and Randolf went for a walk, and every time I got close enough to hear, they sped up."

Serena nodded. "He knew."

"Serena," Alvie pleaded, "please try and find out

from Nicholas where they are going to duel. He will tell you. He loves you."

"No," Serena said, an odd look entering her eyes. "He does not love me. Far from it."

"He must love you." She giggled. "No matter what you do to him, he still persists in courting you."

"He does not court me because he loves me," Serena said. "H-he does it for another purpose."

"He wants to marry you," Alvie said. "Surely it's because he loves you. I mean, I've never seen him behave like this with any other woman. He made a dead set for you the moment he saw you. And you cannot deny that you swooned when you saw him."

"I grew sick, if that is what you mean," Serena said, her tone dry. She looked at Alvie. "I don't think we can stop this duel. You . . . you are not aware of all the circumstances."

"Perhaps I am not, but I don't care. All I know is that I don't want either of them hurt. Please, Serena, try to do something. Please!"

Serena's face darkened. Then she shrugged her shoulder. "If I see Nicholas tonight, I might try. I doubt I will learn anything, however."

"Oh, thank you," Alvie said, springing up and rushing over to hug Serena. "I knew you would help. And I shall try to do what I can, as well."

"That should be enough in itself," Serena chuckled.

"No," Alvie said, grinning. "If anyone can change Nicholas's mind, you can. I just know it."

"And I know better than that," Serena said, her tone brisk. "Now, do not fret so. I assure you, I shan't."

Alvie frowned. "You won't?"

Serena tossed her head. "Of course not."

"I see," Alvie said, her tone mild. She adored Serena, but sometimes she didn't understand her at all, especially in regards to her brother. She refused to believe

Serena was as cold-hearted as she appeared. "I guess I . . . I better be going now."

"Do," Serena said. Her green eyes twinkled. "Else I'll put you to work mopping the floors."

Alvie giggled. "Yes, mum." She dipped a curtsy and sped from the house, her agile mind moving directly onto a new plan.

"Sparrow?" Robby called, searching through the house. He could not find her anywhere. Worried, he finally asked one of the servants where he could find Sparrow's quarters. He hesitated only briefly, before knocking on the door and entering. He discovered her, sitting upon the chair, wringing her hands.

"Sparrow?" Robby asked, confused and a little shaken. Except for those few early days of Sparrow's recovery, she had always been a calm woman, one who never became ruffled. "What is it?"

She looked at him. Her eyes showed fear.

"You've been having those nightmares again, haven't you?" Robby asked, frowning. "Thought you had gotten over them."

Sparrow looked away and shook her head.

Robby sighed and walked over to the bed and sat down. "Come here, Sparrow."

She looked up at him, and shook her head. "Come now, Sparrow." He reached out his hand. Sparrow, not looking at him, rose and walked over to him. He pulled her down to his lap, and loosely encircled her with his arms. "Now, there," Robby said, his tone avuncular. "You've got to stop thinking about those things. They are all in the past. You've got your Robby to take care of you." Sparrow suddenly hid her head upon his shoulder and he heard a slight sob. He stiffened.

"Something truly has you in a pother." He patted

her shoulder. "Just remember, you are in England now. You're safe. Ain't no one going to hurt you while I'm around." Sparrow lifted her head and stared at him. Tears drenched her large eyes and trickled down her cheek. He lifted his hand to her face and brushed a tear away.

"Here, now. Don't cry." She continued to stare at him, wide-eyed. Robby drew in a breath. An undefined emotion passed through him, and suddenly he wanted to lean over and kiss every tear away. He shook his head to clear it. Gads, what was the matter with him? He stiffened, and the urge only became stronger. It was because she was crying, he told himself quickly. Crying women were always dangerous to a man's state of mind. He forced a quick smile. "Here, now. Got just the thing to cheer you up." The look in Sparrow's eyes deepened. "We can play chess! Yes, that's it. We can play chess."

Sparrow started, and she paled slightly. Shaking her head, she sprung from his lap and moved away from him.

Robby felt totally baffled. "You don't want to? But you always like to play."

Sparrow refused to look at him, only shaking her head again.

"How about cards?" Robby asked quickly.

Again Sparrow shook her head.

He rose, and said, smiling, "I know, we could go for a walk."

She shook her head yet again, still not looking at him.

"Don't you want to do anything with me?" Robby asked.

It was only another shake of her head.

"Very well," Robby said, shifting upon his feet. "I—I guess you want to be alone."

This time she nodded her head in agreement.

"I see," Robby said, for some reason his heart sinking. "Then I'll leave you alone. But if you want to do anything," he added more hopefully, "you just let me know."

Sparrow nodded her head.

Robby walked to the door with what he hoped was a jaunty step. He left Sparrow, his mind in turmoil. Never had she turned down a game of chess with him, or cards for that matter. Something was wrong with Sparrow, something she wasn't sharing with him. He frowned. He didn't like it. Didn't like it one whit.

Randolf sat slouched in the chair in his hotel room, his jacket off, his cravat loosened. He stared off into space. Tomorrow he would kill the man who had murdered his brother. He would take revenge, the revenge which had burned in his heart and had kept him living. He had lost so much, so very much. The dream of revenge had been the only one which had driven him, given him purpose. Now doubt frayed the edges of that pristine quest. Could Nicholas St. Irving be telling the truth?

Randolf could not be certain, and it tore at his soul. The man was strange, very strange, but he also seemed to be a man of honor. Randolf ran his hand through his hair in agony and bent his head. He had come to England to claim retribution and lay to rest the ghost of his murdered brother. Instead, he had found another ghost. He could have sworn he had seen Angelica. She had not been dressed as she should, but rather dressed in an ugly brown garb, but still he thought it was her. Had it been a dream? Or was it an omen?

A knock sounded at the door. "Who is it?"

"The maid, sir," a voice called out.

"Enter," Randolf said, sighing.

The door opened and the maid entered. Randolf did

not look up until he realized the maid stood directly before him. He glanced up and his mouth fell open. "Mademoiselle! Wh-what are you doing here?"

"I must speak with you," Alvie said, moving to him.

Randolf sprung from his chair, quickly putting it between them. "But you should not be here. It is improper." He frowned, distracted a moment. "Why are you dressed so?"

"It is a disguise," Alvie said, a charming smile peeking out. "Do you not like it?"

She indeed seemed fetching. "Yes," Randolf said. "I mean, no! You should not be here. Not when I meet your brother to . . ." He halted.

"Yes," Alvie said, her lip pouting out. "You duel with Nicholas tomorrow." A delicate hand fluttered to her chest. "And I cannot bear the thought. To envision you tomorrow morning? In the cold dawn?" She gave a small, strangled sob. "You shooting my brother dead."

"Non," Randolf exclaimed, horrified. "I will not shoot him."

"Then it is foils?" Alvie questioned, her tone excited.

Randolf's eyes widened, shocked. "Mademoiselle, a lady does not ask these questions. This is an affair of honor. I will not speak upon it."

"Oh, please," Alvie begged, clasping her hands together. "Tell me. You meet with Nicholas tomorrow morning at dawn, and it will be swords, upon . . . upon the Commons. Yes?"

"No," Randolf said, almost in a daze. "That would be t-too common."

"What?" Alvie asked, frowning.

He blinked and focused upon the beautiful girl before him. "Y-your brother said it would be too common and something about a minx. A she?" He started. "You are that minx, the she, *non?*"

Tears welled up in Alvie's eyes. "I only ask, because I do not want you killed."

"Me? Killed?" Randolf drew himself up to his full height, outraged. "I—I will not be the one to die. I am most accomplished with the foils, mademoiselle."

"But so is Nicholas!" Alvie cried. "Oh, why didn't you choose pistols?"

"Mademoiselle," Randolf said, his male dignity truly wounded, "I see you think I am an incompetent. What you say . . . a . . . a nincompoop?"

"No," Alvie cried, shaking her head vehemently. "I think you wonderful!"

"Well, I am not a nincompoop!" Randolf shouted. "I shall run your brother . . ." He gurgled to a halt. "Y-you think me wonderful?"

"Yes," Alvie said, walking toward him, a worshipful look in her eyes.

"Non," Randolf said, backing up.

"But, yes," Alvie said.

"Non," Randolf said, flushing. "Y-you should not say that. I duel with your brother tomorrow."

"I know," Alvie said, tears glistening in her eyes. "And I am wretched." She burst into heartrending sobs.

"Mademoiselle," Randolf cried, rushing to her and clasping up her tiny hand. "Please do not cry. I promise you, I shall not kill your brother."

"B-but you said you are accomplished with the f-foils," Alvie wailed.

"Yes, yes. But I shall only, ah . . . wound him, yes?" Randolf said in desperation. "Please, do . . . do not cry."

"You promise?" Alvie asked, her tears abruptly disappearing.

Randolf lifted his chin. "I give you my word. And Randolf Dorvelle does not break his word. Never!"

"And you will be careful?" Alvie asked with a sniff.

"Of course," Randolf said, offended once again. "I will not be killed."

"Oh, can't you tell me where you duel?" Alvie asked. She suddenly threw herself into his arms.

"I cannot," Randolf said, shaking. "Y-your brother did not tell me."

Alvie drew back, her eyes wide. "What?"

"He would not tell me," Randolf said. Then he coughed. "N-not that I would tell you, mademoiselle, even if I knew."

Alvie sniffed and looked down. "Forgive me. It . . . it was unpardonable for me to ask. Y-you must think me terribly forward and . . . and unladylike."

In truth, Randolf had been stunned by her actions. Yet holding her, warm, soft and fragrant in his arms, he found it hard to think. *"Non.* Y-you are very much the lady."

"Truly?" Alvie's eyes lighted. "Then will you kiss me?"

"Mademoiselle?" Randolf asked.

Alvie's lashes fluttered down demurely. "W-we may never see each other after tomorrow."

"Yes," Randolf said, his heart failing. "This is true."

"We are star-crossed lovers," Alvie sighed.

"What?" Randolf asked, blinking.

"Could not you kiss me once," Alvie whispered in a heart-broken tone. "For goodbye."

Randolf's gaze, despite his best efforts, focused on Alvie's trembling, sweet lips. "W-we cannot." He gulped. "Y-you are sister to the man I must fight to-morrow."

"Yes," Alvie whispered. She stood upon tiptoe and placed her lips to his. Randolf groaned and soon discovered he could very much kiss the sister of the man he would fight tomorrow. Indeed, he could kiss her wildly and passionately.

Alvie pulled back finally, her face shining and flushed. "Goodbye," she whispered, and left the room.

Randolf stared after her. He could not think of death, anyone's death, nor of revenge, or laying ghosts to rest. He could only think of life and how he had felt it all with that vibrant, confusing girl within his arms.

"Serena," Lady Lucille's voice said, "do you feel all right?"

"What?" Serena asked, jumping. She found she gripped her fan so tightly she heard the ribs snap.

"I asked if you feel all right," Lady Lucille repeated, studying her closely.

"Of course, why shouldn't I?" Serena pinned a smile upon her lips. Lady Lucille's eyes narrowed and Serena looked out across the crowded ballroom. The note from Alvie crackled in her glove, taunting her. Alvie had learned the duel would be tomorrow at dawn, but she could not discover the place. She begged Serena to either find out that piece of information or induce Nicholas to withdraw from the duel completely. Either request was asking for the moon.

"I don't know," Lady Lucille said. "You seem on the fidgets tonight."

"Do I?" Serena asked and trilled a laugh. It sounded rather pitiful, even to her own ears. "I guess I am tired."

Lady Lucille laughed. "Perhaps if you weren't so busy running from St. Irving, you wouldn't be so tired."

"I'm not running from St. Irving," Serena said, lifting her chin.

"No?" Lady Lucille asked. "Why don't you forgive him? So the man pretended to be a servant. And though you'll not speak on it, I don't doubt he had a good reason." She shook her head. "I must hand it to Nicholas. He fooled me as well, and I even knew he had St. Irving blood in him. I just didn't know he was the earl. But that is neither here nor there. The man is still perfect for you."

"He is not," Serena snapped angrily. "He deceived me, in more ways than one. And . . . and he shows me no respect."

"Of course, you show him such respect yourself," Lady Lucille said, her tone dry.

"He thinks to rule me," Serena said. "And that he'll not."

"Give up the battle, Serena," Lady Lucille said, sighing. "Or you both will lose. You are both throwing away a splendid passion by this petty fighting."

"Petty?" Serena gasped.

"It is beneath both of you," Lady Lucille said sternly. Then as she surveyed the crowd, she smiled. "Here comes Nicholas, my dear." She rose and smoothed out her skirts. "Take my advice. Give up the fight. Let yourself be caught, and let it be soon."

Serena didn't even notice her departure, so intent was she in watching Nicholas as he crossed the ballroom toward her, making greetings and salutations as he came. Something in her heart twisted. She could not let herself be caught. The man thought too little of her, and what he did think of her, he wanted to change. She'd not give herself over to such a man's rule.

Again pain wrenched at her, so cruelly as to bring tears to her eyes. Neither could she think of this man dying. He still approached her, the handsomest man in the room, wearing the air of one without a care in the world. She couldn't imagine him dead or forced to flee the country, to never have him demand a dance from her again, or to catch her up and kiss her again.

"Hello, my love," Nicholas said, sitting down beside her. "Beautiful evening, isn't it?"

"Indeed," Serena said, forcing a coolness.

"Would you care to dance?" Nicholas asked.

"No," Serena answered. Nicholas's eyes darkened. "Let us just sit for the nonce."

Nicholas frowned. "Very well."

Serena drew in a deep breath. "You know, I was thinking."

"Were you?" His tone was amused.

"Yes." Serena lifted her chin. "I think it would be nice if we were to ride in the park tomorrow."

"It would?" Nicholas asked, his brows rising. "Is this an invitation?"

"Yes." Serena looked away. She attempted an innocent voice when she spoke again. "I think it would be nice if we rode very early, before the park grows crowded. Perhaps at dawn?"

Nicholas frowned. "At dawn? You never rise that early."

Serena shrugged. "Everyone says it is the best time. You yourself have told me I lose the better part of the day sleeping in so late. Let us ride at dawn tomorrow."

Nicholas shook his head. "I am sorry, I would like to do so. But I have . . . a prior engagement."

Serena gazed steadily at him. "You cannot break it?"

"No." Nicholas sounded regretful. "We could ride later."

Serena lifted her head. "No. I wish to ride at dawn."

"I cannot," Nicholas said, his voice firm. "It is impossible."

"Is it?" Serena asked, suddenly angry. "You say that you wish to marry me, yet the one request I make, you deny." She stood, holding tightly to her skirts. "You say you court me, but 'tis always on your terms. I must dance with you, when you wish it. You force me to accept your flowers, because you wish it."

"Damn it, Serena," Nicholas said, standing. "You do not understand."

"Oh, I understand," Serena said. "Trust me, my lord. I understand."

"Serena," Nicholas begged, reaching out and clasping up her hand.

She began to shake. "Do not think to detain me. Do not think to show me greater disrespect than you already have."

She jerked her hand away, and fled across the ballroom.

Nicholas watched in frustration as Serena headed toward Lady Lucille. Confound it! Why did Serena finally, upon her own free will, ask for his company, and it be the only time in the world he could not accompany her. Why did it have to be tomorrow morning, at dawn, the same time as the duel? Nicholas stiffened. Serena knew, that was why. He cursed. She'd made him feel guilty, played upon his emotions, when all the time she had been doing nothing more than trying to manipulate him.

His temper boiling, Nicholas strode up to Lady Lucille, only a minute after Serena had left her and departed the room. "Where is Serena going?"

"She says she has the headache," Lady Lucille said, raising her brow. "She is going home."

"Is she?" Nicholas said through gritted teeth. He stepped past her. "We shall see about that."

"Nicholas!" Lady Lucille exclaimed.

He halted a moment. "What?"

"She is truly overset," Lady Lucille said, her eyes concerned. "Cannot you leave this for another day?"

Nicholas clenched his hands. "No. No, I cannot."

He strode through the ballroom and out of the house. Serena was just then entering her carriage.

Swearing, Nicholas ran to the carriage, barely springing into it before the coachman started it up.

"Get out of this carriage," Serena ordered in a low tone as Nicholas settled in beside her. She shifted as far away from him as possible.

It angered Nicholas all the more. "You don't really want to go riding with me tomorrow morning at dawn, do you?"

Serena's eyes widened and she looked away. "I'm sure I don't know what you mean."

"You know about the duel, don't you?" Nicholas accused. She remained silent. "Don't you?"

"Very well," Serena sighed. She shrugged a shoulder, looking indifferent. "Yes, I know about the duel."

"Alvie told you," Nicholas said, nodding. "I don't know how she discovered the time, but she did. Now she's sent you to interfere."

"I told her it would be to no purpose," Serena said, her tone bitter.

Nicholas stiffened. "No, it wouldn't. But why the ruse? Pretending that you wished to ride with me tomorrow. Why didn't you just ask me?"

Serena's gaze turned cool. "If you will not go for a ride with me when I ask it, why would you abstain from a duel if I ask it?"

Nicholas laughed. "I see. I should withdraw from a duel of honor, merely for the favor of riding in the park with the lady Fairchild."

"I told Alvie I couldn't stop you," Serena said, looking away.

"Not for a mere ride in the park." Nicholas gazed at Serena. She was so utterly beautiful in the moonlit carriage, a cool and distant ice queen. A fierce need rose in Nicholas, a need to melt that ice, to once more find the fire in the woman. "We are talking about the fact that I may die tomorrow, Serena. Or kill my man and be forced to flee all that I know and love. If you offer me something more, something warmer, perhaps I might change my mind."

Serena glared at him. "Don't be disgusting."

"Is it disgusting?" Nicholas asked sharply. "Is it too much for a man to ask a kiss from his lady before he faces danger or death?"

"I'm not your lady!" Serena shouted, her eyes flashing.

"Are you not?" Nicholas asked, his voice lowering.

"No, I'm not," Serena said. "And I don't care if you die."

"Truly?" Nicholas asked with a growl. Angered, he reached out and pulled her to him.

Serena did not fight him, but she turned her head quickly away from him, as if to say he might hold her, but never would he have her kisses. "Nor do I care if you flee the country."

"You'd not miss me?" Nicholas asked.

"I wouldn't," Serena said, shaking her head.

It was her undoing, for Nicholas captured her lips in that unguarded moment. She struggled against him, but Nicholas held the kiss, fierce in his need to drown out the words she had spoken. Passion, as raw and jagged as the pain she'd caused him, flared high within Nicholas. Instinctively, he knew when it had caught hold of Serena, for her hands no longer pushed against him, but gripped his shoulders. Her kiss was no longer cold, but heated as she met his with equal fever. Triumphant, he tore his lips from hers and demanded, "Tell me you'll care if I die. Tell me you will miss me if I leave."

Serena's eyes were dark pools, shimmering with tears. It seemed the whole world lay hidden in their depths, his world.

"I . . ." She stopped and shook her head mutely.

"Damn you, Serena," Nicholas muttered, his voice hoarse.

A tear slipped down her cheek, and then she lifted her lips to his. They were soft, yielding, and Nicholas tasted the salt of tears upon them. He groaned, a shiver wracking him. Yet he remained still, awed by the sweet warmth of her kisses. He had no need to take. Serena gave. Her body melted into his, fitting as if it were but his other half and not a different body. Nicholas, with shaking hands, caressed every fluid curve of Serena. An emotion as strong as passion, but so tender it shook him to the very core, filled Nicholas.

"My beautiful Serena," Nicholas whispered. "My lady." He kissed the hollow of her throat, feeling the rapid pulse beneath his lips. Serena moaned and Nicholas pushed her back against the cushions, covering her body with the strength of his.

The rocking of the carriage stopped, and the coachman's voice invaded the warmth of their passion, "We are here, my lady."

Nicholas started and then he sat up. Serena slowly followed. For a moment they stared at each other, the emotion still wrapped about them in the darkness of the carriage.

"I . . ." Nicholas halted. "I will not die. I will not leave you."

Serena stared at him, tears still glistening in her eyes. She lowered her gaze and merely nodded. She started to move past him.

"Wait," Nicholas said softly.

"What?" Serena asked.

Nicholas found he couldn't speak. He gently reached out and smoothed a strand of hair back from Serena's forehead. She sat still, watching him. It was as if both feared words. He reached out to touch her cheek, but quickly pulled his hand back.

"Good night, Serena," Nicholas whispered.

"Good night," Serena said. "My coachman will take you wherever you want." Then she moved past him and alighted from the carriage. Nicholas absently told the coachman to take him to his house. Then he settled back, feeling as if he were a totally different man. He loved Serena. When she had given him that kiss, he knew it.

He groaned and lowered his head into his hands. He had been the very fool Serena had called him. Until now he had been trying to win her, control her unconquerable will, force her to the aisle out of sheer determination and pride. Now he knew he wanted more. He wanted her to willingly give to him, as she had given tonight. He wanted her to come to him in trust, not broken spirit. He wanted her to love him, too.

Eight

"Are you satisfied with the blade, Dorvelle?" Nicholas asked, grasping his own lightly. They stood in a small field, jackets removed. Robby had already inspected the foils and grounds, attesting to the fitness of both. Now he conferred with the surgeon. It seemed to Nicholas Robby had taken unnecessary time in both processes. Nicholas glanced at the pink sky to judge the hour. Never had he been more impatient to end an affair. Honor demanded the duel and he'd see it through, but his heart wasn't in it. Not anymore.

"Yes," Randolf said, slashing through the air with his foil. "It is a very fine one."

"Thank you," Nicholas said, nodding. "Then let's get this done."

"Yes," Randolf agreed with just as brisk a nod. He lifted his chin. "I only wish to say—"

"Dorvelle," Nicholas warned, "if you're going to make a speech, save it until later."

"I was not going to make a speech," Randolf said, his face clouding. "I only wish to say that since I have come to England, and have met you, I find it very difficult, I mean more difficult than I expected, to—"

"That sounds like a speech to me, Dorvelle," Nicholas interrupted.

Randolf blinked. *"Non.* I only wished to . . ."

"Dorvelle," Nicholas said, his tone impatient, "I have Alvie locked in her room for the nonce. I'll not guarantee her remainder there, so do let us proceed with haste."

Randolf started, his face darkening. "You . . . you locked Mademoiselle in her room! *Sacrebleu!* That is the most cruel, the most . . ."

"Did you wish her to be here?" Nicholas asked curtly. "She would have followed us if not confined."

"I see," Randolf said. His face paled. "*Non.* I . . . I would not wish that. No, that would be most terrible."

"Very well then. Let us get on with this." Nicholas waved at Robby. "We're ready."

Robby walked over, his demeanor quite formal for such a carefree man. "Gentlemen, take your places." Randolf and Nicholas obliged, stepping back and falling into the proper stance for the duel. "The rules shall be—"

"Must we go through them all?" Nicholas gritted out.

"*Non,*" Randolf said, shaking his head quickly. "We do not need them. Let us proceed."

"What?" Robby's mouth fell open. "But if this is going to be a fight to the death—"

"Oh, yes, I forgot," Nicholas muttered. He cast a steady look at Randolf. "Are we fighting to the death?"

Randolf lifted his head. He appeared the perfect picture of nobility, though something was lacking in his pose. Perhaps it was his customary fire and fervor. "If you wish it."

"No," Nicholas said, narrowing his eyes. "You're the one who started this. It is your choice."

"*Non,*" Randolf said, a flush covering his features. "You may decide."

"No. That is your call."

"*Non,*" Randolf refuted. "You must decide."

"It's your choice," Nicholas said curtly. "Just make it, and make it quickly."

"I will let you choose," Randolf insisted, his tone stubborn.

Robby, whose head had swung back and forth like a weathervane between the two disagreeing men, exclaimed, "Will someone bloody well make a decision! I thought this would be a fight to the death. Now is it, or isn't it?"

Randolf looked away. "It shall be . . ."

"Very well," Robby said, nodding, "a fight to the death."

"If Monsieur St. Irving wishes it," Randolf added.

"What?" Robby exclaimed. He looked helplessly to Nicholas. "What's it going to be, Nicholas?"

"For God's sake, Dorvelle!" Nicholas cried, throwing his foil down and stalking toward him. "You are the one who hounded me all the way to England, you're the one who demands satisfaction. I'll fight it whichever way you wish, just make up your infernal mind. But once this is done, I want it to be done."

"I give you the choice," Randolf said. He threw down his own foil. Clenching his fists, he stepped forward, glaring at Nicholas. "You make the decision. It is you who—"

"Stop!" Robby shouted, waving his hands in the air. "This is supposed to be a duel, not a brawl. Now, both of you pick up your blasted foils and get back into position."

For a moment both men stood frozen, glowering at each other. Finally Nicholas muttered a curse and spun around. He paced back, snatched up his foil, and assumed his position. Clenching his teeth, he gritted, "What's it to be, Dorvelle?"

"For Gads sake," Robby exclaimed, "don't start the

damn thing all over. Why not toss a coin? Heads it's to the death, tails it's the first blooding."

Randolf's eyes widened. "I beg your pardon? Toss a coin?"

"Well," Robby said, his tone exasperated, "it's as good as any other way, since you two can't come to an agreement."

Randolf's face darkened. "I will not toss . . . the coin! Ridiculous. This is a duel!"

"It won't be if we don't get on with it," Nicholas said. "What's it to be, Dorvelle?"

Randolf's face was closed. He shrugged. "Whatever Monsieur wishes. If you wish first blood, then let it be first blood. If you—"

"First blood it is!" Robby exclaimed quickly. "We have a decision."

Randolf's face darkened. "I did not finish! If . . ."

"Don't need to finish. It's first blood," Robby said. "Since neither of you gentlemen seem to be of a mind to make the decision, I will. Besides," he said, returning a glare at both men, "I ain't waiting for you two to come to fisticuffs over it again."

"First blood," Nicholas nodded and raised his foil. "Engarde."

"Engarde," Randolf nodded, swiftly raising his foil up.

"What ho!" Robby jumped back with a yelp as Nicholas charged at Randolf with a swift fervor. Randolf's blade met Nicholas's just as quickly. He proved to be a very worthy opponent, with a lightness on his feet and a surety with the foil that could only impress. Nicholas was not in the mood to be impressed, however, nor did he possess the patience. Knowing himself to still be the better swordsman, Nicholas attacked with one direct purpose. He found his chance within the first two minutes. He coolly slipped past Randolf's guard, his foil tip flicking up Randolf's left arm.

"*Merde,*" Randolf gasped.

Nicholas adroitly drew the foil back. "Are you satisfied, Dorvelle?"

"*Mon Dieu,* yes," Randolf said, dropping his sword to clutch at his arm. He actually grinned. "This was much easier, yes, than the race we ran yesterday?"

Nicholas laughed, striding to Randolf. "Is it bad?"

"*Non,*" Randolf shook his head. "You are most excellent. But it bleeds much."

"We must get you back to the hotel," Nicholas said, frowning as the surgeon approached.

"Yes," Randolf nodded. His face suddenly blanched. "Let us hurry. The mademoiselle, she waits. When you go to her, will you tell her for me that . . ."

"I'll have the door unlocked and have her informed you are safe," Nicholas said in a heartless tone. "But after that, I'll have no more to do with it. I have my own lady to attend." He glanced up at the lightening sky. "It can still be considered dawn, don't you think?"

Serena sat in lone estate at the breakfast table. She had thrown her entire household staff into a dither upon not only arising shockingly early, but demanding breakfast as well. Ordering food had not been a wise choice, however. It now sat cold and congealed on the plate before her.

She dropped her napkin over the defeating sight, telling herself it was simply because she never could eat so early in the morning. However, that could not explain away the large and painful knot in her stomach. Or why her heart pounded so erratically and she felt compelled to glance at her pin watch every few seconds. Nor why visions of Nicholas lying dead tormented her until she thought she'd go crazy. At that moment Nobles entered the breakfast room.

"Yes, Nobles?" Serena asked, before the butler had a chance to speak. She found her heart migrating to her stomach, vying for room next to the large knot already residing there.

"My lady, a visitor has arrived," Nobles said in his ever steady voice.

"Yes, yes," Serena said, clenching her fists tightly. "Who is it?"

"The Earl of Claremont," Nobles announced, blinking.

"Nicholas!" Serena shouted in pleasure. He had not died! He had not left her! She sprung from her chair so fast that it toppled back.

"My lady?" Nobles asked, his eyes widening.

Serena flushed. The man must think she was insane. Lord, but he was probably right. She attempted a more dignified pose, even though every nerve in her body tensed. "I mean . . . I see. H-how does he look?"

"My lady?" Nobles asked.

"How does he look?" Serena asked more fiercely.

"Why, he looks quite well," Nobles said in a considering tone.

"Thank God," Serena murmured. Her knees were suddenly desirous of giving out.

"Yes," Nobles said solemnly. "The jacket he wears today must be by Weston. I have noticed his lordship does not curry to such blatant fashions as what Shultz tailors. And his cravat I believe is tied in the Waterfall . . ."

"What?" Serena asked. The incongruity of his words versus the train of her thoughts stunned Serena. She fell back into her chair. Or what should have been her chair. Since she had already toppled that over, her posterior hit the carpet in the general position the chair should have been.

"My lady," Nobles cried, rushing over. "Are you all right?"

"Yes, I'm all right." Serena scrabbled from the carpet and pinned a murderous look upon her butler. "Nobles, I don't give a damn about what Nicholas is wearing. I want to know if he is injured or not."

"Injured?" Nobles asked, blinking. He thought a moment. "I believe he cannot be injured, for he wishes for a ride in the park with you."

"What?" Serena exclaimed.

"Yes, that was the full message I was to impart," Nobles said, his tone hurt. "However, my lady did not permit me to . . ."

"Yes, yes," Serena said curtly. She was beginning to positively loathe her new butler.

Suddenly the import of Nobles's "full message" struck Serena. Nicholas had come to claim his ride in the park with her as if naught had happened. He'd fought his duel against her wishes, and put her through a torment so great that no one would ever imagine. Now he wanted his ride in the park. The man thought to have his cake and eat it, too. Serena stiffened and turned a steely eye upon Nobles. Serena Fairchild would be no man's "cake."

"Tell the earl that . . . that I am still abed and will not receive him," she said coolly.

"My lady?" Nobles's eyebrows shot up.

Serena gripped her hands together. "Just tell him that."

"Er, yes, my lady," Nobles said. He bowed and departed.

Serena paced quickly around the breakfast-room table. Every fiber in her body screamed to go to Nicholas. She wanted to see for herself he was safe, she wanted to hold him, and kiss him, and tell him . . . She halted. Good Lord, she didn't even want to think of what she wanted to tell him. She dared not. She couldn't believe it herself. Didn't want to believe it herself. No, going to him in such a manner would be fatal.

After all, Nicholas had only done what he'd always done. Nothing had changed. Except her own silly heart, she feared. Once again, he'd done exactly what he wanted and now came to her in his usual cavalier and brash manner, clearly thinking to brush past her reserves and wishes. She flushed hot. She was in a sad state, but certainly not that sad of state. She'd not let the man treat her so. She must keep her stance.

Serena paced over to her chair, righted it, and sat down to wait. Nicholas would not welcome the news she was still abed. She wondered what action he would take. Her heart pounded far too alarmingly. Drawing in a deep breath, she quickly smoothed her hair back and straightened the folds of her gowns. She never doubted he'd take some kind of action, and she'd be prepared for the battle.

"Yes, Nobles?" Nicholas asked, pacing across the parlor. "What does Serena say?"

Nobles stiffened. "My lady bade me to tell you she is . . . still abed and she will not receive you."

"What?" Nicholas asked, exploding. "She is still asleep?"

"She . . . she will not r-receive you," Nobles said, stepping back.

"Damn it!" Nicholas said, hurt and rage bursting like a volcano within him. Last night she had said she did not care, but her kiss said differently. "We'll just see about that!" He strode with determination toward the door.

"My lord," Nobles cried, scurrying after him. "Where are you going?"

"To roust my lady from her sleep," Nicholas said angrily, stalking out of the parlor. He'd just engaged in the shortest duel of his life because of her, and Serena was damn well going to know it. How dare she sleep when she knew he was out fighting for his life. It didn't matter that the affair hadn't transpired in any such manner, she couldn't have known that.

"You cannot do that, my lord!" Nobles exclaimed, his voice rising.

"I most certainly can," Nicholas said.

"You cannot," Nobles said. "She is not there."

Nicholas halted abruptly. He glared at the butler. "What?"

"She is . . . not abed," Nobles said, his face turning a dull red.

"She isn't?" Nicholas asked in a dangerous tone.

"No, my lord," Nobles said. "Sh-she is in the breakfast room."

Nicholas studied the butler. "She is?"

"Yes, my lord." Nobles coughed. "She has been there since quite early. But she . . . she does not wish to receive you."

Nicholas stared at the butler. A slow smile crossed his lips. "The vixen. So that was the game. She's still in the boughs, is she?"

"I could not say." Nobles frowned. "She is acting in a very confusing manner. Quite odd, in fact."

A weight seemed to fall from Nicholas's shoulders. "There is hope yet."

"My lord?" Nobles asked.

Nicholas grinned. "Thank you, Nobles."

Nobles's brows arched. "For what, my lord?"

"For not letting me go off half-cocked." Only last night he'd sworn to himself he'd not lose his temper with Serena, or force his will upon her in any way. He'd earn her love. Yet at the first sign of a skirmish, he'd almost failed in his resolve. He smiled wryly. "Please tell my lady I send my regards and hope to see her at the Sheridans' ball this evening."

"Yes, my lord," Nobles said, bowing.

Nicholas, quite pleased with his newfound patience, left the house whistling.

Serena waited in the breakfast room. In a short while, Nobles entered once more. His face was quite void of expression.

"Yes?" Serena asked quickly. "What did he say?"

Nobles coughed. "My lord sends his regards and hopes to see you this evening at the Sheridans' ball."

"He does?" Serena asked, frowning. "Was that all?"

"Yes, my lady," Nobles said, nodding.

"Oh," Serena said, nonplussed. For some reason she expected more, certainly something more. She lifted her chin. "Well, you can tell my lord that I do not intend to attend the Sheridan ball."

"I am sorry," Nobles said. "But my lord has already departed."

"What?" Serena asked. "H-he already left?"

"Yes," Nobles said. "You had said you would not receive him."

"Of course I did," Serena said. "But . . ." She halted. She wasn't about to say that when Nicholas wished to do something, he would, no matter what she said. Evidently, this time he didn't care that much if he saw her or not. "Oh, never mind."

She rose from the breakfast table, feeling very much as if Nicholas had pulled the rug out from under her, but not knowing exactly how he'd done it. Worse, disappointment and regret burrowed deep within her heart. She had wanted to see Nicholas, how she had wanted to see him. Now he was gone.

Randolf lay back against the bed pillows, his left arm bandaged the entire length. His pride, in truth, had taken the greatest cut. He was no fool. If St. Irving had chosen to fight him to the death, Randolf knew he'd be resting in a casket now, rather than in a pleasant hotel suite.

Worse, Randolf realized that he had unwisely called out an innocent man. He could no longer believe St. Irving would have ever shot his brother in the back. Not only did St. Irving appear a man of honor in all ways, but with his skills, there would be no need for him to kill dishonorably when he could do it so swiftly with honor.

Randolf sighed and closed his eyes. He had caused much grief to an innocent man and his dear family. He had shown himself a fool. All he could do in restitution was to depart for France as quickly as he could. Never would he trouble the St. Irvings again, never would he see them again.

He heard a sound at the door, and snapped his eyes open. He started up, wincing. "Mademoiselle, what do you do here?"

Alvie, dressed in a yellow jonquil gown and looking the breath of spring, blithely entered, as if his hotel room were nothing less than her own. "Oh, dear, are you badly hurt?"

Randolf stiffened. "No, mademoiselle, I assure you I am not. Your brother but scratched me."

"Thank God," Alvie said, and walked over to sit down directly upon the bed beside him.

Randolf blinked. "Mademoiselle, y-you should not be here, it isn't proper."

"I know," Alvie said, a dimple peeking out. "Mama thinks I am at the lending library with my friend, Charlotte." Her brown eyes darkened. "But . . . but I had to come to see if you were well."

"Of course I am well," Randolf said. He tore his gaze from her. "Now you must go, please."

"Go?" Alvie's eyes widened. "But I just arrived." She looked down demurely. "Do you not wish to see me?"

"Non," Randolf said, shaking his head. "But I have lost the duel to your brother . . ."

Alvie smiled. "Which I am forever grateful to you for doing."

Randolf frowned. "You cannot respect a man who loses the duel."

"Pooh," Alvie said. "I certainly couldn't lov—I mean respect a man if he had wounded or killed my brother. Now could I?"

"Non. I would think not."

"There, you see." Alvie sighed. "I am so glad it is all over."

Randolf gazed at the girl beside him with sadness. "Yes, I am sure. I have . . . caused you and your family great distress."

"Well, it has been quite dramatic and exciting," Alvie agreed, nodding. "But now that it is over, we can settle down and become real friends, can't we?"

Randolf's mouth dropped. "Friends?"

"Of course," Alvie said in a happy tone. She gazed at him with the most innocent of expressions. "Don't you want to be my friend?"

"Mademoiselle, I—I w-would like that very much, but it cannot be so. After all the pain I have brought to your family . . ."

"Oh, no." Alvie shook her head. "If you mean Nicholas, he never holds a grudge. And as for Mama, she doesn't have an inkling of what transpired, you know. She rarely ever knows what is going on."

"This I can believe," Randolf said, frowning. "She does not watch you properly. A *jeune fille* sh-should not be permitted to . . . to visit a gentleman in his rooms."

"Yes," Alvie said, her lip pouting out. "But I am only visiting you."

Randolf stiffened. "I beg your pardon."

"You wouldn't hurt me, would you?" Alvie asked, fluttering her lashes.

"Non, mademoiselle. But . . ."

"Then what is there to be concerned about?"

Randolf stared and shook his head. "I—I do not know."

"See." Alvie smiled. "Besides, now that we are friends, I am anxious to make your stay here in England pleasant."

Randolf frowned. "I do not stay in England."

"You can't mean to travel with that arm!" Alvie gasped. "I know you say it is but a scratch, but, indeed, it could grow worse if you travel. Then I truly would be downcast."

"Forgive me," Randolf said. "But I cannot remain . . ."

Sudden tears sprung up in Alvie's eyes. "Then you are still angry with us."

"Non," Randolf said quickly. "I am not. I would wish with all my heart I could stay . . ."

"Good!" Alvie's tears miraculously disappeared. "I am so glad to hear it. Now, what would you like to do? Do you play chess, or cards, or should I read to you?"

Randolf stared at the bright, merry girl, and with a helpless shrug, said whatever she wished to do would be fine with him. He was a man of honor and knew all that was proper, but when he was around this sprite, he found the path of nobility not only topsy-turvy, but totally impossible to pursue.

Serena thanked Lord Dorington for the dance and returned to her seat. She had noticed Nicholas across the room. She attempted not to follow him with her gaze, but found it difficult. He had been in the ballroom well nigh over an hour and had not approached her. She sniffed. She was sure she didn't care if he ever came to see her. She glanced once more over toward him and realized he was finally heading in her direction.

Serena snapped open her fan and waved it before her face. In truth, she was suddenly flushing. She attempted a surprised expression when she finally looked up to see Nicholas before her.

His brown eyes sparkled as he performed a bow. "Good evening, Serena. Do you mind if I sit next to you?"

Serena lifted her chin. "I am sure I do not care."

Nicholas laughed and sat down. He gazed at her, his eyes embarrassingly warm. "I must apologize for this morning."

Serena looked at him suspiciously. "Indeed?"

"I did not mean to have your butler wake you so early," Nicholas said, a thread of amusement in his voice. "I hope I did not disturb your slumber too much."

Serena narrowed her eyes. "No, of course not. I slept quite famously, I assure you."

"I am pleased to hear it," Nicholas said, his lips twitching.

"What do you find so humorous?" Serena asked sharply.

"Nothing," Nicholas said quickly. "Nothing at all."

"Good," Serena said fiercely.

"Would you care to dance?" Nicholas's eyes still sparkled.

"No, I would not," Serena said, enraged. Clearly he laughed at her. Worse, she was unsure as to why he laughed at her. She stood quickly. "Now if you will excuse me."

"Serena . . ." It appeared Nicholas wished to say something, but then only smiled. "Perhaps later you will permit me a dance, if you find one open upon your dance card."

Serena stood flabbergasted as Nicholas rose, then bowed and strolled away. He stopped next to a young debutante. She saw the silly girl flush and then nod her head. Nicholas was going to dance with the little twit!

Serena glanced quickly around. Unfortunately, many observed her, as was their wont these days. She pinned a wide smile upon her lips and walked as nonchalantly across the ballroom as she could. She would play cards rather than dance.

She entered the card room, determined to forget about everything and enjoy herself. To that purpose she sat down with old Lord Alvany, Lady Dearhearst, Lady Slade, and the baron Clayton, a young man just up from the country.

"What are the stakes?" Serena asked as a servant brought her a glass of wine.

"Nothing to speak of," Lord Alvany said gruffly. He was an inveterate gambler, and it was clear to see the game was far too tame for him.

"Well, then, let us raise them," Serena laughed. She cast a teasing glance around the table. "Will that be acceptable?"

"Oh, I say," Baron Clayton agreed. "That would be dandy."

"As long as Amelia Sheridan doesn't catch wind of

it," Lady Dearhearst chirped. "Sheridan himself won't take snuff, but Amelia is quite a Methodist."

Lady Slade's eyes glinted. "Never mind that, if Serena wants to lose some of her fortune to us, I'll not complain."

Serena rarely played cards, but she knew herself to be very competent. In truth, at the moment it didn't matter as long as she found something to divert her attentions. "We can claim it a charity function then. Amelia surely can't object to that now, can she?"

The small group roared with laughter. Very much like truant children, they raised the stakes by denoting the sums with far greater value than said. At first they played in hushed voices, so as not to attract attention. However, the game grew more and more reckless. Soon they called out their wagers in actual pounds. True to Lady Slade's prediction, Serena went down heavily. Yet the challenge invigorated her, drawing her on all the more.

"Well," Serena quipped as Lord Alvany won another hand. "That is more money out of the vault. Soon, my lord, I'll be seen dressed in rags. Just how does one set a fashion with rags, I wonder?"

"I don't know, but I don't doubt you'll find a way," Lord Alvany said, snorting. He shook his head. "Bedamn, don't know if I enjoy winning the money as much as watching your grand style of losing it, Serena."

"Yes, my lady," Baron Clinton said, his gaze shining with appreciation. "You are the best sport."

Serena winked at him. "You only say that because you took that last hand of mine."

He flushed. "No, no, I truly mean it. I've never met a lady like you before."

"Serious, serious," Lady Dearhearst murmured, her gaze droll upon Serena.

"Never," Serena laughed, gazing steadily back at Lady Dearhearst.

She nodded and then pinned a maternal gaze upon the baron. "Beware, my boy, you may win at cards with Serena, but never at love."

Serena smiled and looked sincerely at Baron Clinton. "As the adage goes, lucky at cards . . . unlucky at love."

"Then you are lucky at love tonight, Serena?" Lady Slade asked, her tone dry. "For the cards are surely against you."

Serena paused. She cocked her head to one side as if in consideration. "Why, no, I'm not!" She performed such a look of mock indignation, everyone laughed. She rapped on the table. "Hand me those cards again. I declare, I am the one who should be winning!"

"Good," Lord Alvany said. He glared at Lady Slade and Dearhearst from under bushy brows. "Was afraid this was going to turn into a ladies' tea for a moment."

"Fie, my lord," Serena said, shuffling the deck. "Just for that, I'm raising the stakes again."

"Bedamn," Lord Alvany hooted. "Talk about anything you want, ladies, for I like the play."

Once more the table returned to the matter at hand. Their banter while playing at such daredevil stakes attracted no small attention. More and more people slipped into the card room to observe. Where the watchers themselves were quiet, the players were not. Serena refused to let it be otherwise. She desired laughter above all else, laughter to prove to the world she cared naught for anything, and laughter to prove to herself she was still her own woman.

The next game fell rather unevenly, and Baron Clinton, for once, remained in for the count. All folded, but for Serena. Hers was not a strong hand. She studied the young baron, trying to decide if he truly held the cards or was merely bluffing. She'd noticed he'd attempted to bluff quite a few times that evening, generally to his loss.

"Well, my dear Baron," Serena said, her eyes glinting. "Shall you raise the stakes once more? I am already designing in my mind a ball gown made of burlap."

He looked at her, his face flushed with wine and adoration. He caught his breath. "I'll raise the stakes, but it won't cost you a pound. If I win, I take a lock of your hair."

Those who watched gasped. Lord Alvany groaned. "Don't do it, boy. We're playing cards, for God's sakes."

Lady Dearhearst threw up her hands. "Serena, you've done it again!"

Serena gazed at the now blushing baron. He was more than out of line, but having just arrived in town, if she rejected him, he would most certainly not live it down. She had not been watching closely, and never expected him to come to such a pronouncement, but he was young. She smiled. "And what do I gain if I win?"

"Anything," the baron said hoarsely. "Anything you wish."

She thought a moment and then grinned. "If I win you shall . . . buy me a bolt of burlap."

Lord Alvany nodded and muttered, "Good show."

The baron's eyes widened. "Is that all?"

"Of course," Serena said, smiling. "Now, sirrah, I call. Lay down your cards."

Baron Clinton laid down his cards. Serena grimaced. He had not been bluffing. The room watched quietly as she showed hers. "You win, Baron," she said in a nonchalant voice. "Who has a pair of shears?"

"I do," a deep voice said. Serena's heart sank as the onlookers swiftly parted and Nicholas strolled forward. "Well, actually I don't. But I do have a blade."

The crowd all muttered and Serena paled.

"Now, Claremont," Lord Alvany said, rising quickly. "Don't be hasty."

Nicholas reached into his vest pocket. The room fell silent. He drew out a small pen knife. The room broke into titters and sighs of relief. Nicholas held the tiny knife out. "Here you are, Serena."

The baron Clinton, evidently confused, stared at Nicholas. "Who are you?"

Lord Alvany groaned. "Damn, boy, don't ask."

Nicholas smiled. "Just a friend." Serena flushed and took the pen knife. She found her hand shook for some unknown reason as she snatched up a lock. "Here, my dear," Nicholas said, leaning over. "Permit me. You wouldn't want to cut yourself, would you?"

"Thank you," Serena said, blushing. She remained still as Nicholas took the small blade and cut a tress. He turned and offered it to the baron. "Here you are . . . Clinton, is it?"

"Just take it," Lord Alvany hissed to the stunned baron.

"Th-thank you," the baron said, his eyes flicking back and forth in nervous hesitancy.

"Now." Nicholas smiled at Serena. "I came for the dance you promised me." His eyes actually lighted. "Which I advise you to accept, before you become totally shorn in this game." Everyone laughed. Once again, it seemed as if it were from nervous relief more than anything else.

Serena flushed, but rose. She presented a brave smile, though inwardly she cringed. Nicholas appeared sanguine, but she never doubted he'd ring a peal over her head. "If you will excuse me."

Her new friends were all too eager to wave her on, assuring her they understood. It was clear they didn't wish to become involved in a confrontation. Head held high, Serena followed Nicholas out of the room and back into the ballroom.

"Ah, it is a waltz," Nicholas murmured. Taking up

Serena's hand, he swept her onto the dance floor. For a moment, they danced in silence. Serena, stiff and tense, waited for Nicholas's impending explosion.

"You dipped pretty heavily in there, didn't you?" Nicholas finally said.

"Yes," Serena said, raising her chin. "But I can afford it."

"True." Nicholas chuckled. "It was quite amusing to see everyone in here create excuses to go to the card room."

Serena glared at him. "You mean I put on quite a show."

He grinned. "In your own inimitable fashion."

Serena gazed at him narrowly. Nicholas, however, said nothing else. Somehow it unsettled her all the more. Finally she sighed in exasperation. "Oh, just have done with it, my lord. Say what you intend."

Nicholas looked down at her. "I've said what I've intended. What more should I say?"

"I'm sure you have plenty more to say. Something along the order, no doubt, that I made a spectacle out of myself. I lost a small fortune playing at stakes that were against the rules of the house. And I was fast and loose in allowing that poor boy to win a lock of my hair."

Nicholas shook his head, his eyes darkening. "I didn't say those things."

"But you are thinking them," Serena retorted.

"Serena," Nicholas said, almost with a helpless chuckle, "you have often declared we fight too much and that I show you too little respect. Now, how am I to show you respect if you will not permit it?"

Serena gazed at him suspiciously and then looked away. "I know you do not respect me."

"I am sorry you believe that." Nicholas's tone sounded so sincere, Serena's gaze flew to his in astonishment. He smiled, his gaze warm. "Let us call a truce, shall we? We may disagree on various issues, but I do respect you in many ways, Serena."

Something deep and almost fearful inside Serena forced her to say, "Yes, but you'd not respect such behavior in your wife, now would you?"

"No. I must confess, I would prefer that a wife of mine would behave more circumspectly." An irrepressible smile suddenly crossed his lips. "But then again, perhaps I am not one who should speak. If I had been the baron I wouldn't have asked for a lock of hair."

Serena raised a brow. "You wouldn't?"

Nicholas leaned down and his breath tickled Serena's ear. "I would have asked for your garter, my dear."

Serena choked, and her eyes widened. She broke into laughter. "No, my lord, I don't think you are one to speak."

"Then I won't." Grinning wickedly down at her, Nicholas pulled her far closer than proper, and swung her expertly around. Serena knew she should object, yet she could not deny the pleasure of his arms, nor the strange, sweet comfort of merely being with him, without a need for words of defense or excuse.

The strains of music finally died away. Serena looked up to Nicholas. His face held the gentlest of looks and he smiled as he released her. "Thank you, my lady, for the pleasure of this waltz."

With that, Nicholas bowed and once more left her. Serena gazed after him, feeling oddly bereft and extremely confused. His behavior was so completely different from his usual manner, it frightened her.

Nine

Lady Lucille, Robby, and Serena sat at the breakfast table the next morning. Lady Lucille studied her two amazingly silent partners. She shook her head. "Is everything all right, Robby?" she asked.

Robby looked up from the plate of beef and eggs on which he was bending a dire frown. "Oh, yes. Yes, of course."

"Good," Lady Lucille murmured.

Robby let out a sigh of exasperation. "Do you think something is wrong with Sparrow?"

Serena looked up from the tea and toast she had been glaring at. "What?"

"Haven't you noticed she ain't acting normal?" Robby asked.

Serena's eyes widened. "No, I hadn't noticed."

"You must have," Robby said, frowning. "I mean, she's turned so quiet." Lady Lucille and Serena only stared at him. He flushed. "What I mean is, she's staying to herself. Don't want company." He looked down. "At least, she don't want mine."

"Perhaps she just needs time to adjust to her new life here," Lady Lucille suggested.

"Yes," Serena said. "Though I'm pleased at her abilities. She is an excellent ladies' maid. You were right, Robby, her fashion sense is superior."

"Thought she'd do good," Robby said, nodding. He sighed. "Just wish she'd . . . well, if you say nothing is wrong, I guess nothing is wrong."

Once again the table fell silent, Robby returning his frown to his beef and eggs, and Serena her glare to her tea and toast. Lady Lucille hid her smile. "Serena dear, you seem distracted as well. You aren't fretting over your losses from last night, are you?"

Serena shrugged. "No, of course not."

Robby looked up. "What losses?"

"Serena played high stake poker last night at the Sheridans' ball," Lady Lucille said dryly.

"What?" Robby's eyes widened. "Didn't know they'd permit it. That's why I went to my club instead."

"We hadn't exactly intended for the play to go so steep," Serena said, flushing. "It just . . . happened."

"Oh, it did?" Robby asked, his eyes narrowing.

"Yes," Lady Lucille said, chuckling. "Serena dropped a pretty bundle, as well as losing a lock of hair to a young baron."

"What?" Robby exclaimed.

"It was nothing," Serena said, her tone pettish.

"Nothing?" Robby frowned. "Losing money at play is nothing, but losing a lock of your hair? Well, it ain't proper. Hope Nicholas doesn't get wind of this. For the baron's sake as well as yours."

"Nicholas was there," Lady Lucille said.

"What?" Robby exclaimed. He sighed a sigh, which sounded long-suffering. "All right. You might as well tell me the whole of it here and now, before I go to the club. They'll roast me no end, I don't doubt."

"Nothing happened, I tell you," Serena said.

"Gammon," Robby retorted. "You said Nick was there. You two must have had a row. Or was it worse than a row?"

"No, there was no commotion," Lady Lucille said,

since Serena seemed unwilling to answer. "In fact, Nicholas was so kind as to assist Serena in clipping the lock of hair to give to the baron."

"The devil," Robby said, staring. Then he shook his head, his face turning morose. "I guess it's all for the best anyhow."

"What is for the best?" Serena asked.

"Would have liked him for a brother-in-law, but there you have it," Robby muttered, more to himself than anyone else.

"Whatever are you talking about?" Serena asked.

Robby frowned. "Why, I'm talking about Old Nick drawing back. He wouldn't have taken that lying down if he cared. Not him."

Lady Lucille noticed Serena's face turned pale, even though she said, "I'm sure I don't care."

"Yes," Robby said, sighing. "But . . ." He halted under Serena's threatening look. "Oh, never mind."

At that moment Nobles entered the breakfast room. "Pardon me, my lady, but Miss St. Irving has arrived and wishes to speak with you."

"Indeed?" Serena's face brightened. "Do bring her here."

"Yes, my lady," Nobles said. He bowed and departed the room.

Within seconds Alvie rushed into the room. "Serena, I came as soon as I heard."

"About what?" Serena asked, frowning.

"Why, about last night," Alvie said, taking up a chair immediately. "Mother told me all about it." She flushed. "I—I would have been there, but I was . . . visiting a sick friend."

"Oh, that," Serena said, her tone light. "Such a to-do over nothing."

Alvie frowned. "Then you truly don't mind?"

"What should I mind?" Serena asked.

"Why, that Nicholas has given up!" Alvie exclaimed. She immediately bit her lip. "Oh, I'm sorry. I didn't mean that. It may not be so. Forgive me."

Serena's smile seemed weak. "It is of no significance."

"Of course not," Alvie said, her tone bracing. "Perhaps we have all misread the situation."

"I'm sure it doesn't matter." Serena's laugh was brittle. "Your brother did speak of crying a truce."

Alvie's face fell even more. "I see. Well, then that means we all can still be friends? Right?"

"Of course," Serena said.

"Good." Alvie drew in a deep breath. "Because I was hoping you would accompany me this afternoon for a ride in Hyde Park."

"Certainly," Serena said, frowning.

"And perhaps you too, Lady Lucille?" Alvie asked, her voice appealing.

"I would be delighted."

Alvie seemed to hesitate. "I would particularly like to introduce you to Randolf Dorvelle then."

"What!" Robby exclaimed. "You mean the Frenchie who—"

"Yes," Alvie said quickly.

Serena's brows rose. "You cannot wish an acquaintance with him after . . ." She stopped.

Lady Lucille looked at the three. They had all fallen quickly silent. "Who is this Randolf Dorvelle I am to meet?"

"H-he's visiting here," Alvie said. She looked sincerely at Lady Lucille. "He and Nicholas had—had an argument. But they have settled their differences." Robby snorted. "No, indeed they have. I assure you, Nicholas doesn't hold a grudge against Randolf anymore, nor Randolf against him. I—I would just like it to be pleasant for Randolf, and for him to meet my friends."

"I'll be all too glad to meet this Randolf," Lady Lucille said, very intrigued.

Alvie looked at Serena. "And will you come as well?"

Serena sighed. "Yes, Alvie, I will."

"Excellent," Alvie said, rising. "I'll bring Randolf here and we can all go together. Now I must be going." Before anyone could say another word, she departed the breakfast room.

Lady Lucille chuckled. "That child is a minx, if I've ever seen one."

She received no answer from her two partners, both of them already having fallen back into their private reveries. Lady Lucille sighed. Youth truly was wasted upon the young.

Serena sat beside Lady Lucille in the open carriage. Alvie and her Frenchman sat across from them. Randolf Dorvelle, his arm in a sling, was indeed a romantic sight. It was clear Alvie was head over feet in love with him. It was rather strange, for Randolf seemed to be the pattern card of propriety and his social graces were par excellence, as was obvious as he met the cream of the ton on strut. Alvie, on the other hand, was pert, pernicious, and her graces were not social, but completely hers and hers alone.

Serena studied Randolf covertly. This was the man who had thirsted for Nicholas's blood, who in fact had sent him into hiding. This was the man who had also sent two idiot assassins into their lives to cause havoc and pain. Now he sat across from her for a ride in the park. Life was indeed convoluted. It changed so rapidly one soon became confused about who was really a foe or a friend. Or perhaps they were neither, but merely another human, equally tossed by life's wicked sense of humor.

"Oh, look who is here!" Alvie exclaimed and waved to someone.

"Could she have managed to finagle an appearance from Prinny, do you think?" Lady Lucille asked.

Serena chuckled. "I don't know. But she's certainly introduced Randolf to everyone else of consequence today."

"You mean we have," Lucille said, her tone wry. She frowned. "Just who is this man? I don't believe for one moment his wound came from Mohawks."

"No," Serena admitted, her chest tightening.

"Nicholas gave it to him, didn't he?" Lady Lucille asked. Serena looked at Lucille, debating what she should say. Lucille laughed. "You don't have to tell me. They dueled, did they not?"

"How did you know?" Serena asked.

Lucille chuckled. "Two and two does make four."

"Nicholas!" Alvie suddenly cried out. She jumped up and down in her seat and waved madly. "We are over here!"

"Oh, my God," Serena gasped, before she could stop herself.

"Nicholas?" Randolf asked, frowning.

"She's a marvel," Lady Lucille breathed.

Alvie cast an innocent gaze upon them all. "I'm sorry, I forgot to tell you he might be here."

"Did you?" Serena asked, casting Alvie a narrow look. She noticed Randolf's expression was no more pleased than her own. The group fell notably silent as Nicholas approached. Serena found that for some reason she couldn't meet Nicholas's gaze directly when he reined in his horse beside the carriage.

"Good afternoon. How is everyone?" Nicholas asked, his brown eyes sparkling. Fortunately, his attention went to Randolf first. "Hello, Dorvelle. Alvie told me you intended to remain in town for the moment."

"Yes," Randolf said, looking singularly bemused, as if he himself found it a surprise. Then a flush rose to his face. "If, that is, Monsieur does not find it offensive."

"Of course Nicholas doesn't find it offensive," Alvie said quickly. "Do you, Nicky?"

"Of course not," Nicholas said, his tone dry. "Why ever should I?"

"If you do . . ." Randolf began, his tone stiff and formal.

"But I don't." Nicholas grinned. "However, old man, don't expect me to show you around the town. I believe that must be Alvie's . . . affair, as it were." Before anyone could comment, Nicholas turned his gaze upon Serena. "And how are you today?"

"I am fine," Serena said, telling an outright lie. She wasn't fine. Ever since this morning, she had found herself in an unsettled mood. No, in truth, ever since last evening she had been agitated. She winced. No, it went further back. Ever since she had kissed Nicholas in the coach her world had been overturned. Something had happened in that moment. Or it had for her.

What had it done for Nicholas? That was the question that ran through her mind and taunted her. He was acting so differently. Panic rose within her. Could Alvie and Robby be right? Had Nicholas finally lost interest? What a dreadful jest that would be. She had fought so long, but that night in the coach, despite herself, she had lost her heart. He had promised her he would not die and that he would come back to her. He'd kept both promises, but had he stopped caring because of it?

Serena suddenly realized Nicholas had asked her

something. She blinked and forced a smile. "I'm sorry, what did you say?"

His gaze turned quizzical. "I asked if you plan to attend the Farthingates' assembly tonight?"

"Oh." Serena looked away quickly. She simply must regain her equilibrium. "No. I—I believe I wish to remain at home tonight. I am . . . rather tired."

"Under the weather," Lucille said, "as well as under the hatches."

"For shame, Lady Lucille," Nicholas chuckled. "Serena didn't lose *that* much last night."

"Of course I didn't," Serena said, lifting her chin. Unfortunately, she hadn't even considered the money. It was the other things she might have lost which weighed on her mind. "As I said, I am merely tired and would like an evening of quiet."

"But you'll feel better by tomorrow morning?" Alvie asked, her face showing concern. "Won't you?"

"I imagine I will." A qualm shot through Serena. "Why?"

"I thought we might get up a riding party." Alvie's tone was eager. She turned to Randolf. "That is, if your arm will permit it?"

"But, yes," Randolf said, his face taking on an imperious look. "This is a mere scratch." His glance skittered to Nicholas. "That is, it does not pain me."

Nicholas only laughed. "I am glad to hear that." He looked at Serena, amusement clear within his eyes. "Then you think you'll be rested enough to join our party tomorrow?"

Serena hesitated. "I—I don't know."

"Oh, please do," Alvie said. "We are all friends now, aren't we?" Nicholas's brow shot up. Serena almost groaned. Alvie, curse the child, persisted. "I mean, you and Nicholas have cried a truce, haven't you?"

Nicholas nodded. A smile hovered upon his lips. "I know I've laid down my sword."

"Sword?" Randolf exclaimed. Confusion washed his face. Then his eyes widened and flew to Serena. *"Mon Dieu!* You are the woman who duels with monsieur, *non?"*

"I beg your pardon?" Serena asked, stunned.

"The one who throws the pink punch and challenges him, yes?" Randolf asked. He gazed at her as if she had suddenly sprouted two heads and four arms, all of them purple at that. Serena colored up despite herself.

Nicholas laughed. "Dorvelle, I didn't mean that! At least, not at the moment. Not that Serena can't throw a good punch."

"And they've cried a truce," Alvie said, nodding her head.

Randolf himself colored up. "Forgive me, mademoiselle. It is only I did not understand the customs in England. That the woman, she can duel with the man."

"Tsk, Lord Dorvelle," Lady Lucille said, laughing. "They do it as well in every country. Perhaps not as openly as Serena does, but they most certainly do."

Randolf frowned. "Pardon?"

"But that doesn't matter. They are friends now," Alvie repeated her now well-worn, and well despised, refrain. She smiled and fluttered her lashes. "Just as you and Nicholas are friends."

Randolf flushed. "I see."

"So that means we all can go for a riding party tomorrow."

A fraught moment passed. Then everyone laughed.

"I told you, Monsieur Dorvelle," Lady Lucille said with a chuckle. "Every woman duels in one manner or another." She turned a glittering gaze upon Alvie. "Dear, have you ever thought of marrying a diplomat? England could use you in that position."

This time it was Alvie's turn to flush. "No, no, of course not."

"But you do wish to improve foreign relations, do you not?" Serena asked. She couldn't resist the remark. Not after all the hot water Alvie was splashing so liberally about upon everyone else.

Alvie frowned at her severely. Then she giggled, her dimples appearing. "Yes, indeed. I believe in peace."

"Very well," Nicholas said with a nod. He cast a teasing glance at Serena. "Since we are all under a diplomatic sanction, will you ride with us tomorrow morning?"

Serena laughed. "I fear I must."

"Would ten be a good time?" Nicholas asked.

"Ten?" Alvie frowned. "But that is so late. The park will be quite crowded by that time. I thought perhaps we could go much earlier."

"No." Nicholas's gaze still rested upon Serena. "Serena does not rise at dawn. No matter what transpires. Even if it's a life and death matter."

"Oh, I see," Alvie said, her face falling.

Serena lifted her chin. "No, I shall come."

Nicholas smiled. It held that hint of a secret which was starting to drive her mad. "I begin to like this truce more and more." His gaze flicked past her a moment. He seemed to stiffen, but then he smiled. "Well, it seems you have others wishing the pleasure of your company."

Serena looked in the direction he was gazing. Young Baron Clinton was clearly making his way toward them, astride a mettlesome mare, which he didn't appear to have much success in keeping under control.

Nicholas's brow rose. "He sits a horse well, does he not? No doubt he is one who would ride roughshod over anyone." Serena frowned at him severely. He merely laughed. "I believe I'll make my departure before young Clinton arrives upon his trusty steed." He nodded and turned his horse away from them. He threw over his shoulder, "I'll see you all at dawn tomorrow. Try not to lose any more locks of hair, Serena."

The ladies, except for Serena, all laughed. Randolf once again appeared confused. "Locks of hair?"

"She lost a lock of hair to Baron Clinton," Alvie whispered.

Randolf stared at her, blinking. Then he nodded. "Ah, another duel, yes?"

"No, merely cards," Lady Lucille murmured. "At which she still seems to be losing."

Serena glared at Lucille. At that moment, young Clinton arrived, his mount almost ramming into the carriage. Serena sighed. Unwillingly, her gaze drifted to watch Nicholas riding off, as if he had not a care in the world. He might be pleased with the truce, but she certainly wasn't.

Alvie and Randolf said their goodbyes at Serena's. Alvie all but skipped down the townhouse steps toward their awaiting coach. She felt as if she were living in a dream, a delicious dream. Randolf had charmed the ton. Better yet, it seemed Randolf had been charmed by the ton. He could be happy in England. She just knew it.

Alvie turned to Randolf. "You did enjoy the day?"

For the first time, Alvie saw Randolf truly smile. It was the most enthralling smile she'd ever seen. "Yes. I have always heard the English, they are cold. I do not see this."

"No, no we are not," Alvie said, feeling all too warm as they halted a moment. "Once you come to know us."

Randolf gazed down at her. Still smiling, he reached for her hand. "I—I am pleased to know you, mademoiselle." He bowed and lightly kissed her fingers. A tingle shot through Alvie, all the way to her toes. She closed her eyes from the thrill of it.

"My God," Randolf said, his voice hoarse.

"Yes," Alvie murmured. He must have felt it as well, this strong emotion.

"Angelica!" Randolf cried.

"What?" Alvie's eyes snapped open. She blinked. Randolf wasn't gazing down at her in the throes of enchantment. Rather, he stared completely past her, his face as white as a sheet.

"Angelica," he repeated. His grip on Alvie's hand tightened painfully.

"Ouch!" Alvie exclaimed.

Randolf promptly dropped her hand. With no apology, he bolted past her, running into the street. "Angelica! Wait!"

"Randolf!" Alvie called out. "Wait! Who is Angelica?"

Randolf cleared the street and ran full tilt toward the townhouse upon the other side. Alvie, muttering an unladylike oath, picked up her skirts and chased after him. He swerved to the side of the townhouse, disappearing through the plush bushes that grew there. Alvie, all the more determined to catch her dashing swain and see this Angelica, dug in her heels and picked up her speed. She crashed through the thickets, emerging with a coating of twigs and leaves. She skidded to a halt. Randolf stood before her, a frozen statue. He was quite alone. Alvie glanced around the neat side yard. "Where is she?"

Randolf turned wild eyes upon her. "You saw her?"

"No," Alvie said, irately. "Now, where is she?"

"Sh-she's not here." Randolf sounded dazed. "But I saw her. I saw Angelica."

"And just who is Angelica?" Alvie asked, jealousy shooting through her.

"M-my fiancée." Randolf almost moaned.

"Your fiancée!" Alvie cried, stunned. "Y-you never told me y-you had a fiancée. You should have told me you had a fiancée."

Randolf blinked. "But I don't! She is dead."

"Dead!" Alvie exclaimed. She paled. "But y-you were just chasing her . . . weren't you?"

Randolf ran a shaking hand through his hair. "Yes. I saw her. I saw my beloved Angelica."

"Your beloved?" Alvie asked. Pain sliced through her.

"I am going mad," Randolf groaned. He paced away. "But I . . . I saw her. Just like the other day. I saw her."

"You can't have seen her," Alvie said, her heart failing. "If . . . if she is dead."

"I know, I know. But I swear, it was her."

Alvie swallowed hard. "Y-you saw her, but she is dead?"

Randolf's gaze turned dull. "Yes. Sh—she died a year ago."

"A full year ago?" Alvie asked.

"Yes," Randolf said. "She and her family were . . . were killed in one of the last battles before Bonaparte's defeat."

"I see," Alvie said. Suddenly tears slid down her face. Real, unwanted, painful tears.

"Mademoiselle," Randolf said, rushing to her. "D-do not cry. It . . . it was sad. Very sad, but please, do not cry."

"I'm not crying because of that," Alvie choked out.

"Then why?" Randolf exclaimed.

"Because . . . because . . ." Alvie burst into sobs.

"Because I love you and you . . . you love a dead woman."

"Y-you love me?" Randolf stammered. His face twisted and he shook his head. "Y-you cannot love me, *ma belle*. We . . . we have just met."

"I loved you the instant I saw you," Alvie sniffed. "What does time have to do with it? I loved you within moments of meeting you. You still love a woman after she is dead a year." She spun and started walking away. "You should have told me."

"But . . . but how could I?" Randolf cried, following after her. "Angelica is dead!"

"Not to you she isn't," Alvie sniffed, dashing her tears away and hastening her steps. "You're still seeing her everywhere."

"Not everywhere!" Randolf objected. "Only once . . . I mean twice."

"I'm sure I don't care," Alvie said militantly. "If you want to . . . to chase after a ghost, then do so."

"Mademoiselle, stop!" Randolf cried. "Alvie! Please!"

Alvie halted, but only because she had reached the thickets. Randolf, following closely behind, ran directly into her. *"Sacrebleu!* All this running. I—I am not accustomed."

"If you hadn't been chasing your dead Angelica," Alvie said angrily, "you wouldn't be so tired."

"But . . . but I am running after you now," Randolf exclaimed with heat. Alvie froze and stared up at him with glistening eyes. Randolf appeared stunned. Then his dark eyes flared. "I am running after you, mademoiselle."

Abruptly, with no preamble, he hauled her to him. Even with one arm, his manly strength awed Alvie. He captured her lips in a swift, fierce kiss. Alvie, with only the smallest cry, melted into his arms. All thoughts of dead fiancées flitted away in the glow of passion.

"Miss Alvie!" a disembodied voice called out. Alvie frowned slightly, still clinging to Randolf. It couldn't be the dead Angelica, for the voice was deeply male. "Where are ye?" The bushes rustled and suddenly a third body crashed into Randolf and Alvie. Alvie squeaked. Randolf muttered something totally Gaelic.

"Oh, lud," Alvie's coachman said, skittering back. His broad face turned a bright red. "I'm sorry, miss. But I was that worried, what with you just running off after . . . er, Lord Dorvelle."

Alvie disentangled herself from Randolf quickly. She attempted to catch her breath. "No, that's quite all right, Hinklemire. Randolf thought he saw . . ."

"Nothing," Randolf said quickly.

Alvie looked hastily at him. His dark gaze was steady upon her. Once again, the smile, which was so new and intriguing to her, crossed Randolf's lips. "I saw nothing."

"Er, ye saw nothing?" Hinklemire asked, frowning.

Alvie's heart glowed. "That's right, he saw nothing."

"Then why did you go haring off like that?" Hinklemire asked.

Randolf stiffened and became very much the aristocrat. "It was for . . . exercise. It is very good for a person. Now we shall go, yes?"

Alvie nodded quickly, all too glad to be leaving. It hurt her to know the ghost of a past beloved haunted Randolf. Yet she shored up her own spirits. The woman was dead. While Alvie was alive. By that right alone she should be able to win Randolf's love.

With that comforting thought, Alvie turned and made her way through the bushes once more. It was a far easier task this time, since there was now a gaping hole from the passage of so many bodies through it. Randolf politely followed behind her.

Hinklemire came behind both of them, muttering

that he didn't see why people would want to exercise that way.

Robby strolled through the servants' hall, attempting to appear nonchalant, and feeling totally idiotic. Faith, he was beginning to positively haunt the servants' quarters. Yet, he couldn't help himself. Sparrow never seemed to be around anymore. The few times he saw her, she was always distracted, and jumpy. He couldn't help but be concerned. After all, he had brought her to England, and, therefore, was responsible for her. He heard a noise and looked up eagerly. Sparrow came rushing down the hall from the opposite direction. She halted the moment she saw him.

"Hello," Robby said, smiling. Then he frowned. Sparrow's hair was in wild disarray. It looked as if there were twigs and leaves within it. "What is that?"

Sparrow's face paled. Suddenly she spun and ran in the other direction. "Sparrow! Stop!"

Robby bolted down the hall after her. Sparrow reached her room and darted into it. Robby arrived just as the door slammed shut. He heard the grate of a key.

He stood stupefied with shock. Sparrow had actually run from him and locked him out. Anger swiftly rose to replace his confusion. He'd have none of that! He pounded on the door. "Sparrow! Let me in!" He banged once more. "Let me in; blast it!"

He waited a moment. Finally, he heard the key grate once more and the door opened. Frowning darkly, Robby entered. "Now what in blazes is going on here?" He glared at Sparrow, who had backed away. Her eyes were large in a parchment white face. "Why did you lock me out, and why do you have twigs in your hair?"

Sparrow only lowered her gaze and shrugged.

"Confound it, Sparrow!" Robby exclaimed. "Something is going on and I want to know what it is."

Sparrow shook her head quickly, though her eyes appeared frightened.

"Yes, there is something going on," Robby persisted. "You ain't been acting like yourself. You're never around anymore. And now you've got leaves in your hair." She stared mutely at him. "What could you have been doing to get leaves . . . ?" Robby suddenly stiffened. A totally unworthy and very male thought passed through his mind. "You . . . you ain't been, er . . . well, is it a man?"

Sparrow's eyes widened and her complexion flushed to red. She shook her head vehemently.

"Good," Robby sighed. Then he himself flushed. "I mean, well, damn it, I don't know what I mean. I'm only trying to help, that's all. But if you don't tell me what's wrong, I can't help you! And something is wrong, that I know!" He looked at Sparrow once more. Tears were welling in her eyes. He groaned helplessly. "Sparrow, please. What is it?"

Sparrow let out a small sob. Suddenly she flung herself at him and kissed him strongly on the lips. Robby was so stunned that he tottered back. Fortunately the bed was directly behind, and they fell upon it. He meant to exclaim, but Sparrow's kiss distracted him. Truthfully, it did more than that. It drew out his very soul. Mixed with an electricity was a feeling of utter rightness. Her lips should have always been upon his because they spoke of life itself. His arms should have always been around her, because her body belonged against his. He groaned from the shattering knowledge.

Just as suddenly as she had kissed him, Sparrow withdrew. She tore her lips from his and scrambled from his hold. Stunned and bereft, Robby sat up. "Sparrow?"

She would not meet his gaze. She dashed from the

room. Robby stared after her. Then he fell back upon the bed. He blinked and looked up at the ceiling. Sparrow had kissed him. In one moment his life had totally expanded and he had felt the rightness of it. Yet the rightness itself was confusing, so very confusing.

He frowned. He still didn't know what was the matter with Sparrow. Or perhaps he did. It might very well be what was the matter with him. He just hadn't realized it until a moment ago.

Ten

"Robby, what is the matter, dear?" Serena asked, stifling a yawn as she sat down upon the parlor's settee. She frowned as she noticed the cuff of her riding habit was quite undone. Strange, Sparrow never missed such particulars.

Of course, Serena didn't wonder why she herself had overlooked it. She knew the answer. It was far too early and her quiet night at home hadn't given her much rest. It had only caused her mind to run in circles, all of them revolving around Nicholas and his confusing behavior. She also couldn't help but feel she'd taken the coward's way out in avoiding Nicholas. She forced her mind away from such depressing thoughts. She'd turn it all about, sooner or later, somehow or some way. With that nebulous decision made, she focused upon her brother, who had supposedly joined her for breakfast, and who now paced restlessly around the room.

"Hmm, what?" Robby asked as he circled a table.

"I asked, what is the matter?" Serena repeated, quickly doing up her cuff. "You didn't speak at all during breakfast and now you are pacing like a caged tiger."

Robby halted, a flush covering his face. "Oh. I see."

He stalked to a chair and threw himself into it. He sighed heavily. "It's nothing."

"Is it Sparrow?" Serena asked. Even in her own confused state, she was fairly positive about his answer.

Robby jumped. "No, of course not!" His voice came out in a squeak.

Serena hid her smile. "It isn't?"

Robby glanced at her, his eyes tormented. "It's Sparrow."

Serena suddenly tensed. The look of pain that streaked through Robby's eyes was swift. It hurt her to see it. Clearly, this was no small matter. She forced a smile. "I own I may not be the best person to speak with, not if it is in regards to . . . relationships, but I would like to help if I could."

"Serena . . . I . . . I think I . . ." Robby halted.

"Yes?" Serena asked in an encouraging tone.

"I think I love Sparrow," Robby blurted out.

Serena started in astonishment. Then she almost laughed at herself. It's not as if she shouldn't have known that Robby was in love. In truth, she had known it, underneath. She had merely been so selfishly involved in her own life that she had not considered Robby's. She nodded her head. "Yes, I think you do."

"You don't understand," Robby said, bolting from his chair again. "Serena, I love her, really love her. I—I just didn't realize it. Not until. . . . well . . ." He looked down and then continued in a gruff voice. "I kissed her."

"You kissed her?" Serena asked, her brows rising.

"Well, I think she kissed me first," Robby said. "I—I don't know."

Serena studied her brother. He appeared so mortified, a sudden fear struck her. "Robby, is that all you did, kiss her?"

"Yes! I swear it!" he said quickly. Then his eyes filled

with wonderment. "But that was enough, Serena, more than enough." He groaned and walked back to the chair and flung himself into it. He ran his hand through his hair. "She's grown to be the very best part of me. And all this time, I've taken it for granted. I've been such a block. What am I going to do?"

Serena gazed at Robby. Suddenly he was a little boy again to her, her younger brother whom she'd always thought of as hers and hers alone. She blinked and her heart twisted as the vision cleared. He was not a little boy, nor was he hers alone anymore. Somehow it made her want to cry. No doubt it was because she was tired.

She forced a smile. "As I said, I'm not sure I'm the one to advise you. It is unfortunate Lady Lucille has already gone out."

Robby shook his head. "No. She only knows about . . . affairs and . . . and dalliances. This is love."

"No, she does know about love," Serena said, a sadness entering her. Why, oh why, hadn't she listened to Lady Lucille. "More than you think."

Robby drew in his breath. "Serena, I don't want to just . . . dally with Sparrow."

"No, of course not," Serena said, her smile wavering.

"Then what am I to do?" Robby asked, his voice tormented.

"Well," Serena said, keeping her tone light, "I'd imagine the first thing in order would be to tell Sparrow that you love her."

"Yes, yes, of course," he said with a flush. He looked at her, his heart in his eyes. "And then what?"

Serena sucked in her breath. She knew what he asked. It hung in the room, waiting. Her answer would matter, matter to them all. She said slowly, evenly, "And then you ask her if she will marry you."

Love and gratitude leapt into Robby's eyes. "Could I?"

"I don't know why not," Serena said, attempting a nonchalance.

"No, you do know why," Robby said, his face hardening and his eyes turning bitter. "She's not from our class." He barked a laugh. "She's not even from our country."

Serena found herself choking. How the fates played and toyed with one. Not so very long ago, she'd had a love for a servant, yet she couldn't admit it. She'd preferred to dally.

She paled and shook her head. No, it wasn't the same. Nicholas hadn't been a real servant. Nor had their relationship been the same as Robby's and Sparrow's. Theirs was love, not just passion and battling wills. She forced her thoughts away from that deep and dark coil. It did cause her to say with a newfound sincerity, "If you truly love her, Robby, marry her."

"But the scandal," Robby groaned. "Sparrow don't even speak."

Serena laughed, despite herself. "Robby, our family is well versed in scandal. In fact, I certainly wouldn't mind it at all. It's high time someone else other than I caused a stir. A changing of the guards, as it were."

"By gads, you're right," Robby said, his eyes flaring bright. Then once again they darkened.

"But how could I put my Sparrow through it?"

"That would be Sparrow's choice," Serena said. "All you can do is ask her."

Robby stared at her. Suddenly the silliest of grins crossed his lips. "By Jove, I will." He sprung up. "That's exactly what I'm going to do." He charged toward the door but halted straightaway, spun back around, and returned to Serena. He bent down and placed a loud kiss upon her cheek. "Thank you. I love you, Serena."

He pivoted and was gone from the parlor in a flash. Serena felt the sting of tears. She loved him, too, and she prayed all would work out. Surely at least one member in the family deserved to find and keep a true love.

Robby strode through the townhouse toward the servants' quarters, his heart pounding. In fact, it felt as if it would explode with his newly accepted love. He'd combed the house already and had asked every staff member where he could find Sparrow. He hoped she was still in her room and not out upon some errand. Now that he had decided to ask her to marry him, he didn't think he could wait another moment to profess it. He couldn't wait another moment to know that Sparrow would be his.

He reached her door and rapped upon it. "Sparrow? Are you in there?" He tried the door and found it unlocked. He cracked it open, peering within. He caught a glimpse of Sparrow moving about. "There you are!"

He swung the door open and entered. Sparrow stood in the middle of the small room. She spun to him, though her hands were behind her back. Robby didn't notice her posture as much as he noticed her expression. Her eyes seemed alarmed. He flushed, sudden anxiety overcoming him.

"Ahem." He shifted on his feet. "I'm sorry to burst in like this. Only . . . only . . ." He halted, his throat suddenly dry. He expelled a breath. "Only, well . . . I want to tell you that . . . that . . ." He looked at Sparrow, and his confidence returned, shaped with the strength of his love. "I love you!"

Sparrow's eyes widened and then she seemed to jerk as if he had shot her. Robby flushed. "Oh, blast it. I'm sorry. That ain't the way I should have done it." He smiled sheepishly. "Only, I've never done this before." He stepped quickly forward and fell to one knee. Robby gazed up, his heart in his eyes. "Sparrow . . . would you . . . would you marry me?"

Sparrow didn't move. Her face turned to parchment, and tears swelled up in her brown eyes. Robby blinked. "What is it, Sparrow?" Fear shot through him. "Don't you want to marry me?"

A sob wracked Sparrow. She shook her head wildly and spun away from him, moving toward the bed. Robby's eyes widened. For the first time, he noticed an open satchel upon it. He actually yelped when he saw what had been hidden behind Sparrow's back. It was a petticoat, which she quickly packed into the satchel.

Robby sprung from his knees. "Sparrow, what are you doing?" The blood froze in his veins and he knew his question had been stupid. "Y-you are leaving."

Sparrow let out a heart-wrenching sob and nodded her head.

"But why?" Robby asked. "Why?" He tried desperately to make sense of it all. "Is it because of yesterday?" He flushed hot. "I'm sorry for kissing you . . . but I thought you kissed me."

Sparrow, crying, closed the satchel shut.

"Here now!" Robby exclaimed. "I . . . I . . . Oh, blast! Don't leave!" He sprung toward her as Sparrow grabbed up the bag. "Please, don't. If it's because I kissed you . . . I'm sorry." He flushed. "Or if it's because of what I said just now . . . well, I take that all back." Sparrow only cried all the more. "I mean, I will if you want me to. You don't have to leave." She tried to step past him. Desperation filled Robby and he grabbed hold of her arm. "Sparrow, you can't leave me! If you don't want to marry me, you don't have to. Just don't leave."

Sparrow attempted to pull away from him, but Robby couldn't release her. If she left, his life left. "Sparrow, I don't understand."

She stopped struggling, but only stood with her head bowed, crying softly. Robby's heart broke. He'd hurt his Sparrow, and he didn't even understand how he had done it. A proposal wasn't supposed to make a woman cry like this. At least, he never thought it should, but what did he know about women?

His heart leapt. That was it, it was a mysterious woman thing, which only women understood. Relief flooded him. "Serena! She'll understand!"

Eagerly he tugged at Sparrow. She shook her head. "That's it. You can talk to Serena," he said with determination. Serena always knew how to arrange things. She never failed him. "You ladies talk. Settle things."

Sparrow dug in her heels, refusing to budge. "Sparrow, please!" Robby cried in desperation. "I won't let you go this way!"

Sparrow shook her head, tears still streaming down her face. Robby stopped and put his arms about her. She sobbed all the more.

Frightened, Robby became a man of action. He scooped Sparrow up into his arms and all but raced through the townhouse. He charged into the parlor. "Serena! You must talk to Sparrow."

Serena looked up from where she still sat upon the settee. Her mouth fell open. "Robby, what on earth are you doing!"

"I proposed," Robby said, panting and out of breath. "And . . . and she started to cry." His voice rose in panic. "She was packing. She was going to leave me! And she won't stop crying!"

"Faith," Serena exclaimed. She sprung up. "Well, for goodness' sake, Robby, do bring her here."

"You must talk to her," Robby said desperately. He carried his crying lady over to the settee and set her down. "Sh-she won't listen to me. I don't understand."

Serena immediately sat down beside Sparrow and quickly picked up her hand. "Sparrow, please calm down."

"Promise her anything," Robby said. "Tell her I won't kiss her again. Or I won't propose again. Or . . . or I won't say I love her again. Just make her stay."

"Robby!" Serena said, her voice sharp. "Please be quiet!"

"Oh, yes," Robby said before he clamped his mouth shut. He stared mutely at Serena and then gazed hopelessly at Sparrow.

"Sparrow," Serena said more quietly. "We won't make you stay . . ."

"What?" Robby yelped.

Serena cast him a stern look. "But I think that before you leave, you should becalm yourself."

"Yes," Robby said, nodding. He began to pace the room. "Calm. Yes, that's it. Calm."

"Now, please," Serena said soothingly. "Are you leaving because of Robby?"

Sparrow shook her head no, a vehement no.

"Thank God," Robby breathed.

Then Sparrow nodded her head.

"Oh, God!" Robby cried, his heart sinking.

"Sparrow, I don't understand," Serena said, frowning. "Which is it? Are you leaving because of Robby or not?"

"Don't try and force her," Robby said. "She can't answer the question that way."

"I'm not forcing her!" Serena exclaimed. "You are the one who literally carried her in here."

"Yes, but . . ." Robby said. Suddenly Sparrow jumped up and darted toward the door. "Sparrow!" Robby called out and dashed after her.

"Robby!" Serena cried and sprung up.

"Sparrow, wait." Robby never imagined Sparrow could move so quickly. He was still four paces behind her when they entered the foyer. Sparrow arrowed directly toward the large doors. Robby's heart failed, until he saw that Nobles stood at the gates of escape. Robby cursed, however, when he realized Nobles was actually reaching to open the door. "Nobles, blast it, don't!"

"I beg pardon, my lord?" Nobles turned a stunned gaze upon Robby. Then he gurgled as Sparrow pelted at him.

"Don't let Sparrow . . ." Robby said, and then groaned. Sparrow had circumvented the befuddled Nobles and jerked open the door. "Go!"

Time suddenly droned into slow motion as Robby watched Sparrow step through the exit. Then it leapt into fast action as Sparrow immediately appeared again. She was running back to him. He opened his arms wide and caught her to him. "Sparrow!"

"Angelica!" a male voice shouted. Randolf Dorvelle charged through the entrance. His face was wild and his gaze was directly upon Sparrow.

"Angelica?" Alvie St. Irving cried, appearing through the portal. Her face was pale as she, too, stared at Sparrow. "Y-you are Angelica?"

"Who is Angelica?" Serena asked, coming up from behind.

"Yes, who is Angelica?" Nicholas asked as he, too, appeared.

"You're not a ghost!" Alvie stammered, gazing at Sparrow with wide, wide eyes.

"Course she's not a ghost," Robby exclaimed, holding Sparrow protectively. He could feel her shaking. He didn't know how everyone had suddenly come to be in the foyer, or why they all stared at Sparrow, but he wished they'd leave. "What are you all doing here?"

"We came for Serena," Nicholas said. "We're going for a ride in the park."

"Oh, I see," Robby said. He didn't like the frozen attention, which was focused upon Sparrow, or how she cringed in his arms. "Then go." No one moved. "You may go!"

"Yes, sir!" Unfortunately it was only Nobles who consented and obeyed.

"I wasn't seeing things," Randolf said lowly. "It is you. You are alive."

"She's alive," Alvie said, tears springing into her eyes.

Robby frowned, somehow feeling offended. "Course she's alive. Why shouldn't Sparrow be alive?"

"Sparrow?" Randolf started back, appearing offended. "That is a bird, yes? You cannot call Angelica a bird! *Mon Dieu!*"

"I'm not calling Angelica a bird," Robby said in exasperation. "I don't even know who Angelica is."

Randolf pointed a shaking finger at Sparrow. "She is Angelica."

"No, she ain't!" Robby retorted. He felt Sparrow push gently at him. He looked down at her. His heart gave a lurch at what he saw in her dark eyes. "Are you?"

A tear slipped down Sparrow's face. She nodded her head in consent.

Robby's arms fell from her in shock. He stared at her. "You're Angelica."

"My Angelica," Randolf breathed, walking slowly toward her. "I thought you were dead."

"Here now, what are you doing?" Robby asked, stepping quickly in front of Sparrow. He glared hard at Randolf.

Randolf stiffened. His eyes shot sparks back. "Monsieur, you have no right to keep me from her. She is my fiancée!"

"Your fiancée!" Robby shouted.

"My Lord," Serena breathed out.

Robby spun toward Sparrow. "Is that true, Sparrow?"

"Of course it is true!" Randolf cried, stepping forward with a dark frown. "Angelica, why have you not told him this? And why do you permit him to call you a bird?"

"Because she can't speak," Robby said angrily. "That's why. And I like the name Sparrow. What's wrong with it?"

"What's wrong with it?" Randolf exclaimed hotly. "One does not call the Countess of Landour a bird! It is not . . ." Randolf halted. "She cannot speak?"

"Countess?" Robby asked at the same time.

Everyone paused a silent, pregnant moment, all eyes turned upon poor Sparrow-Angelica, the Countess of Landour.

"Good Lord," Serena said with a shaky laugh. "Not again. Not another aristocrat in disguise. It's impossible!"

"Apparently not," Nicholas murmured, amusement threading his words.

"It's not funny," Alvie said, her voice full of pain. "I want to go home."

Randolf turned to her. His face had been parchment white. Now it turned red, and his brown eyes pleaded. "Alvie . . . I mean . . . Mademoiselle St. Irving."

"No," Alvie said, shaking her head and slowly backing away. "You have found your b-beloved. I—I wish you well." She turned and dashed to the door, disappearing.

"If you will excuse me," Nicholas said quietly. "I must take Alvie home." He turned and followed his sister.

Robby swallowed hard. Alvie St. Irving had done the only thing possible. He gazed at the woman he loved. She was not his Sparrow. She was an engaged woman and a countess. "I'm sorry, I did not understand. I—I wish you well."

He turned and walked away in a daze. He heard Serena call to him, but he kept walking.

Randolf stood rooted to the floor, immobilized by confusion. He stared at the woman whom he had thought dead, the woman he had mourned for over a year. Yet all he could think of was Alvie leaving. He shook his head to clear it.

Angelica studied him with serious eyes. He flushed. "Y-you cannot speak?"

She lowered her gaze, and nodded her head.

He walked up to her. "I—I thought you were dead."

She nodded and then shrugged.

He studied her. She was much thinner, and her face far older. She had always been so vibrant. So beautifully dressed at all times. He stiffened as he realized his thoughts. Forcing a happiness to his voice he said, "But you are not, *Mon Dieu*. It . . . it hard to believe."

Angelica looked at him and offered him a quivering smile.

Randolf forced a smile as well. "It is very hard to believe. But n-now we have found each other again, we can . . ."

Angelica shook her head and walked up to him. She gently put a finger to his lips. Randolf fell silent. Her eyes seemed far too knowing and understanding. She removed her finger and pointed at the door.

Randolf flushed. "Y-you wish me to go?"

She nodded. Then a smile, so very similar to the one

he had always remembered, crossed her lips. His breath caught. "I love you, Angelica."

She nodded, but pointed toward the door once more. Randolf realized he could not deny it anymore. He desperately wanted to rush out that door and go after Alvie. "Can you forgive me?"

Angelica nodded and leaned up and kissed him on the cheek. Then she grabbed hold of his arm and led him toward the door. Randolf began to laugh. When she opened the door for him, he knew he could walk out of it without guilt or regret. There was no longer a ghost to haunt him, for she was literally pushing him forward to go to his true beloved.

Randolf pounded eagerly upon the St. Irving door. It finally opened. Hobson stood in the entrance. His proper butler demeanor melted away and an open look of dislike appeared on his face. "Oh, it's you, is it?"

"I wish to see, Mademoiselle," Randolf said, raising both brow and chin.

"Do ye now?" Hobson said in a pugnacious tone. "Well, ye can't. She's laid down to rest, and ain't receiving."

"I wish to see her," Randolf said, just as pugnaciously but far more autocratically. "I demand you go and ask if she will receive me."

"I told you," Hobson said. "She ain't receiving. And certainly not the likes of you."

"I will see her," Randolf said. "You shall not stop me."

Hobson actually dropped into a fighter's stance. "You ain't getting past me this time, Frenchie. I've got your measure, I do."

"I will see Alvie," Randolf ensured. He charged at the butler. They both tumbled into the foyer. Hobson indeed was better prepared than last time, or else Randolf's bandaged arm hindered him, for Hobson succeeded in landing a good left to Randolf's jaw. Randolf, grunting, swiftly dealt Hobson a telling blow with his good fist. The butler shouted, toppled back, and lay unmoving. Randolf swiped at the trickle of blood he felt at his mouth and winced from the pain in his other arm.

"Brawling with my butler again?" Nicholas's voice asked.

Randolf looked up to see Nicholas coming down the stairs that flanked the left side of the foyer. He stiffened. "I have come to see Alvie."

"Have you?" Nicholas asked, his voice amused.

Randolf glared at him. "I intend to propose to her."

"Do you?" Nicholas asked. "Forgive me, but aren't you engaged already?"

"Non," Randolf said. "Angelica has . . . has set me free. I come to propose to Alvie." His eyes flashed. "I will not permit you to stop me."

Nicholas threw his hands up. "Save your fervor for Alvie. I have no intention of fighting with you. These days I have become a man of peace. I strive not to fight with anyone."

Randolf looked suspiciously at him. "You will not fight?"

"No. I have no doubt my dear sister would run a blade through me if I did," Nicholas said. He shook his head. "Are you sure you want to become a member of this family?"

"Yes," Randolf said, placing his hand to his chest. "With all my heart."

"Very well," Nicholas said. He glanced at the still unmoving Hobson. "Though if you do, I must demand you resist from milling down my butler in the future. He's been in our family for years."

Randolf smiled and bowed. "I promise, monsieur."

"Very well," Nicholas said. "I shall retrieve Alvie. She is in her room."

"No," Randolf said, what could only be called a "whim" taking hold of him. "Please. I would like to go to her myself. If . . . if you will give me the directions to her room."

Nicholas raised his brow. "I beg your pardon?"

Randolf smiled. "I am to become a member of the family, *non*? I must not be so proper. Mademoiselle Alvie, she has taught me this, yes?"

"Has she?" Nicholas asked, his eyes narrowing.

Randolf nodded. "She has visited my room. I shall visit hers."

Nicholas frowned. "You'd better propose to her, else I might have to duel with you after all."

"*Non*, I am a man of honor," Randolf said quickly. "I would never take advantage of a lady. Mademoiselle Alvie, she is the innocent." He grinned. "But in this, I do not wish to be proper."

"Very well," Nicholas said, a glint in his eyes. "You may very well do better for Alvie than I first thought. Besides, I would not like to join the fate of my butler. Alvie's room is down the hall and to the right."

"Thank you . . . brother," Randolf nodded. He bolted toward the stairs, passed Nicholas, and rushed up them. He only halted when he reached the door he believed was Alvie's. He straightened his jacket and then opened the door, entering quickly. He saw Alvie, lying across the bed. Randolf heard her sob. "Mademoiselle, you should not cry!"

Alvie squeaked and scrambled to a sitting position. Her eyes, red-rimmed, widened. "Randolf. Wh-what are you doing here?"

He grinned. "I am the maid, *non*?"

Alvie giggled. Then she frowned. "You are hurt."

Randolf shrugged. "Your butler . . . he would not let me in. I fear I . . . er, milled him down?"

"You did?" Alvie asked, sighing. That charming, impish smile peeked out. "You really shouldn't have. Poor Hobson."

Randolf lifted his chin. "Yes, I should have. He would not let me see you."

Alvie glanced down, a delightful blush painting her cheeks. "Why are you here? You . . . you should be with Angelica."

"*Non,*" Randolf said, his voice low. "She did not want me."

Alvie's eyes flew to his. "What?"

"And I did not want her," he said, walking toward Alvie. "I want you."

Alvie jumped up from the bed, her eyes wide and wondrous. "You do?"

"I do," Randolf said. He solemnly knelt before her. "Mademoiselle . . . Alvie . . . will you marry me?"

"Oh, yes!" Alvie cried. She promptly threw herself at him. "Oh, yes!"

Randolf swiftly caught her, though he could not maintain his balance. They toppled to the floor. Randolf laughed. His life would be so different with this wild, improper girl. He had come to England to kill a man, instead he had found his life. He swiftly kissed Alvie with a fervor, his passion unrestrained.

It was Alvie who drew back first, her face flushed. Randolf gazed at her. A surge of male pride rushed through him. "I have shocked you, *non?*"

"Yes," Alvie said, blushing to a brighter hue.

Randolf laughed. "At last! I have shocked you! Many times you have shocked me. Now, I shock you! I will do well in your family, *non?*"

"Yes," Alvie breathed. "Oh, yes." Then she kissed him. Her lips were so sweet. Yet the sweetness turned far too quickly to heat. Randolf suddenly groaned and rolled away from Alvie. He stood quickly, sucking in his breath.

Alvie sat up. She gazed at him, her eyes dazed and loving. "I have shocked *you.*"

Randolf shifted uncomfortably. *"Non.* But I have promised your brother that I would be an honorable man."

Alvie rose quickly, all but tripping on her skirts. "You are an honorable man."

"Yes," Randolf said, the desire rushing through him anything but honorable. He bowed quickly. "Thank you. Now I must leave."

"But . . . !" Alvie exclaimed.

Randolf spun on his heel and bolted toward the door. "We shall marry soon. Yes?"

He didn't wait for Alvie's reply, but hastened from the room. He already knew the answer after all.

"I'm sorry, Robby," Serena said softly as they sat in the library.

Robby sat in his favorite large chair, a bumper of brandy in his hand. He felt as if a mule had kicked him in the stomach. He looked at Serena and shook his head, feeling dazed. He didn't doubt that the pain would grow worse. He took a swift pull of his brandy, hoping to start the anesthetizing process early. "Now I know how you felt when you discovered Nicholas wasn't . . . wasn't who you thought he was."

"Yes," Serena said. She bit her lip. "But we don't know why Sparrow behaved the way she did. She can't tell us. I'm sure she had her reasons, just as Nicholas had his."

Robby shivered. "She's engaged, Serena."

"I know," Serena said, the look upon her face rather

helpless. "But Randolf also thought her dead for over a year. Something happened to her Robby."

"I know," Robby said in anguish. "God, I know that. My poor Sparrow. A countess and lady. You don't know in what condition I found her. And I treated her as . . ." He halted and laughed bitterly. "Well, as what I called her. Sparrow. A bird. While all the time, I've loved her."

"Robby, you didn't know," Serena said. "What if you hadn't found her? Have you thought of that?"

"Yes," Robby said, sighing. "And I—I can't bear the thought." He looked at Serena. "I'm not sorry I found her. I'm sorry I . . ." He shook his head and sighed again. "What does it matter?"

At that moment the door to the library opened. Sparrow entered silently. Robby stood immediately, almost spilling his drink in the process. "Sparrow . . . I mean, my lady."

Serena rose to her feet as well. She smiled. "If you will excuse me. I have . . . have some things I must do."

Robby didn't even note her departure. He could only stand, staring at Sparrow, or Angelica, that was. It didn't matter. He loved her and didn't know how he'd live without her now.

Angelica smiled at him and motioned for him to sit down. Robby, not knowing what else to do, sat. Angelica walked quietly over and shifted the ottoman beside the chair even closer. She sat down upon it. Robby's heart wrenched. They had sat thus, so many times.

He forced a smile, gripping his glass of brandy. "Y-you could have knocked me over with a feather out there. I—I didn't know that . . . well, all that." He laughed. "Well, of course I didn't know. Dorvelle's right. Guess I shouldn't have called you Sparrow." He glanced at Angelica. Her gaze was lowered. He flushed. "Now I can understand why you wanted to leave. I mean, you have a different life than . . . what you have here. You're a countess, after all, and engaged. Now that you've found Dorvelle again . . ."

"I love you," Angelica said softly.

"You'll want to . . ." Robby halted. The glass slid from his fingers. He didn't even regard the splashing brandy, or the glass rolling to the carpet. "D-did you j-just speak?"

Angelica lifted her gaze to him, her eyes warm but frightened. "I love you."

"Sparrow!" shouted Robby, reaching out to clutch her shoulders. "You spoke. You really spoke. You . . ." He sucked in his breath. "You love me?"

"Yes," Angelica said in a wonderfully soft, warm voice, "I love you."

Robby found himself grinning ridiculously. All he could do was stare, dumfounded. "You love me . . . and you said it!"

"Can you forgive me?"

"Hmm?" Robby asked, still taken by hearing her voice. It fit her perfectly. Her accent was so very light, her words so beautiful.

"Can you forgive me?" Angelica asked again.

Robby's eyes widened, finally gaining focus. "Forgive you for what?"

Angelica's eyes darkened. "I have been able to talk for . . . for a time now."

Robby's hands fell from her shoulders. He blinked. "You have?"

"Yes," Angelica said. She clasped her hands together and looked down. "I—I was frightened to speak."

"Why?" Robby asked, shaking his head in a daze.

Angelica twisted her hands. "When you found me, I—I couldn't talk. I don't know why." She shrugged. "Perhaps I didn't want to talk. I know I didn't want to live. But you . . . you were so kind to me. I started to want to live again. Soon I knew I could also speak again." She lowered her gaze. "But I didn't. I couldn't."

"Why not?" Robby asked.

"If I started to talk, you would ask me about my life. I knew I couldn't lie to you, so I remained silent."

"It wouldn't have mattered what you told me about your life."

"Yes, it would have," Angelica said softly. "For you did exactly what I was frightened you might do. I knew you would expect me to go back to my . . . my past life." She looked at him, tears in her eyes. "But there is no past life for me. It is all gone."

"My poor Sparrow," Robby said, anguished.

She sprung up and moved away from him. She wouldn't look at him. "I am the Countess of Landour, now that all my family is dead."

Robby shook his head. "But . . . but how . . . how did I come to find you the way you were? I thought you a . . . a peasant."

Angelica looked up, a sad smile upon her face. "I am that, too."

"I don't understand," Robby said.

She drew in a breath. "My . . . my family, my real family was killed. Or executed, I would say, by Napoleon."

"I see," Robby said, wincing.

"My father believed in Napoleon at first. He was one of his best men. But . . . but the more power hungry Napoleon became, the more he led our poor country into war for his own glory, the less my father accepted him. He openly opposed Napoleon."

She shrugged. "He and my mother were killed for it. I escaped. I had been wounded, but I escaped. If it weren't for a peasant family who took me in, I would have died." She moved as if she were sleepwalking, and settled upon the ottoman once more. "I lived with them. They became my family. It was not as if I could claim my title again."

She looked down. "Nor did I really think about Randolf. He was part of my past. I—I fear I did not love him enough to wish to return." She smiled sadly. "Even when Napoleon was defeated and sent to the island, I chose to remain with them. I owed them my life, and even though it was a harder life, it was a simpler life. Away from the intrigue. Away from the war. Or so I thought."

A cold, deadened look crossed her face. "Then Napoleon escaped and returned. We had moved to a small village on the outskirts of Paris by then. My family was caught in a battle between the royalists and Napoleon's return to Paris."

"My God," Robby whispered.

"I had two families and he took both of them."

Robby swallowed hard. "Can you . . . would you accept another family?"

Tears welled in Angelica's eyes. "I would do anything to be with you."

Robby gulped. "Then why . . . why were you leaving me?"

"I was frightened," Angelica said. "Randolf had seen me. When I realized h-he was close to your family, I knew it would be only a matter of time." She flushed. "I didn't want to leave you, but I didn't want you to discover who I was. I didn't know . . . never thought you could love me as I loved you. When I—I kissed you, it was for goodbye. And because I—I wanted to kiss you just once."

Robby shivered. How close he had come to losing her. What a fool he had been! Then he shivered again. "But this morning. When I proposed . . ."

Angelica smiled, a hurt, bruised smile. "You still didn't know the truth. I—I have lost so much. To have you say you would marry me, and then have you discover who I was." She shook her head. "I wanted to escape before that happened. Before my . . . my lives collided and . . . and . . ."

"And you lost once more," Robby said softly.

"Yes," Angelica said, nodding her head. "Can you forgive me?"

"Always," Robby said. He opened his arms wide. Angelica shifted so quickly and easily from the ottoman onto his lap and into his arms, Robby thought he was dreaming. Their lips met in a slow kiss. Love flooded through Robby. "You will marry me, Sparrow? I mean, Angelica."

"I like the name Sparrow," Angelica said softly. "And all I want is to marry you."

Eleven

"My, it is positively a French invasion," Lady Witherington said with a laugh. "I do hope Napoleon will not be as successful in his efforts."

"I doubt it," Lady Lucille said, fanning herself negligently as she looked out across the ballroom. "But then, Napoleon isn't as dear and sweet as Angelica is. I'd say we've got the best of the best."

"I certainly didn't mean to cast dispersions," Lady Witherington said quickly. "Indeed, I think it quite romantic, the story of Angelica and your Robby. Only, it does astound one so. Robby Fairchild is to marry a Frenchwoman, and Alvie St. James is to marry that dashing Frenchman, Randolf Dorvelle. It seemed to happen so fast. None of us knowing the better."

"Love happens that way sometimes," Lady Lucille said.

Lady Witherington trilled a laugh. "And you would know, wouldn't you, Lucille?"

Lucille smiled pleasantly. "Yes, I would."

"It's strange," Lady Witherington said, her tone dry. "To be here for an engagement ball for Robby Fairchild, rather than Serena. You know we all thought it would be she and Nicholas first with an announcement." She sighed. "Now there is an affair which seems to have died."

Lucille cast Lady Witherington a cool look. "Yes, so it would appear."

"Of course, one can't be surprised, can one?" Lady Witherington tittered. "They truly were an unmatched couple."

"Perhaps," Lucille said, tamping down her rising anger. Amelia Witherington was such a cat.

"In a way, it is a shame," Lady Witherington said. "We poor, dull ones simply have no more entertainment. Serena and Nicholas did enliven things when they were . . ." She halted then continued, "Well, I guess you can't call it courting, now, can you?"

"You may call it whatever you wish," Lucille said. "Which I'm sure you will."

"Well, no matter." Lady Witherington waved a hand. "We'll just have to look elsewhere for entertainment, won't we?" She smiled. "Though it seems Serena and Nicholas have settled down and are at least amiable to each other. They are friends now, I assume?"

Lady Lucille narrowed her eyes. "Why do you ask?"

"Oh, nothing," Lady Witherington said, though her eyes shifted.

Lucille lifted her brow and repeated, "Why do you ask?"

"Very well," Lady Witherington said, tittering once more. "I suppose I can tell you. I doubt you'll be shocked."

"Of course not," Lady Lucille said.

"Well, you know how men are . . ." Lady Witherington lowered her voice. "They do like their little wagers. Lord Witherington has a bet at White's that Nicholas will still bring Serena to the altar. Of course, he placed it quite a few weeks ago. I told him he should withdraw the bet, as many others have, but the silly man still persists. Indeed, he is taking all odds." She leaned forward. "What do you think, dear Lucille? Is there still a chance?"

Lucille smiled. "I certainly couldn't say. But they do seem to have become merely friends."

"Ha!" Lady Witherington exclaimed, nodding. "I have told Lord Witherington that, over and over again." She rose. "If you will excuse me, I believe I see . . . Lord Witherington beckoning me."

"You must certainly go to him then," Lucille said. She watched as Mrs. Witherington wended her way through the crowd, Lord Witherington nowhere in sight. She shook her head and smiled. She never knew Hubert Witherington was so perspicuous. She would still lay her money on Serena and Nicholas becoming a match. Though she'd never tell that witch, Amelia Witherington. Let Hubert listen to his dear wife and lose a bundle.

Lucille frowned. She knew better than to meddle at this stage of the game, but sometimes she just burned to take both the silly children in hand. Nicholas was clearly playing the low suit, quite the supportive friend rather than ardent lover. Indeed, Nicholas and Serena were being so wondrously amiable to each other as to be positively sickening. Lucille shook her head. She hoped they'd not play the game too long. In truth, neither were of the "amiable" persuasion.

Nicholas watched as Serena danced with Lord Farrington. He bit back a smile. The man was known as the most fiddle-footed dancer amongst the ton. Tonight, Lord Farrington was far surpassing his acknowledged talent. Serena was manfully attempting to keep her feet free from the gentleman's heavy tread.

His smile turned gentle. For all that the ton thought Serena heartless, if one watched her closely, one could see acts of sheer kindness. Indeed, he had seen her be far kinder in the past few weeks than he would have ever imagined. He held back the sudden surge of desire and told himself to be patient. In truth, it should be enough they had grown to be on friendlier terms, but it wasn't. He wanted more, much more.

Serena herself seemed calmer, and quite willing for his company. Even through the preparations for the engagement ball, they'd not fought. Not that there weren't occasions when his blood boiled, or jealousy overcame him, but it seemed the lighter he held the reins with Serena, the better for them both. She was changing, clearly changing. He laughed slightly. Perhaps it was merely he who was changing. Or perhaps not. Perhaps it was just that he was growing to love, an emotion now he knew he had never really experienced before.

He frowned as he noticed Serena and Lord Farrington suddenly stumble. Serena righted herself and so did Lord Farrington, but Serena hadn't moved or entered the dance again. Nicholas, without conscious thought, moved directly toward them. He forced a smile as he approached, though Serena's pale face let him know she had suffered an injury.

Nicholas tapped the man upon the shoulder. "Excuse me, Farrington."

"Heh, what?" Lord Farrington asked, looking around.

"I'm afraid I must steal Lady Fairchild from you for a moment," Nicholas said. "It seems her butler requires her surveillance in regards to the . . . late supper."

"Does he?" Lord Farrington asked, frowning.

"Yes," Nicholas said adroitly but determinedly, drawing Serena from out of Farrington's arms.

Serena's smile was grateful. "If you will excuse me."

"Are you all right?" Nicholas asked lowly as she grasped his arm and leaned heavily upon it.

"I'm not sure," Serena said with a small laugh. "It's my foot. I—I don't know if I've sprained it or not."

"Should I carry you?" Nicholas asked in concern.

"Heavens no!" Serena answered quickly.

Nicholas laughed. "Why not? It's not as if I have not done so before."

Serena flushed and looked away. "I don't wish to make a spectacle of myself tonight. Not at Robby's engagement party."

Nicholas wanted to tease her, but something in her closed expression made him bite back his words. "No, of course not. Let us go for some fresh air." He directed her toward the balcony doors. Serena sighed in obvious relief when he led her over to a stone bench. She sat down rather abruptly.

"You were brave to dance with Farrington," Nicholas said, his lips twitching.

"No, I was a fool." Serena shook her head with a laugh. She moved slightly and winced.

"Here," Nicholas said, and knelt before her.

Serena's eyes widened. "What on earth are you doing?"

"Seeking a peek at your lovely ankles, my dear."

Serena's eyes widened, and a flush covered her cheeks. "That won't be necessary."

Nicholas smiled wryly. "You still don't trust me. Do you, Serena?"

Serena looked down. "What does trust have to do with this?"

"Plenty," Nicholas said softly.

"Very well," Serena said, her tone light. "I trust you."

Nicholas's heart beat faster. "Good. Now permit Dr. Nicholas to look at your ankle."

Serena chuckled. Amazingly it sounded breathless.

She lifted her skirts very slightly. Her one foot peeked out.

Nicholas reached over and gently took her foot in his hand. He felt it tenderly. He heard Serena's small moan. Of a sudden, his own hands trembled. He forced himself to focus upon the foot itself. It didn't help. Her ankle was trim and neat. Nicholas almost groaned. He was actually becoming heated over a woman's ankle. His hand itched to slide past that ankle, to smooth along the calf of her leg. He swallowed, trying to gain control of himself. "Does that hurt?" His voice came out far huskier than he intended.

"Yes," Serena said, her words but a whisper.

"I'm sorry." He couldn't seem to release her ankle. Serena blinked. "No. I meant no."

"I see," Nicholas said. He quickly directed his attention back to his supposed doctoring. He moved her foot slightly to the left and to the right. "Does that hurt?"

Serena shook her head, her green eyes dark. "No."

"It's not sprained then." Nicholas looked up at her. How he would like to topple her from the bench and take her right there. How he wanted to command and demand the passion which lurked within her eyes. It had been far too long since they had kissed or touched. He swore he couldn't remember the last time. Unfortunately, he could remember. It was the night he had realized he loved her and known he wanted her to give her love to him freely in return. He quickly released her foot. "Th-that is fortunate."

"It m-must be only bruised," Serena said, leaning over to cover her foot with her skirts.

"Serena . . ." Nicholas's voice was soft as he bent closer.

"Yes?" she asked, moving even closer. Their faces were mere inches apart.

Nicholas realized it was a moment of decision. Part

of him wanted to simply succumb to the desire, forget what he was fighting to gain, kiss Serena soundly and tell her she would marry him post haste. He drew back quickly, stiffening. He'd not lose what he had accomplished. When he proposed the next time, Serena would know he was asking, not telling. "Nothing." He saw the spark die in Serena's eyes. "Serena . . ."

"Nicholas!" a voice all but screeched from behind him.

Nicholas started, looking behind him. Alvie and Angelica stood not far from them. He'd not even noticed their arrival. No doubt an army could have camped on the balcony and he wouldn't have noticed.

Alvie's face was alight and excited. She clapped her hands together. "You are finally proposing!"

"No, I'm not," Nicholas said curtly. He'd just drawn back from an unfitting proposal. He'd not permit Alvie to force him into one now. He stood up quickly and glanced at Serena. Her gaze was lowered, her face flushed with what actually appeared embarrassment. Upon Serena it was an unusual sight.

"Oh," Alvie said. Her voice sounded dejected. "I'm sorry. I only thought . . ."

"Yes," Nicholas said grimly. "We know what you thought."

Alvie frowned. "But then what were you doing?"

"I was only checking to see if Serena's ankle was all right," Nicholas said. "Lord Farrington struck again."

"You mean stepped again," Serena murmured.

"I see," Alvie said. Her face didn't exactly portray either understanding or belief.

Angelica hastened forward. "Are you all right?"

"Yes," Alvie said, crowding closer. "I do hope you are. It is time to announce the engagement."

"I'm fine," Serena said, rising. She sucked in her breath. It was clear she favored her injured foot.

"No, sit down," Nicholas insisted quickly. He realized he sounded brisk. "Please sit down again."

"But I must have Nobles prepare the champagne," Serena objected.

"I can do that," Nicholas said. She looked at him hesitantly. He grinned. "Certainly you know I am capable of overseeing your household."

Serena, rather than laughing as he had expected, only flushed. "Of course."

He smiled. "Remain out here while we make the final preparations."

Serena sat down slowly. "I—I think I shall."

"Good," Nicholas said. He looked to Alvie and Angelica. "Ladies, shall we?"

"Yes." Alvie glanced at Serena with concern. "If you are certain?"

"Please, do go," Serena said, her tone sounding odd. "I shall be there in the nonce."

Nicholas bowed slightly. With a wry smile he said, "Your servant, my lady."

With that Nicholas herded Alvie and Angelica back toward the ballroom, though his thoughts were still upon Serena. He could wait no longer. He must propose and propose soon for his own sanity's sake.

His mind immediately turned toward the preparations. He had a ring to choose and a honeymoon to prepare. He thought about the kiss he had denied himself. Perhaps a special license would be in order as well. He definitely didn't want to suffer a long engagement.

Serena prepared herself for bed. Exhaustion sapped her. Tandy, once again her dresser, rattled on and on. About what, Serena didn't know or care. Her mind, unlike her body, whirled. It flashed images continuously before her. Images of Nicholas kneeling at her feet. Images of Nicholas when he sprung up as if he had been shot when Alvie asked if he were proposing. Then the image of Robby and Angelica as they stood beside each other, glowing with love when they received a toast upon their upcoming marriage.

A knock sounded at her door. Serena sighed. She didn't relish company. "Who is it?"

"Serena," Angelica called. "It's me. May I come in?"

"Yes," Serena said, sighing again. She only wanted quiet. However, Angelica had just announced her engagement this evening, and every lady deserved to be able to talk about it afterwards.

The door opened and Angelica entered. Her face was solemn and her eyes concerned. "How are you feeling?" she asked.

Serena smiled. "My foot is fine now."

Angelica nodded, then glanced toward Tandy. "I wonder if I might speak to you in private?"

"Certainly," Serena said, raising her brow. She nodded to Tandy. "You may leave now, Tandy."

"Yes, mum," Tandy said. "Oh, I mean, my lady. Now, you all have a good coze. Reckon you have a lot to talk about after the ball. Ma always said that be the best part of a celebration. Having a good gossip afterward. Though I'd think wearing the pretty dresses would be the finest thing . . ." She dipped a curtsy and meandered from the room, leaving some involved sentence dangling.

Serena and Angelica shared a look of amusement. Serena shook her head. "I am quite pleased you will be my sister-in-law, but I own I miss you as my dresser."

Angelica chuckled. She walked to a chair and sat down in it. Her face turned wry. "I do not know if you will care for me as a sister-in-law after I speak."

"Why?" Serena frowned in concern. "What is it?"

"You are not happy," Angelica said directly, her voice quiet.

Serena stiffened in astonishment. "I am happy. Quite happy."

"I do not feel that you are," Angelica said, still with a steady gaze.

Serena flushed and shook her head. "Angelica, I am very pleased with your engagement to Robby. Surely you do not think I object to . . ."

"That is not what I meant," Angelica said. She cocked her head to one side. "You love Nicholas, do you not?"

Serena started. She forced a wry laugh. "I believe I liked it better when you could not speak." A flush washed Angelica's cheeks. "No, forgive me," Serena said quickly with contrition. "I did not mean that."

"Yes you did," Angelica said, the slightest smile playing upon her lips.

The two women gazed at each other and laughed. Angelica had become a perpetual and pleasant surprise ever since she began to speak. Serena said in a teasing tone, "Perhaps you are right."

"You must forgive me," Angelica said softly. "But I have discovered that when one does not talk, or is expected to talk, one can discover much."

"I see," Serena said, her heart failing her. "And you believe I love Nicholas."

"Yes."

Serena debated for only a moment. She sighed. "Yes, I do. But he . . . he does not love me." She performed a semblance of a smile. "You saw how he acted when Alvie asked if he were proposing."

Angelica shrugged. "No man likes to be surprised. Miss St. Irving has many fine qualities, but delicacy is not among them."

"True." Serena's heart tightened. "But I don't think that is the case this time. Nicholas doesn't love me."

"I think he does," Angelica said softly. "He has grown . . . very kind to you."

Serena flushed. "Yes, he has grown . . . kind." Never passionate. Never jealous. But certainly kind. She could not admit it was his kindness that hurt the most. She had come to need that kindness. She had come to love him more and more because of it. Yet he no longer kissed her, or tried to kiss her. He no longer talked of marriage. She noticed Angelica watching her with that silent, penetrating look that surely had caused Robby to bequeath the name Sparrow upon her. She shook her head. "Nicholas and I are friends now, I believe. Nothing more."

Angelica frowned. "Are you certain?"

"Yes." Serena flushed. For a moment tonight, she had thought Nicholas would kiss her. How desperately she had wanted him to kiss her. Then he had drawn back. "He . . . does not desire me anymore."

"But he did once," Angelica said. Serena's eyes widened. Angelica's tone was apologetic. "You must forgive me, but Robby has told me."

"Oh, God," Serena said, mortified. "Of course he would have. I—I hope it did not shock you . . . or give you a disgust of me."

Angelica merely waved her hand, as if brushing away an inconsequential gnat. Her serious look did not waver. "If Nicholas desired you once, he can desire you again."

"What?" Serena asked, stunned.

Angelica smiled. "You have not tried to see if he still desires you?"

"Of course not."

"Then how do you know he does not?" Angelica asked in a perfectly reasonable tone. "Or how does he know?"

Serena gazed at Angelica in amazement. "Are you suggesting that I—I . . . ?"

"Seduce him," Angelica said, nodding.

A surprised laugh escaped Serena.

Angelica smiled. "A Frenchwoman, she is taught differently than an Englishwoman. Seduction should not always be the . . . the choice of the man. They do not always understand what they feel. You must show them."

"You believe this?" Serena asked.

Angelica shrugged. "That is what I was taught." Her eyes grew dark. "But I have learned more than that. I almost left my love, because I would not speak to Robby of it."

"You would not speak at all."

"Yes," Angelica nodded. "And it caused much pain for both him and me, because I would not tell him the truth."

Serena thought a moment. She shook her head. There had been too many battles, too many games for control, between Nicholas and her. "No, I could not do that."

Angelica rose with a sigh. "I understand. I am sorry if I spoke when I should not have."

"No, it is all right," Serena said. "I—I thank you for your concern."

Serena smiled bravely, but only felt at ease once Angelica had left. A laugh escaped her then. Robby had misnamed Angelica when he called her Sparrow. Sparrows did not so calmly suggest seduction.

Serena winced. The notion was preposterous. She could never try to seduce Nicholas. It would be too mortifying if she were rejected. As of speaking of love to him, impossible. Her heart quailed at what he might say if she confessed she loved him.

She stared into space, depression darkening every

crevice of her soul. Yet then her spirit began to rise in rebellion. She clearly was not French. She'd not risk all in a seduction. Or worse, a confession of love. However, she was Serena Fairchild, and Serena Fairchild did not sit around crying because a man did not want her. Serena Fairchild did not give up the battle so easily.

She squared her shoulders. She knew how to bring men to their knees, and that was what *she* had been taught. She knew the games and knew the ploys. She'd regain Nicholas's attention in her own way. Her heart silently sighed in relief. She'd bring Nicholas back to heel. She'd regain the advantage, and she'd not have to bare her soul to do it.

Serena was enjoying herself immensely. Or she told herself she was enjoying herself immensely. Of course it had only taken four glasses of champagne to ease her nerves into such a state. She had worn her most dashing dress. The sapphire one, in fact, over which Nicholas the footman had fought with her. That in itself should make him sit up and take notice. Nicholas had been jealous before when she wore it, he could be jealous again.

That was, if he were there. They were a full two hours into the ball already and he hadn't appeared. Serena had prepared for battle, to captivate and conquer, and she couldn't even find her quarry. Where was Nicholas? Originally he had promised to escort her. Then he'd sent a message around saying he was detained and could he meet her at the ball? Now it appeared he intended to deny her completely.

Serena sipped the last of her champagne and flashed a brilliant smile at the men surrounding her. She could count a good eight of them. Not a shabby court at all. She still had the knack. A small, almost bitter laugh escaped her. She was certainly bringing the men to their knees, but not the one she desired. She tossed her head and held up her glass of champagne. "Gentlemen, it is tragic. I have no more champagne."

"I'll fetch you another," young Clinton said quickly. He turned and bolted through the group. The rest of the men laughed.

"Good," Lord Waverly said. As one of her favorite and longtime admirers, he possessed one of the seats of honor beside her. "It's one less of us here." He smiled, looking deep into Serena's eyes. "It's good to have you back, Serena."

Serena started. "What do you mean?"

He grimaced. "You must forgive me, but it's been too long that you've been . . . otherwise engaged." He lowered his voice. "St. Irving wasn't worthy of you."

A knot formed in Serena's throat. It was unfortunate Nicholas wasn't present to hear that. "Thank you."

He grinned. "But that's over with now, isn't it? It's good to have the old Serena back."

"Yes," Serena said quietly. But she wasn't the old Serena, she realized, and it frightened her. In truth, she didn't want or need all these men about her. Before, she had always enjoyed having a large court. She thrived on the attention. It kept her from becoming bored.

This time, it was different. This time she had only drawn them to her side to make Nicholas, even a non-present Nicholas, jealous. It hurt to be so honest with herself. In fact it hurt so much that ire for the man who had caused her to change, to lose the thrill of it all, welled within her.

"Here's your champagne!" Lord Clinton's voice shouted out. He shoved through the throng of men and offered her the glass.

"Ah, nectar from the gods," she quipped.

"No, ambrosia for a goddess," Clinton said, his voice high.

"Lord," Lord Waverly murmured.

Serena chuckled. It died abruptly. The men about her had shifted, and through the gap, she saw Nicholas enter the ballroom. Her heart skipped a monumental beat. Why did he have to be the handsomest man in the entire room? She returned her gaze to the men about her, her body tensing. The moment had come, and now she wasn't sure what to do. Fortunately, the orchestra began tuning up for the next dance. Lord Clinton exclaimed that it was his dance.

Serena rose and permitted him to lead her out, determined to show her gaiety and unconcern. Indeed, she proceeded to show it all the way through the country dance. She laughed. She sashayed. She flirted with every fiber of her body. She also became very dizzy.

When the dance was over, she covertly glanced about, even as Lord Clinton led her back to her chair. Nicholas was now across the room, talking to a far too buxom, far too beautiful, and far too young redhead. Serena, jealousy exploding within her, accepted another glass of champagne. She drank it swiftly.

The men once again navigated to her. It showed her talent that she quipped with them and laughed with them, even while her vision became blurred and she was seeing two and three of everybody. It made the room extremely crowded, and the cortege of men about her a regular battalion. The only person she saw one of was Nicholas. And, of course, the hussy beside him. It wasn't fair. She had a battalion of men to make him jealous. He had but one chit to make her jealous.

The orchestra once again began to play. This was going to be a waltz. Strong determination filled Serena. She was not about to let that redheaded chit dance with Nicholas. This was her night to conquer!

"If you gentlemen will please excuse me," Serena said, right in the middle of what conversation she didn't know. She dropped her empty glass into Lord Waverly's lap and rose. The men's objections were but a dull buzz in her ears as she walked away from them. She crossed the ballroom, noticing the floor was heaving. Very much like her emotions were. She staunchly ignored it as she halted directly in front of Nicholas and his red-headed chit.

"Good evening, Nicholas." She smiled and batted her lashes. "So you have just arrived."

Nicholas gazed at her, a considering look in his eyes. In truth, it was a rather solemn look. Serena gritted her teeth. A look of adoration would have been good. Even a look of jealous anger would have worked. The look of quiet reserve in his eyes was not acceptable.

"I arrived quite a few minutes ago," was all Nicholas said.

"Did you?" Serena laughed. "I hadn't noticed. I've been having so-o-o much fun."

There was but the slightest twitch to Nicholas's lips. "Yes, I can tell."

"Can you?" Serena trilled another laugh, though her gaze narrowed darkly upon the redhead. She had no problem with her vision there. The child had a chest upon her that was indecent. "I am surprised." The girl's eyes widened into those of a frightened doe. Ah ha! Big bosomed, but a lightweight, Serena thought with malicious satisfaction. She looked back to Nicholas and smiled. "At least you have arrived in time for our waltz."

Nicholas's brows rose. "Have I?"

Serena held out her hand imperiously. "Yes. And we must hurry." She grinned rather evilly to the girl. "You will excuse us, won't you?"

Nicholas paused a moment, frowning. Then he

turned to the . . . the child. "If you will excuse me, I evidently forgot that this was Lady Fairchild's dance."

"Yes, of course," the girl said, flushing a deep red. She spun and bolted. No doubt running to her mother's side. Where she should rightly be, Serena thought. Pleasure rose within her. That had been an easy battle. Age still had its benefits.

Laughing, she grabbed up Nicholas's hand and drew him onto the dance floor. It was far from her usual behavior, but tonight it didn't seem to matter. She smiled up at Nicholas as he took her into his arms and the music began. " 'Tis a shame you are s-s-o late, Nicholas. It's been a de-lightful ball."

"I'm sorry," Nicholas said. "I was detained. I had a certain matter I was attending."

Green jealousy rose within Serena. "And what matter might 'she' be?"

Nicholas's brow rose. Then he laughed. "It's not what you think, Serena." His lips twitched. "In fact, when I tell you, you will find it amusing."

Serena bared her teeth. "Then tell me now. I l-love to be amused."

"No," Nicholas said. That irritating solemn look entered his eyes again. "When I tell you, I want you sober."

Serena grimaced. He was already sobering her, in a most disheartening way, in fact. "But I am sober."

"Serena," Nicholas said, laughing, "don't try that one with me. Just how many glasses of champagne have you had?"

"Evidently not enough," Serena said, seething.

"I'd say you have." Nicholas's eyes showed concern. "Don't you think you should slow down?"

"Are you telling me what to do?" Serena asked. The fighting fumes rose within her.

Nicholas paused. "No, I'm advising you."

"No, you aren't," Serena said angrily. "You are telling

me. Like you are always telling me. Well, I don't have to listen to you. Not ever."

"Very well." Nicholas's eyes darkened now. "Continue to drink. I'll scrape you off the floor later and make sure you arrive home safely."

"No, you won't," Serena said, swiftly retreating to obstinacy. "Because I'm not drunk."

"Yes, you are."

"Ha," Serena said, hurt and self-pity welling up within her. "Other men find me captivating and charming. You . . . you only find me drunk!"

Nicholas's eyes flared. "I am not other men."

Serena laughed bitterly. "Oh, no. You are most definitely not."

Nicholas's eyes narrowed. "What do you mean by that?"

"What do I mean?" Serena retorted. "I mean that no matter what I do, you find fault with me, that is what I mean."

"No," Nicholas retorted. "No matter what I do, you refuse to take it in the proper way."

"But that's because I am *not* proper, am I?" Serena shot back.

Nicholas almost growled. "No you are most definitely not proper."

"And you are rude and officious," Serena snapped. Tears formed at her eyes. She had wanted to bring Nicholas to his knees. Instead, it seemed it was she falling down, falling down fast.

"Is that what you think?" Nicholas pulled her tightly to his chest, his eyes blazing. "Is that what you *still* think?"

"Yes," Serena said. "No!" She choked slightly. "I don't know what I think."

"Damn it, Serena," Nicholas growled. "What do you want from me? Tell me! What do you want from me?"

Serena gazed up at him helplessly. God, she *was* drunk. She wanted to become a blithering idiot. She wanted to cry that she wanted him to love her, to accept her, to marry her. She strove for control the only way she knew how. She shoved at him. "I don't want anything from you. Nothing at all."

"Serena!" Nicholas cried, his voice a rasp.

"Just let me go!" Serena shouted in desperation. She loved him, and he didn't love her. She had to get away. "I don't ever want to see you again."

"No," Nicholas said. "You don't mean that!"

"Yes, I do!" Serena sobbed, struggling. She freed her one hand and slapped him sharply. Nicholas didn't even flinch. He paled, his eyes black with fury. Serena felt the tears slipping. "Just let me go!" She pushed at him. Nicholas didn't resist. His arms fell from about her.

For a moment they stared at each other. As did everyone else. Serena wasn't *that* drunk. She heard all the whispers. In fact, they all but pounded in her ears. "She slapped him!" "They're at it again!" "Why does he tolerate it!" "The shrew!" "Poor man!"

Serena, choking on a sob which welled up to burst the very seams of her heart, spun away. Everything was whirling. All was washed by a blur of tears. She careened into a body. She looked up as two arms came about her. She blinked away her tears.

"Oh, God!" Serena moaned. She prayed her vision was wrong. She could swear she was seeing her ex-fiancé Darrell Appledorf . . . no, Appletime . . . no, Applesomething before her misty gaze.

"Hello, Serena," Darrel said. He looked far stronger and nastier than she had ever seen him, or imagined to see him.

"Darrel?" Serena asked, determined he was just a champagne figment of her imagination.

"Remember me?" Darrel asked. He looked past them. "No, I suppose not." He barked a laugh. Clearly not a humorous one. "You have another poor fool already in your toils, I see."

"He's not in my toils," Serena said. Lord, but that was a joke!

"Yes, he is," Darrel said, his fingers digging into her arms.

"Let me go," Serena hissed. It was fortunate she was drunk, considering the manhandling she was receiving.

"I've tried to let you go," Darrel said, almost shaking her. "I've tried and I can't."

"Serena said to let her go!" Nicholas's voice cracked like thunder from behind.

"Why?" Darrel asked. "So you can have her? Well, you can't. You can't hold her any more than I could!" He had an angry, wild look to him. The world had clearly gone mad. Darrel, The-Dull-Stick-Lap-Dog-Darrel, was looking wild. "She's a bitch! She'll ruin your life, like she did mine."

"Don't call her a bitch!" Nicholas roared.

"She is a bitch!" Darrel shouted. He flung Serena aside. Serena, dizzy and still stunned that the world had turned so crazy, twirled and then toppled to the floor. Shaking her head, she groaned and sat up. She blinked hard several times.

Darrel, The-Changeling-Never-Underestimate-Man-Darrel had charged at Nicholas. Nicholas met him with one swift, shooting fist to his face. Darrel jerked once. Then he capsized backward. He fell, full length, as stiff as a board, in front of Serena. Serena nodded. Now, *that* did make sense. She looked up at Nicholas.

He stood, his face rigid fury, his hands clenching and unclenching. He looked her directly in the eye and said lowly, "I'll fight for you no more, Serena."

Serena's mouth dropped, as did her heart. "Nicholas!"

Nicholas merely turned and walked through the surrounding crowd, which parted for him with mutters and nods of approval. Serena scrambled to her feet. She lifted her skirts and bolted over the supine Darrel, chasing after Nicholas and calling out his name. She managed to catch up with him just outside the ballroom. "Nicholas!" she cried, panting. "Stop!"

He spun around. His gaze was solid and unwavering. "No, Serena. No more!"

"What do you mean no more?" Serena asked desperately.

He stalked up to her. "I'm done fighting, Serena. I'm not going to fight against you anymore. Or for you anymore."

Serena swallowed hard. "Y-you haven't been fighting for me. Well, except for Darrel."

"No, Serena," Nicholas said. "I've been fighting for you."

"How?" Serena asked. "How?"

"You asked me to show you respect. Well, I've tried. I've tried to be your friend, to show you that a marriage between us would be good. I've changed, but you haven't noticed. I thought you had changed, but you haven't. What you ask from me, you will not give." He laughed bitterly. "I wanted you to come to me in love. I didn't want to force you to it. I wanted you to give it." He shook his head. "Instead it is you who have forced me to realize that will never happen. You've won, Serena," he said in a suddenly sad and tired voice. "You've won." Unaccountably, he reached into his pocket and withdrew a small box. "Here. You might as well have this. That's why I was late." He handed the box into Serena's shaking hand. "Consider it the spoils of war."

Without another word, he turned and walked away.

"Nicholas!" Serena cried, gripping the box in her hand with a sick premonition. "Wait." He kept walking. Fear made her desperate. "Nicholas! Come back here this instant!"

He spun, his gaze cold. "You forget, Serena, I'm not your servant anymore. Nor will I ever be." He turned and continued to walk away.

Serena knew better than to call him back. Silently, tears in her eyes, she opened the box. A beautiful, marquise-cut diamond glittered up at her. It should have been an engagement ring . . . not the spoils of war.

Twelve

"Serena, this has got to stop," Lady Lucille said, her tone exasperated. "Where is your fighting spirit?"

"It is quite gone," Serena responded in a calm tone as she looked through a ladies' magazine. She chuckled, though it hurt her. "The battle is over."

"But that doesn't mean life should be over," Lady Lucille said. "You've locked yourself up in this house for two weeks now. You must . . ."

"I know," Serena sighed. "I should go out and be seen. I should act as if nothing has happened."

Lady Lucille's gaze turned serious. "Yes."

Serena tossed the magazine down. "I can't. Not this time."

"But you must," Lucille said. "You are committing social destruction behaving like this. By not going out or receiving anyone you are letting the world know you accept the blame."

"And why not?" Serena asked angrily. She sprung up and paced to the fireplace. "It is my fault."

"Yes," Lady Lucille agreed baldly. "But there is no reason to turn tail and run like this. Look at Nicholas. Thank God he has the presence of mind to continue to see and be seen. He is acting like it was nothing. Just the way you should."

"I'm sorry." Serena's chest tightened. "But I can't do it."

"I've never known you to be a coward before."

Serena laughed. "Well, now you do." She shivered. "I simply can't face Nicholas. Not after I humiliated him like that."

"Serena," Lady Lucille said, throwing up her hands, "don't make this a Chetleham tragedy. You and Nicholas have had scenes before this one. Many that I personally felt were far worse. So why should this one be different?"

Serena remained silent. She wouldn't say that this time it was worse because she had a ring to prove it. She had sent the ring with a note of apology to Nicholas. The ring had been returned to her with no other response. Just as had all her other notes of apology been returned. This time Nicholas wouldn't forgive her. He'd be her servant no more.

A commotion sounded outside the parlor door. Serena turned as Robby and Angelica entered. Alvie and Randolf came in directly behind. "Hello. How was the morning ride?" she asked.

Alvie's face was flushed. "Oh, it was fine."

"Er, yes, it was." Robby walked over to take up a seat. Angelica moved to sit next to him.

"I'll order some tea," Serena said, going to the bell pull.

"Th-that would be nice." Alvie's gaze flickered to Randolf.

"Yes, it would," Randolf said. He did not say it with enthusiasm.

Serena laughed. "Then do have a seat."

"Yes," Alvie said. She scurried to take up a seat. Randolf walked over stiffly and sat down next to her.

The room fell amazingly silent then. Serena noticed that four pairs of eyes gazed at her with an alarming amount of solemnest. She laughed. "What is it? Why is everyone looking at me?" She glanced down at her dress. "Is something wrong?"

"N-no, of course not," Alvie said quickly. Her fair face flushed to a deep red. "Well, not with your dress."

Serena raised a brow. Everyone still watched her. "With my hair then?"

"No," Randolf said, shaking his head vehemently.

Serena, feeling the first real qualms, looked to Robby. "Then what is it? I know I haven't grown two heads yet."

Robby sighed. "Don't know if you care to hear. I mean, will want to hear."

"Most likely not." Serena forced a laugh. "But it surely will be better than you all looking at me as if I'm a monster or something."

"No," Angelica said quickly. "No. We never meant that."

"Then what is it?" Serena persisted.

"Nicholas is leaving for the Continent," Robby blurted out.

Serena stiffened as if she'd been shot. "I see." She shook her head. "Perhaps I am a monster after all."

"No," Alvie said. "You're not. W-we just didn't know if we sh-should tell you or not."

Serena attempted a shrug. "Why shouldn't you tell me?" A swift fear entered her and she looked at Robby. "He's not going to—"

"No," Robby said. "He's not going . . . er, to do service or anything."

"He says he just feels like traveling," Alvie said. She looked down. "He intends to leave in two days."

"I see," Serena said, a numbness invading her. How strange. She hadn't seen Nicholas. Had avoided it at all cost. Yet to know he was leaving, wouldn't even be in the same town as her, cut deep. Very deep.

"He's promised to remain for Mother's ball, since it is the last in the season and she sets such store in it," Alvie's voice sounded unusually hesitant. "But then he intends to leave. H-he says he doesn't know when he will return."

"I see," Serena said again.

"I'm sorry, Serena," Alvie said quietly.

Serena fabricated a shadow of a laugh. "Whatever for?"

Alvie flushed. "Well, for . . . for . . . well, I'm just sorry."

"Perhaps if you were to see Nicholas," Angelica said. "He would not go."

"Yes," Lady Lucille said softly. "At least appear in public with him."

Serena laughed bitterly. "Oh, yes. I'm sure that would help. No doubt it would send him tearing off for the next ship out of here to any region unknown." She paled. "No. There isn't anything to be done. And . . . and at least there won't be another scene."

"Serena may be right," Robby said, his expression serious.

"Robby, no," Angelica said softly.

"Well," Robby said, his tone defensive. Or perhaps it was protective. "Ain't no use in Serena trying to jump a fence that she can't. I mean, I've tried to talk to Nicholas about it. He won't. He won't even speak Serena's name."

"See," Serena said, clasping her hands tightly together and attempting to act calm. She laughed. "As Lucille was just telling me, there isn't any reason to make a Chetleham tragedy over the issue."

"That is not what I meant," Lucille said, her tone dry.

Serena shrugged. "No matter. If Nicholas feels like

traveling, he feels like traveling." She lifted her chin. "Let us speak about other matters."

"Of course," Robby said quickly.

"Oh, yes," Alvie said, nodding.

Everyone promptly began talking at once. The dialogue was certainly not brilliant, but every inane subject which any of them could muster up was diligently discussed.

Serena awoke with a start. She was bathed in sweat. She groaned. She was redreaming the last scene with Nicholas, as she had every night for two weeks. Why couldn't she let it go? One would have thought, as drunk as she had been that night, that the scene would have been blurred and hazy. Rather it had become sharper and sharper within her mind, and in her dreams.

Nicholas had wanted her to come to him in love. And she had fought him all the way. She had humiliated him. She had shown him no respect. Now he was leaving. Her heart ached. How was she going to live with the continual, raw pain?

He said she had won, but she had lost it all. Regret filled her. If only she had listened to Angelica. She should have gone to him with love. Rather, she had tried to bring him to heel. She had played the games she knew so well, and had lost because of them.

Suddenly her heart flipflopped. She couldn't let him leave. Not this way. She really had nothing else to lose. But she had something to give. Even if Nicholas rejected her, she could at least, for once, give him the respect he deserved.

* * *

"You did a wonderful job, Angelica," Serena said, studying the outfit that lay upon the bed.

Angelica, dressed in a beautiful rose ball gown, glanced to the outfit on the bed. She then looked Serena in the eye. "You truly are going to do this?"

Serena smiled. "Yes, I truly am."

Angelica shook her head. "I do not think I would be able to do so."

"This from the lady who advised me to seduce the man."

Humor traced through Angelica's eyes. "Yes, but I didn't mean for you to do it in public."

Serena shook her head. "I've made a mockery of Nicholas in public. It's only right that my apology be in public." She swallowed hard. "Besides, you say Nicholas intends to leave tonight directly from the ball. This will be my last chance."

Angelica nodded. Then she smiled. "I wish you the best of luck."

"I don't need the best of luck," Serena said softly. "I need the best of love."

Serena stood just outside the doorway to the ballroom. The noise and music flooded forth. She smoothed down the fabric of her outfit. In truth, the colors of the St. Irving livery suited her well. Angelica had indeed done an excellent job in tailoring the jacket, with its stark lines and laced cuffs. The only jewelry Serena wore was a fine gold necklace, the diamond marquise ring its only pendant.

Serena drew in a deep breath. Silently she entered the ballroom. Spying a servant carrying a tray of champagne, she strode directly up to him.

"Excuse me," she said. "Could I please have that tray?"

"Pardon?" the servant asked, glancing at her. His eyes immediately popped wide and his tray listed at a sharp angle. "Gore!"

"Let me assist you," Serena said, swiftly reaching out. She took the tray from the man's slackening hands, just barely saving the four glasses of champagne upon it.

"Yes . . . m-my lady," he stammered.

Serena noticed she had already gained the attention of the people around her. If she hadn't, the shrill shout of "Serena!" in Alvie's ringing voice would have clearly done the trick. She glanced up to discover Alvie, her eyes the size of saucers, dashing toward her. "What . . . what are you . . . ?"

"Hello, Alvie," Serena said with a determined calm. She held out her tray. "Would you care for a drink?"

Randolf, who came in a close second behind his beloved, nodded his head. "I would." His stunned gaze appeared permanently focused upon Serena's britches. She herself thought Angelica had tailored them particularly well. *"Mon Dieu."*

"Here," Serena said, maneuvering the tray and lifting a glass. Randolf had the presence of mind to at least hold out his hand. She rammed the glass into his frozen fingers. Then she glanced quickly around. "Where is Nicholas, by the by?"

"H-he's over th-there with Mother," Alvie stammered. She waved one hand to the left, while she snatched at a glass from the tray with the other. She gulped the champagne down.

Serena looked in the general direction of Alvie's wild wave and finally caught sight of Nicholas. He stood clear across the ballroom. She sighed in resignation. It *would* have to be that way. She drew up her courage, even as the hum of voices elevated, her name definitely floating to the top. "Thank you."

Serena began her trek, keeping her gaze straight and

her walk stately. She soon had an entourage in tow behind her. Not only did Alvie and Randolf follow her, but anyone else who spied her did the same. She was only halfway across the room when she heard another familiar voice raised in alarm.

"What the devil!" Robby bolted through the crowd. Angelica trailed behind him at a more discreet pace. Robby's frown was marked. "Serena! What in blazes are you doing now?"

"Leave her be, dear," Angelica said, placing a gentle hand upon his arm. "Serena knows what she is doing."

Robby looked down at Angelica, his expression stunned. "She does?"

"Here, dearest . . ." Serena held out her tray once more. "Take a glass. But only one. You and Angelica must share it. The other is reserved for Nicholas."

"I s-see," Robby stammered. Then his eyes shuttered wide and a grin cracked across his face. "Damn! I do see." He took the glass quickly and raised it in a toast. "Here's to you."

"Here's to us, I hope," Serena said, a nervous laugh escaping her. Ignoring her bejeweled and chattering followers, who sounded suspiciously like magpies to her, Serena once again set her course toward her final destination. Or what she prayed was her final destination, rather than her final downfall. Robby and Angelica, as well as Alvie and Randolf, proved an excellent vanguard, banding closely around her and insulating her from the gawking crowd. No matter what happened, Serena knew now she had a group of dear and loyal friends. She only hoped she wasn't forcing them to support her in a futile cause.

Serena's heart leapt and pounded so heavily she thought it would lose its moorings. She had successfully traversed two thirds across the ballroom. People were now parting quickly to the side for her, creating a clear aisle as it were. The gossip had apparently already raced ahead.

Yet their gaping faces, titters, and whispers didn't even faze Serena. They didn't matter. What mattered was what Nicholas would do. Would he accept her or reject her? One face in the crowd did make Serena halt, however. Lady Lucille stood to the right. True to that woman's superb nature, she had not even called out.

"Hello, Lucille," Serena said, smiling.

"Hello, dear," Lady Lucille said, her eyes full of laughter. "So you took my advice to get out in public again, I see?"

"Yes, and I intend to take your other advice as well."

Lucille shook her head, her eyes rueful. "I'm sorry I ever called you a coward."

"No, I *have* been a coward," Serena said softly.

"Well, you are certainly making up for it now."

"We'll see," Serena said, drawing in a deep breath. She nodded to Lady Lucille and then proceeded. It seemed the last final steps came far too quickly. Her heart almost failed her when she met Nicholas's gaze. His dark eyes were impenetrable, but she could read the tension in every line of his body.

Forcing a smile, and dredging up the rest of her courage, Serena walked directly up to him. The room had fallen suddenly quiet, the kind of silence required to hear the proverbial pin drop. No doubt even the musicians were now in the crowd and ready for the show.

It was Nicholas's mother, standing beside him, who first spoke, a look of utter bafflement upon her face. "Serena, dearest, is this a new fashion? You look like a servant. One of *my* servants!"

"Not your servant, my lady," Serena said. "But your son's." Her gaze fixed upon Nicholas, she slowly knelt to one knee and held out the tray. She waited a moment for the gasps and shouts to die down. "My lord, as your servant, may I offer you a glass of champagne."

Nicholas remained stiff and silent one dreadful second. He then shook his head. "No, I do not want a glass of champagne."

The crowd went wild. Serena heard Robby's groan close behind her. Some man, with the loudest voice, shouted, "That's it. You show her, my lord." A ripple of applause even went through the room. Serena flushed deeply. She had risked it all, and lost.

"But!" Nicholas said loudly, his eyes suddenly flashing. "I do want *you*, my lady."

"What did he say?" a voice shouted out from somewhere in the back of the crowd.

"I said," Nicholas repeated, raising his voice, "I want the lady!"

That silenced the crowd promptly. Except for Robby, who shouted hooray and clapped loudly. Other applause started up. Serena didn't need to look to see who joined in. It could only be from her nearest and dearest.

Serena looked at Nicholas with a trembling smile. Her heart seemed to break into ten million pieces, like a star shooting light and sparks. "Thank you, my lord."

"No, thank you, my lady," Nicholas said. He glanced quickly around and then looked at Serena, his eyes warm, and yet, challenging. "I intended to leave England tonight. There is a ship waiting."

Serena laughed, despite herself. "I will gladly go wherever you wish to go."

Nicholas grinned. "Very well." He reached out and removed the tray from Serena's hands. He turned to Lady St. Irving. "Excuse me, Mother, could you please take this?"

"Of course, dear," Lady St. Irving said, blinking in confusion as she received the tray.

Nicholas turned and held out his hand to Serena. She accepted it readily. He drew her to her feet. For a moment they merely gazed at each other. Nicholas then turned his gaze to the onlookers. Serena hid her smile. His look was as autocratic and "bedamned to you" as she had ever seen it. And she had seen it plenty.

"If you will excuse us," Nicholas announced, "my future wife and I are leaving."

It appeared a standoff. Everyone merely gaped.

"The coach is ready and awaiting, Nicholas," Serena murmured quietly to him.

"Then do let us go," Nicholas said, a chuckle rifling his voice.

Serena lifted her chin and donned an imperious look. Together, Nicholas and Serena, slowly and regally, walked through the crowd. Or perhaps it was slowly and cautiously, so as not to precipitate a riot. Either way, the onlookers fell back and let them pass without a word.

Only when they had left the ballroom and stood quietly in a secluded corner of the foyer did Nicholas ask, "Do you truly have that coach waiting?"

"Yes." Serena sighed. "I thought, no matter what happened, an escape would be necessary." She grinned. "I'm glad we're going together."

"Yes," Nicholas said softly. He reached out and silently unclasped the chain about her neck. He slipped the ring off of it and held it up to her. "Will you accept this, Serena? I don't know if it will be a victory for you or not." He grimaced. "Not with what kind of husband I will make."

"Or what kind of wife I will make," Serena said with a shaky laugh. She held out her hand, amazed to see it tremble. Nicholas silently slid the diamond upon her finger. Serena gazed at it a moment. The ring was finally where it should be and what it should be. She clenched her hand, holding it tightly, as she intended to hold their love. She looked up at Nicholas, her gaze solemn. "It doesn't matter if it is a victory or not, what matters is that I love you." She flushed. "I know in the past that I—"

"No, as you said, it doesn't matter." Nicholas looked at her gently. "Neither of us have done well by the other, Serena."

"No," Serena said softly.

He laughed. "But we are a match, my love."

Nicholas placed his hands to her shoulders and drew her to him. Serena moved willingly into his arms, lifting her lips to be kissed. His met hers softly at first, tenderly. Serena breathed a sigh, melding her body to his. Nicholas groaned and pulled her closer, deepening the kiss. Whirlwinds and fires and lightning swirled about them.

Nicholas finally drew back, his arms firmly about her. "Lord, but we are a match."

"Yes," Serena said, still dazed. She blinked, trying to catch her breath. "We just need to tame our passions."

"No, we don't," Nicholas said, frowning. He gave her a dark and dangerous look. "I've waited far too long for you, Serena. I've no intention of taming my passions once we are married, and that I'll warn you of right now."

"No," Serena said, laughing and flushing with heat at the same time. "It's something Lucille said to me once. Something about taming your passions until both run well in tandem and . . . and make a glorious team."

"I see. In that case, I'll agree," Nicholas said. His smile was definitely roguish. "Just as long as *those* are the passions you mean for me to tame, and not the other ones."

Serena pressed against him, returning that look ten fold. "Most definitely."

Nicholas stiffened. He promptly disengaged himself from her, firmly setting her away from him. "If you will excuse me for just one moment."

"Where are you going?" Serena asked, frowning.

"I'm going to my room."

"But . . ."

"And you're not invited," he said sternly.

Serena lifted her brow. Then she laughed. "What are you afraid of? That I'll take it over as you tried to take mine over when we first met?"

"No," Nicholas said, grinning. "I'm afraid we'll not make it out of this house if you come with me. And I'll not have you just dally with me. We'll be securely married before that."

"I see," Serena said with a long drawn-out sigh.

Nicholas laughed. "It won't be that long. I've a special license in my room."

"What!" Serena exclaimed.

Nicholas grinned. "I've had it since the night of the ball. That's why I was late. Dealing with the church takes more time than you think."

"You . . . you had it then?" Serena asked, stupefied.

"Yes." Nicholas nodded. "You were the cause of why I was late."

"Oh, dear," Serena whispered, mortified. Then another thought struck her. "And you kept it?"

"Yes." Nicholas's brown eyes darkened. "I don't know why I did. I think I was hoping against hope you would still come to me." He laughed. "But I never expected you to come to me the way you did. We'll have stories to tell our children."

Serena laughed. "Always."

Nicholas grinned. "Wait only a moment."

Indeed, it was only a moment, or so it seemed to Serena, before Nicholas returned to her. He patted his jacket. "Now we can go." He held out his hand to her. "Ready?"

"Indeed," Serena said, and took his hand.

Hand in hand they walked out of the St. Irving townhouse. True to her word, Serena's coach awaited them. Callen, the minute he saw them, jumped down from the box and went to open the door.

Nicholas suddenly halted. He looked at Serena with glittering eyes. "It's a lovely night. I'll be glad to be coachman."

Serena laughed in delight. It was indeed a lovely night. "And I'll be your partner!" She glanced down wryly. "And manservant?"

Nicholas laughed. He looked at Callen. "You can ride within."

Callen's mouth fell open. "What, my lord?"

"We're the servants tonight," Nicholas said, his lips twitching as he looked at Serena. "Of each other."

"Yes," Serena nodded. "We are."

Callen stared. However, as a servant of Serena, he had learned to not ask questions but to accept. He nodded and climbed into the coach. Nicholas went and slammed the door shut upon the still frowning coachman. He then assisted Serena up to the coach box.

They attracted no small attention as they drove through London, Nicholas the fine aristocrat in his ball attire and Serena beside him, a woman dressed in the St. Irving livery. It wasn't until they left the outskirts of London and Nicholas whipped up the team to a reckless and wild speed that Serena laughed, and laughed aloud. How she loved the wind and the speed and the man beside her.

The course they had run before this had surely been rough and jolting. Yet she looked forward to the future with excitement. Now that they would be running in tandem, she never doubted they would make a wild and glorious team, or that they wouldn't travel many long and wonderful miles together.

WATCH FOR THESE REGENCY ROMANCES

LOOK FOR THESE REGENCY ROMANCES

WATCH FOR THESE ZEBRA REGENCIES

LADY STEPHANIE   (0-8217-5341-X, $4.50)
by Jeanne Savery
Lady Stephanie Morris has only one true love: the family estate she
has managed ever since her mother died. But then Lord Anthony Rider
arrives on her estate, claiming he has plans for both the land and the
woman. Stephanie soon realizes she's fallen in love with a man whose
sensual caresses will plunge her into a world of peril and intrigue . . . a
man as dangerous as he is irresistible.

BRIGHTON BEAUTY   (0-8217-5340-1, $4.50)
by Marilyn Clay
Chelsea Grant, pretty and poor, naively takes school friend Alayna
Marchmont's place and spends a month in the country. The devastating
man had sailed from Honduras to claim his promised bride, Miss
Marchmont. An affair of the heart may lead to disaster . . . unless a
resourceful Brighton beauty finds a way to stop a masquerade and
keep a lord's love.

LORD DIABLO'S DEMISE   (0-8217-5338-X, $4.50)
by Meg-Lynn Roberts
The sinfully handsome Lord Harry Glendower was a gambler and the
black sheep of his family. About to be forced into a marriage of con-
venience, the devilish fellow engineered his own demise, never having
dreamed that faking his death would lead him to the heavenly refuge
of spirited heiress Gwyn Morgan, the daughter of a physician.

A PERILOUS ATTRACTION   (0-8217-5339-8, $4.50)
by Dawn Aldridge Poore
Alissa Morgan is stunned when a frantic passenger thrusts her baby
into Alissa's arms and flees, having heard rumors that a notorious
highwayman posed a threat to their coach. Handsome stranger Hugh
Sebastian secretly possesses the treasured necklace the highwayman
seeks and volunteers to pose as Alissa's husband to save her reputation.
With a lost baby and missing necklace in their care, the couple embarks
on a journey into peril—and passion.

*Available wherever paperbacks are sold, or order direct from the
Publisher. Send cover price plus 50¢ per copy for mailing and
handling to Kensington Publishing Corp., Consumer Orders,
or call (toll free) 888-345-BOOK, to place your order using
Mastercard or Visa. Residents of New York and Tennessee
must include sales tax. DO NOT SEND CASH.*

ROMANCE FROM ROSANNE BITTNER

CARESS   (0-8217-3791-0, $5.99)

FULL CIRCLE   (0-8217-4711-8, $5.99)

SHAMELESS   (0-8217-4056-3, $5.99)

SIOUX SPLENDOR   (0-8217-5157-3, $4.99)

UNFORGETTABLE   (0-8217-4423-2, $5.50)

TEXAS EMBRACE   (0-8217-5625-7, $5.99)

UNTIL TOMORROW   (0-8217-5064-X, $5.99)